W9-CYY-234

LP
F
FRI

43354

Friedman, Mickey

Magic mirror

$18.95 BT

Magic Mirror

Magic Mirror

A GEORGIA LEE MAXWELL MYSTERY

Mickey Friedman

G.K.HALL &CO.
Boston, Massachusetts
1990

Published in Large Print by arrangement with
Viking Penguin, a division of Penguin Books USA Inc.

G.K. Hall Large Print Book Series.

Set in 18 pt. Plantin.

Library of Congress Cataloging in Publication Data

Friedman, Mickey.
    Magic mirror : a Georgia Lee Maxwell mystery / Mickey Friedman.
        p.   cm.—(G.K. Hall large print book series)
    ISBN 0-8161-4823-6 (lg. print)
    1. Large type books. I. Title.
    [PS3556.R53M346   1990]
    813'.54—dc20   89-26754

To Doris Whealton

ACKNOWLEDGEMENTS

THE Mirror and Man by Benjamin Goldberg (University Press of Virginia, 1985) provided me with both inspiration and information.

I am grateful to Thea Lurie, for letting me borrow snippets of her life, and to Priscilla Watson, for help with my research.

I offer profound thanks to my Paris informants: Sam Abt, Alain Audebert, Barbara Bell, Harry Dunphy, Judy Fayard, Mireille Huchon, Dmitri Kessel, Shirley Kessel, Paul La Feuille, Michelle Lapautre, Pierre Ottavioli, Patricia Palut, Adele Robert, Philippe Robert. They are not responsible for my mistakes or misapprehensions, or for liberties I may have taken with the information they so kindly gave me.

A WHIM

I went to live in Paris on a whim. I've always had strong whims.

It isn't that my life in Florida was unsatisfactory. I had my condo at Channel Point, and Twinkie, and my column in the Bay City *Sun* three times a week. I'd even gotten them to run my picture at the top of it, finally: hair artfully tousled, chin on fist, sophisticated smile. Naturally, being society editor, I had more invitations than I could handle—everything from the Rotary dinner dance at the country club to the grand opening of a convenience store on Route 98. A lot of people envied me.

I was close enough to Cross Beach to drive over and see Daddy and Mama pretty frequently. Of course, the talk around there is that I was fired from my job or disappointed in love, or both—preferably both. The ladies at Mama's church circle meeting pumped her good and proper, she said. Half of them didn't even realize I'd gone to live in Paris,

France, and not Paris, Kentucky. When they tried to get her to say why I'd done it Mama told them, "I have no more notion than you do. I never could do a thing with Georgia Lee once she got an idea in her head." And it's true. She never could.

The real story is this. The top brass at the *Sun* were practically on their knees begging me to stay, once they realized I really was quitting. And as for disappointment in love, I had three ardent admirers at the time I chose to leave Bay City. I admit that two of them were married and one—a fellow named Ray—wasn't worth a damn in any way whatsoever, but if I wanted male companionship it was available.

Actually, I left Bay City because of Cecilia Driscoll's daughter's wedding. Cecilia loved to see her name and picture in the paper. Since her husband owned an Oldsmobile dealership whose full-page advertisements were regularly featured in the *Sun*, Cecilia's doings were deemed extremely noteworthy by the powers that be. ("A whirlwind of a weekend *chez* Driscoll," I would write. "Cecilia and darling daughter Debbie transformed the house on Rhododendron Road into a French Provincial bower, with baskets of dried flowers, life-size ceramic ducks, and huge bows of printed fabric everywhere, for a brunch in honor of . . . ," and so on.)

Cecilia started prepping me for the wedding months in advance: the church (Episcopal, naturally, although all Cecilia's people had been hard-shell Baptists); the color of the bridesmaids' dresses (pale lilac); the kind of champagne to be served at the reception (Moët et Chandon); the groom's future employment (high school football coach). Is it any wonder I got a teeny bit bored with it all?

At Cecilia's Christmas eggnog party she took me aside and said, in a conspiratorial tone, "Debbie has chosen Alençon lace for her veil."

I was into my second eggnog, which was definitely more "nog" than egg. Straight-faced, I said, "Can I use your phone? I'd better call and stop the presses."

I thought her smile was tight, but attributed it to her latest face-lift, which I happened to know had been done recently at a private clinic down on Key Biscayne. I had wanted to run the face-lift as a blind item, but the brass said no.

The wedding took place in April, and although we usually write them up from forms, I attended personally, with my notebook tucked into my beige silk clutch. The occasion was typical, with stephanotis, princess necklines, and a toddling ring-bearer who dropped his white satin cushion. Maybe it was newsworthy that the mother of the groom had a run in her hose. I had my photographer (dressed for the occasion in a Hawaiian shirt, jeans, and sandals) take some shots at the reception, and that was that.

I did, I admit it, get a giggle out of the picture of Cecilia. Her collar was ruched up so it looked like she didn't have a neck, and with her eyes half-closed because of the flash she looked like Mama Toad instead of the mother of the bride. But I honestly wouldn't have used that one if the others had been any better. "Deliberate sabotage" is an ugly phrase, isn't it?

The rest was in no way my fault. I turned in a perfectly respectable write-up, but the slot man was out sick and the kid who took his place hadn't mastered the computer system. In the next day's paper three paragraphs concerning a marijuana raid on a cottage at the beach were inserted at the end of the wedding story. It read something like, "The Driscoll family's out-of-town guests included . . . Joe Jones, who police said is wanted in Georgia for trafficking in a controlled substance; Jack Smith, recently released on bail on a similar charge," and on like that.

You can imagine. As soon as the early edition hit the stands Cecilia was in the publisher's office, carrying on like a lunatic. Did he back me up, apologize, smooth it over? After she left he called me in, white as a sheet, and said Cecilia's husband would pull his advertising if I wasn't fired from the *Sun* immediately. I told him I hadn't done anything wrong. He said maybe if I apologized she'd relent. I wanted to ask if Cecilia Driscoll was the boss around here, but the answer was obvious. I said that even though I'd done nothing wrong I would apologize to Cecilia. Then I left and went to the ladies' room.

I stayed there a long time, leaning against the wall, gazing in the mirror. The greenish cast on my face was a reflection from the tile wall, but it made me look as sick as I felt. My hairdresser hadn't had time to give me my auburn rinse the week before, and I could see gray everywhere. Mascara was smudged around my eyes where I had fought back tears of fury. I remembered suddenly and forcibly that I was looking at my thirty-fifth birthday. From there, it was a mere hop down the road to the big four-oh. And where was I, and what had I accomplished? I was in Bay City, Florida, and I had accomplished getting myself into a position where I had to grovel to Cecilia Driscoll.

That's when my whim started. I leaned over and stuck my face so close to the mirror I was nearly cross-eyed. "Georgia Lee," I whispered. "Georgia Lee Maxwell." Georgia Lee Maxwell, I realized dreamily, was not going to apologize to Cecilia Driscoll. Furthermore, Georgia Lee Maxwell was sick of small-time aggravation. If I was going to have aggravation, I would have big-time aggravation.

I was leaving the *Sun*. I was leaving Bay City. The month was April. April in Paris. I was going to Paris.

GOOD-BYE TO CROSS BEACH

IT wasn't as farfetched as it may seem. Thanks to Mama's ideas of refinement, I'd had years of French lessons from Mrs. Desirée Davis, a Parisienne who, by way of marriage to a GI, had ended up in Cross Beach. After countless afternoons slumped over Mrs. Davis's dining table grinding away

6

at verb tenses, then continuing my studies at college, I could read French pretty well. My speech carried over some of its native drawl, but I thought it was passable. Writing was different. I could get along, but I certainly couldn't write the language well enough to go over there and become the society editor of *Le Monde*, even providing *Le Monde* would ever dream of having a society editor.

This was where Loretta came in.

We had been colleagues at the *Sun* some years before, Loretta covering fashion while I covered society. Then, through one of life's ironies, Loretta went off on a trip that should have been mine, and found a new existence.

The trip was to Atlanta. A Bay City majorette was entered in a prestigious baton-twirling competition there, and I was scheduled to go with her and write up her experiences. It was the one and only time the paper ever offered to send me out of town, aside from paying my mileage to Tallahassee to cover the tailgate parties at the FSU-Florida football game.

Two days before I was supposed to leave for Atlanta, I came down with a horrible strep throat, so Loretta got to go instead. While I was fighting a raging fever and taking antibiotics, Loretta went to a Coke party

7

for the twirlers and met a wealthy business-man named Wendell Walker, who was there representing one of the competition's sponsors.

You guessed it. Six months later Loretta married Wendell and went off to live in luxury in Atlanta.

Of course I wonder what would have happened if I hadn't come down with strep. Would *I* have met and married Wendell Walker? I tell myself I couldn't have, since I was married to Lonnie Boyette at the time. (My high school sweetheart. He spent all his spare time in the river swamp, blasting away at innocent wildlife with a shotgun, and loved his bird dog, a bitch named Sukey, better than he loved me. I'm just glad I got it out of the way early in my life.) Still, I *might* have met Wendell, and we *might* have gotten married after I got divorced. It's such an example of the Road Not Taken, isn't it?

Eventually, Wendell was named CEO of his company and transferred to New York City. Loretta called me from there and said, kidding around, "I can't believe it! There's Yankees everywhere!"

"I hear they've even got a baseball team named after them," I said.

"Oh, no! That's one team I could *never* root for."

Loretta did all right for herself in New York. Despite being well-off she had continued to work, and after a while she ended up as executive editor of a glossy women's magazine called *Good Look*. She never forgot her old girlfriend, either. When she wanted a story for *Good Look* that she thought was right for me, she'd call and offer me the assignment. I made a fair amount of freelance money that way, writing pieces about how to tone your calves and thighs by walking through beach sand, a revolutionary new kelp diet, table settings using fishnet with conch shells and driftwood, and recipes for periwinkle stew or sweet-and-sour okra. At the time of my defection from the *Sun*, I'd become a fairly regular contributor to *Good Look*, which was why I felt I could call Loretta with my proposition.

Once I got her on the phone, though, it wasn't as easy as I thought. She commiserated with me heartily about my troubles with the brass and Cecilia Driscoll, but when I put forth my idea there was a good thirty seconds of dead air—at my expense—before she responded.

At last she said, "Well, Georgia Lee, I don't . . . Have you ever *been* to Paris?"

I was miffed. "I certainly have. I went with Daddy and Mama when I was sixteen, and I spent a whole week there on my European tour." (To tell the truth, it was five days, but I thought I had to make as strong a case as I could.)

More silence. I said, "I do speak the language. When I was there, I spoke to all kinds of people." I remembered the conversation I'd had with the tacky-looking man who approached me in the Louvre. I was madly searching for Vermeer's *The Lacemaker*, which was down in my guidebook as a "must-see." I'd understood his suggestions only too well, and after he'd followed me through a few rooms I'd been able to say, "Leave me alone or I'll call the police" in perfect French. Later, I'd had another successful conversation, with a guard who told me the exhibition rooms were being rearranged and *The Lacemaker* wouldn't be available for viewing in the foreseeable future.

"You know"—Loretta's voice had a high, pinched quality—"we have fashion people on our staff who go to Paris twice a year for the *couture* shows, and the *prêt-à-porter*—"

"Naturally," I said. I was being nice as pie, despite my growing annoyance. "I'm not asking to cover the fashion shows. What I'm offering is to do a monthly column about—un—*other* aspects of Paris."

"What other aspects?"

I was up against it, now. I hadn't expected Loretta to be such a tough nut. I tried to summon up articles from travel magazines I'd glanced through lately. I remembered a brightly colored photo of a street filled with stands and stalls. Had it been Paris or Rome? I plunged. "Street markets. Those darling street markets they have, with the fabulous meat and produce. Or facials." I was rolling now. "Where do you get a great facial in Paris? I could test out several places and describe them. Or, say everybody in Paris is wearing high-buttoned shoes—"

"They are?"

"I don't know what they're wearing till I get there. But say it's high-buttoned shoes. I write about that, and I find out where they buy them, and so on—"

"According to the proofs of our next issue, everybody in Paris is wearing metallic-colored pumps."

"Or maybe there's some adorable new restaurant everybody loves, or a book that's making a stir. It could be anything, don't you see?"

"Yes, but Georgia Lee, how are you going to find out about these things?"

"I'm a newspaperwoman, Loretta. *I'll find out.*"

The silence this time had a different quality. I got a few more ideas—jogging in Paris, where to get cut-rate *couture*—but sensed it was time for me to shut up. I heard Loretta take a deep breath. "This would have to be completely on spec, you know. I couldn't put you on the staff."

No health insurance, no retirement package. "How much would you pay per piece?"

She named an obscenely low figure.

"Loretta!"

"Georgia Lee, it's an unknown quantity. If it works out, we'll do better."

"You'll have to do better now! I've got Twinkie to support!"

She came up a fraction and said, "That's the best I can do. My financial people make me toe the line. It isn't all up to me, you know."

My financial people. I'd have to sell the condo, unless I could find somebody to gouge for an unheard-of rent. Maybe somebody new

12

to the area, who hadn't looked around very much.

Between that and depleting my savings, I might just get by. I thanked Loretta with some asperity and got off the phone.

After that, I moved ahead. I did find a tenant, a recently divorced colonel from the air force base who didn't seem to care what he paid, and he took it furnished. I packed a couple of trunks and bought a sturdy carrier for Twinkie. For a healthy fee, an international home-finders organization found me a studio apartment in Montparnasse. One ruinously expensive room, with bath and kitchenette. It seemed a pathetic comedown. I began to wonder, now that it was too late, whether I had made a terrible mistake.

A bunch of my friends gave me a bon voyage bash in a private room at the Sea Shack. On one wall was a caricature of me wearing a beret and waving a tricolor, drawn by the political cartoonist at the *Sun*. A fellow named Dobie, who worked in the art department, dragged me aside. He had lived in Paris once, trying to be a painter. Fervently, he pressed into my hand a piece of paper, saying he wanted me to promise to call his friend Kitty. Equally fervently, I pledged that I would. After we hugged, tears in our eyes, I was dragged away because the group was singing, "For She's a Jolly Good Fellow." I didn't cry during my thank-you speech, but almost.

One afternoon, I went to Cross Beach for a good-bye dinner with Daddy and Mama. The drive had never been more beautiful. In the lowering sun the white sand was luminous, and light-green waves spilled placidly over it, leaving glittering wet semicircles when they ebbed. Sea grasses waved on dunes covered with a tangle of flowering vines. On the hazy pink horizon were silhouetted shrimp boats. Only a fool would leave this.

Mama and Daddy seemed to agree. "I don't know *what* you'll eat over there," Mama said as she served me celery stuffed with pimento cheese to nibble with my cocktail.

"The French are famous for food, Mama."

"They aren't famous for hush puppies," Daddy yelled from the kitchen, where he was deep-frying a batch of them to go with the deep-fried catfish. The whole house smelled like hot oil. He came out in his apron and said, "There must be some kind of trick to getting along with those French people. I remember when we were there they treated us like—"

"I'm sure they can be very nice," said Mama, giving him a look that sent him back to the kitchen.

Daddy is the editor, publisher, ad salesman, janitor, star reporter, and photographer—that is to say, the sole owner and proprietor—of the weekly Cross Beach *Current*. It's because of him, of course, that I became a journalist. The latest issue of the *Current* was lying on the coffee table. I picked it up and leafed through it while Mama tossed the salad. In Daddy's column, "Malcolm's Corner," I found:

Allow me a personal note. The one and only child of Roselle and yours truly, who had been living and working in Bay City, has decided to leave the area and go live in Paris, France. She will be in the Montparnasse district, and I know will welcome calls from her Cross Beach friends who might be traveling out that way. Paris, France, seems like a long way to go, but Georgia Lee says she is looking forward to it. She will be writing a column for *Good Look* magazine. We'll hope she doesn't learn to 'parley-voo' so well she forgets how to speak English!

Roselle and I will miss her. I know her

friends and acquaintances in Cross Beach join me in wishing her well in this new venture.

God bless you, Georgia Lee.

I cried all the way home. The next morning, Twinkie and I left for Paris.

KITTY

I cannot honestly say I took to Paris immediately. Twinkie and I arrived in a freezing rain that felt like the dead of winter to a native Floridian, even though it was June. I had pictured people strolling down a sunlit Champs-Elysées, a cute whirlwind of traffic on the Place de la Concorde, and the Eiffel Tower soaring into the blue, with Gershwin's "An American in Paris" playing in the background. Instead, I got a surly and incomprehensible cabdriver, dripping gray facades, and a wallowing, gunmetal-colored Seine that was practically whitecapping. Twinkie's tranquilizer began to wear off and she started up the most pitiful mewing. Then we ran into an awful traffic jam with police blockades. When I tried, with my jet-lagged tongue and brain, to ask the driver what was going on, he snarled, *"Bombe."*

I sat back. Wonderful. A bomb. Twinkie mewed some more. I felt like mewing right along with her.

The apartment wasn't exactly perfect, although it had its good features. The Rue Delacôte, a narrow, block-long street, runs parallel to the Boulevard Montparnasse between the Rue de Rennes and the Rue de Vaugirard. I was at number three, a graceful old structure of gray-gold stone with black wrought-iron balconies. The one room was L-shaped, the windows tall, the ceiling high and edged with a modest frieze of plaster foliage. I even had a tiny balcony, decorated with two clay pots half filled with damp dirt. Judging from neighboring balconies, I could see the only acceptable flowers to plant in them were red geraniums.

The furniture in the place was sparse and marginal. The modernity of a round butcher-block dining table and four mismatched chairs made an inharmonious contrast to the pseudo-antique sofa upholstered in fading mustard brocade. I couldn't do much about the sofa, but maybe I could get a long, fringed cloth for the table. I wondered how much fringed tablecloths cost in Paris. I wondered how much geraniums cost.

There was no carpet on the hardwood floor, which creaked and reverberated with every step I took. I tore my mind away from the dusky peach wall-to-wall in my condo and inspected the bathroom, which might have been redone as recently as the twenties. The tile was severe white, the footed tub big enough to hold three people, if that were your pleasure. A halfhearted shower had been rigged up with a thin pipe and flat round head, and a stiff blue shower curtain hung on rusting rings from a wire surrounding the tub. There was a toilet, a bidet, a medicine cabinet containing the requisite number of rusty razor blades, and a sink which had separate faucets for hot and cold, something I've always hated. At this point comparisons with my condo became ludicrous, and I gave up making them. With some trepidation I tried flushing the toilet, but it rushed into vigorous action. I filed this under Thank God for Small Favors.

The bedroom "area" contained a sagging bed with a gray mattress and a huge, gnarled-looking armoire. Gazing at the armoire I realized, with a sinking heart, that there were no closets whatsoever.

While I made this preliminary inspection, Twinkie had been howling in her carrier. The time had come to let her inspect her new home. When I released her, she ran directly under the bed. She didn't emerge, except for furtive nighttime trips to the litter box and food dish, for two solid weeks.

Imagine it: Twinkie huddled under the bed, fifteen pounds of terrified calico. Me on my knees peering at her, pleading, "Come on, Twinks. Come on, sweet girl. Come out, sweet baby." All to no avail. It was just as ghastly as it sounds.

While dealing with Twinkie's maladjustment, not to mention mine, I had to do my all-important first column for Loretta. Nothing had ever seemed more impossible. In the first place, my French didn't prove to be as fluent as I'd thought. Yes, I could go to the awning-shaded greengrocer's stand down the street and, with a modicum of prompting from the bustling proprietress, come away with half a dozen juice oranges (from Italy, not Florida) and a head of lettuce. (But what *kind* of lettuce? *Laitue* was the only one variety of leafy green. What about *escarole? Frisée? Endive?*)

I could go to a café and order a *kir* or a *crème*. I could buy an umbrella (a necessary purchase) or inquire where the bus stop was. That was a far cry from being able to interview somebody and actually understand what the person was saying, and I didn't know who to interview anyway. I was paralyzed by culture shock and sensory overload. I started having nightmares about it, thrashing around on my saggy bed, Twinkie a mute witness beneath. At three o'clock one morning I stared up through the darkness at my lofty ceiling and decided this venture wasn't going to work out. I would make reservations tomorrow and crawl back to Cross Beach. I would live with Mama and Daddy, and maybe Daddy would let me work at the *Current*. The idea, which normally would have sent me screaming into the night, brought such blissful relaxation that I fell asleep immediately.

At this low and desperate point, fate gave a sign that my immediate future did not lie in Cross Beach. While contemplating making my return reservations, I came across a piece of paper on which was written the name and phone number of Kitty de Villiers-Marigny, the friend of my friend Dobie at the Bay City *Sun*.

I almost didn't call her. Her name sounded too French and too fancy. Anyway, I wasn't staying, so what was the point? But I remembered promising Dobie, and our tearful hug. I'd ruined my cat's life and my own, but at least I could keep that promise.

Determined, I picked up the phone. I wasn't looking forward to this, since I'd found that phone conversations in French caused me to perspire unduly. I clenched my jaw and dialed, trying to put together the phrases that would explain who I was and why I was calling.

She answered with a French-sounding " 'Allo?" but I hadn't gotten out more than three words when she said, "We can speak English." Her voice was unmistakably American. I told her who I was, and she suggested we meet late that afternoon at her office and go for a drink. I thought she sounded distracted, but I figured I sounded distracted myself.

All that day, I was on the verge of calling the airlines. I put on my heaviest sweater and stood on my balcony in the chilly wind. People passed below me in the Rue Delacôte. French people. Some of them went into the bakery down the way and came out carrying long loaves of bread in their bare hands, without even cellophane around it. Half the time they tore the end off the bread and ate it as they went along. Dogs of every size and breed pranced along on leashes and used the sidewalk for a bathroom at will, although later a man driving a green and white motor scooter cart with a mechanical brush came and swept it up. Little children ran by, yelling at each other in perfect French. Was there a column in any of this? Could I write my first column for *Good Look* about doggy do?

I dragged myself to the Montparnasse Métro station to go to my drinks engagement with Kitty de Villiers-Marigny. It looked like rain. Maybe I could do a column about how damn much it rained in Paris. I found the address she had given me, a nondescript office building on the Rue du Quatre-Septembre, near the Opéra. She had said third floor, end of the hall. The third floor, I noticed on a directory board in the unimposing lobby, was occupied by the Worldwide Wire Service.

The third floor hallway was lit by fluorescent glare and could have been located anywhere from Tallahassee to Timbuktu. The door to the room at the end was ajar. As I approached, I heard gasping, gurgling sounds. My steps slowed. I had done enough gasping and gurgling myself lately to know acute distress when I heard it. I tiptoed up and peeked in to see a broom-closet-sized office which was all but filled by two scarred desks. A woman sat at one of the desks, sobbing, head cradled in her arms. Her hair was carrot red, a wildly curly pre-Raphaelite cascade. She was wearing a shapeless, oatmeal-colored sweatsuit outfit that looked chic and expensive even at this disadvantageous angle. Her shoulders were heaving.

The question was whether to slip away, walk around the block, and return for a fresh start, or barge in and see what I could do. I was debating the point when a masculine voice behind me said, "I was afraid of this."

I jumped a mile. The speaker was a gray-haired, craggy man in his fifties who, I couldn't help noticing even under the circumstances, wasn't bad looking although his clothes were atrocious. His socks were drooping over his Hush Puppies, his pants were unpressed, his shirt bagged over his belt, his loosened tie was twenty years old at least. He smelled distinctly of cigarettes. Obviously, a newsman.

At his voice, the woman looked up, revealing the kind of cheekbones we all long for (wet, at the moment, with tears), green eyes, a generous mouth, and a furious pink facial flush. The man said, "He isn't worth it, Kitty," as he walked past me into the room. I hovered in the doorway, partly out of timidity and partly because there was no room inside for anybody else.

"Don't insult me, Jack," she said in a choked tone of outrage. "Do you really think I'd cry like this over Marc-Antoine?"

"Well, you told me this morning the two of you had split. What else am I supposed to think?"

"Think what wonders it's going to do for my waistline! Who needs a pastry chef hanging around?"

"Why aren't you laughing, then?"

Her face crumpled and she buried it in her hands. "Felicia told me this afternoon she's going back to Barcelona. Carlos finally wrote to her."

The man had worked his way around the desks to the room's one window. He perched on the sill, fished a cigarette out of his pocket, and lit it. "Is that all? You've known for months that was probably going to happen. You'll get somebody else to share the office."

"It isn't just that." Her voice was muffled by her hands.

"What else?"

"Teddy spiked my piece about the *parfumeur*." The sentence ended in a wail and her shoulders started to shake again.

He tapped ashes into his pants cuff and said, "The one about the old guy who mixes the scent especially for each customer? Cute old Monsieur Whatsisname, with his workroom on the Rue St. Sulpice?"

"Yes! Monsieur Dupont will be *so* disappointed. He was really happy about the story, all excited. I could *kill* Teddy. He said it was too lightweight."

You can believe that my hand was sneaking into my purse toward my notebook while I repeated, over and over to myself, "Monsieur Dupont. Rue St. Sulpice." If the old boy could talk slowly enough for me to understand him, he might get his story yet.

"It probably *was* too lightweight for Teddy," the man was saying.

She looked up and said, furiously, "Whose side are you on, Jack?" Her gaze swung toward me. "And why don't you introduce me to your friend?"

They both looked at me. I froze, my hand in my purse, feeling as if I'd been caught picking a pocket.

Jack, of course, said, "*My* friend?" and

25

then I had to step in and explain that I was in fact *her* friend, if anybody's.

That was the beginning. With Kitty's help, I wrote up Monsieur Dupont, the charming perfume-maker, for my first *Good Look* column, and it passed muster with Loretta. After Felicia went back to Barcelona, I moved in to share the broom-closet office. Twinkie came out from under the bed. I bought a fringed tablecloth and a couple of red geraniums. My French improved.

And just when I was starting to get comfortable, I witnessed a murder.

A TAXI RIDE

I was never one of those reporters who pant to be first at the scene of a dreadful occurrence. My kind of journalistic tragedy was two women showing up at a party wearing identical dresses. I hated writing obituaries and wouldn't have dreamed of taking the police beat even if an editor had dreamed of offering it to me. Cold-blooded murder, in other words, was not in my repertoire.

It was October. I'd been in Paris almost four months, and had scrambled for four columns. Since I was still shaky in the language and in my knowledge of the city, I hadn't yet come up with anything too original, but I had learned long ago that writing the same stories over and over is an honored tradition in journalism. I'd done the ice cream at Berthillon and gained three pounds in a week of sampling *chocolat au nougat* and *praliné aux pignons*. To compensate, I'd done Parisian swimming pools. I'd done street markets, tramping up and down the Rue Mouffetard, hovering at the intersection of Rue de Seine and Rue de Buci with a shopping bag too heavy to carry. Fired with misguided enthusiasm, I bought sea urchins at a fish stall. We'd had sea urchins aplenty in Cross Beach. Why had we never thought of eating them? After I made the attempt, the answer was obvious.

Loretta continued to like my columns, but she also continued to be parsimonious. On the other hand, now that "Paris Patter" (the title was Loretta's brainstorm) looked like a going concern, I began to get on the invitation lists for press bashes. Often, in lieu of dinner, I could nibble flaky pastries filled with mushroom purée at parties to celebrate a new sportswear line or a restaurant opening. Still, I was always short of cash. If I were going to get my hair cut at a decent salon and feed Twinkie the best *paté pour chat* money could buy, my scope had to expand beyond "Paris Patter."

It was in the worthy cause of financial improvement, then, that I found myself, that bright October morning, sharing a taxi with a British art conservator named Clive Overton. The worst problem I had in the world was the suspicion that he was going to stick me with the fare. The second worst problem, which promised to be more serious in the long run, was that Overton, a man in his forties who had the general demeanor of a mackerel, was showing no inclination to talk to me.

"He'll probably be one of those really charming British guys with a dry wit and lots of anecdotes," Kitty had said, urging me to take over the assignment. It had originally been offered to her by an American popular science magazine, but she was too busy to do it.

"Yeah, but I don't know anything about restoring damaged art works, and this man is a master in the field."

"So, he'll tell you about what he does. That's the story."

I balked. "I just don't feel right about it."

"O.K." Kitty dropped Overton's bio on

her desk and started to dial her phone. While she waited for whomever she was calling to answer, she mentioned the figure the magazine was willing to pay for the Overton profile.

So here I was in the taxi with Overton who, if indeed he was a charming British guy with a dry wit and lots of anecdotes, was keeping the fact under wraps. When I'd picked him up at his hotel, the Relais Christine, he'd said hello. That was it so far.

We were barreling along the Seine at a speed any non-Parisian would consider excessive. It was a lovely day, by far the prettiest since I'd been in Paris. The river gleamed deep green. Sea gulls wheeled. A barge pushed upstream, a line of laundry flapping from its deck. The sun had started to creep over the stones of the quay. Maybe Overton had simply turned away from me to enjoy the scene in peace. I stared at the back of his neatly barbered blond head and the rolls of pudge above his collar. His hands, I noticed, were clasped together so tightly the ends of his fingers were white.

Maybe the idea of publicity freaked him out. But if so, why had he consented to the story? Why had he asked me to come with him to the museum and watch him in action?

Overton cleared his throat noisily. I leaned toward him eagerly, hoping he was about to speak, but after a couple of final hawks he turned back to the window. At last, unable to stand it any longer, I fished out my notebook, uncapped my pen, and said, "Why don't I ask a few preliminary questions. Can you tell me something about the Musée Bellefroide?"

He looked around at me, bulging blue eyes as shocked as if I'd asked him whether he wore boxer shorts or jockeys. After due consideration he said, "Lovely place."

"I haven't been there, myself," I said. "I haven't lived in Paris very long. I moved over here with my cat a few months ago. I came from Florida, in the southern part of the United States. But anyway, I'm looking forward to seeing the museum."

When I'm nervous, I tend to run on a bit.

Although I hadn't seen the Bellefroide, I had done my homework about it, which meant I'd asked both Kitty and Jack Arlen. Jack, the man I'd met the day I met Kitty, turned out to be the Paris bureau chief for the Worldwide Wire Service. "I think the Bellefroides were bankers. The museum is the former family mansion," Kitty had told me. "It's gorgeous. Walls decorated with carved wood, magnificent eighteenth-century furniture, a marble grand staircase, display cabinets of Sèvres porcelain—all that."

"It's kind of a mixed bag, though," said Jack. "Some of the paintings have been de-attributed, or whatever you call it. You know—'School of Rembrandt' instead of Rembrandt. And each of the Bellefroides had his own interest, so there'll be a case of Japanese netsukes, and then a case of enameled snuffboxes, and then a case of . . . of . . ."

"Dog figurines," said Kitty.

"Yeah. They've got masterpieces and junk side by side, and under the terms of the will, or the trust, or whatever, it all has to be kept together, just as it was when the old man died."

All of this Overton had compressed into "lovely place." I sucked on the end of my pen, and Overton looked out the window.

The taxi was stuck in traffic. Horns blared. The driver's dog, a brown mongrel which until now had been dozing in the front seat, unfolded himself and gave us a pink-tongued, doggy smile. No wonder he was smiling. He didn't have to interview Clive Overton. I

31

tried again. "What will you be doing at the Bellefroide?"

"Altarpiece. Water damage."

I wrote "Altarpiece. Water damage" in my notebook.

Our taxi driver, a woman with short, bleached-blond hair under a checked newsboy's cap, hit the horn. She rolled down her window, stuck her head out, and drew a deep breath. Before she had time to let loose with whatever she'd been planning to shriek, we began to move.

I said, desperately, *"What* altarpiece? *What* water damage?"

"Leak." (That had to be "water damage.") He continued, "Flemish. Early fifteenth century. Madonna and Child. Wood. Porous."

I wrote it all down, but with a sensation of futility. If Overton didn't become more articulate, there wouldn't be a story. Maybe he'd unbend once we got to the museum. By now, we were gliding down the quiet, tree-lined streets of the sixteenth *arrondissement,* the most posh and proper district in Paris. We pulled up in front of a square, solid-looking house of gray stone, chestnut-shaded and discreetly sumptuous behind a hedge. While Overton (to my relief) paid the taxi driver, the massive dark green front door opened and a small, sharp-faced man wearing rimless round glasses emerged.

The day's third problem presented itself. The small man, who had a headful of dark curls and was wearing a nubby brown wool suit too heavy for the weather, shot a disapproving look at me and immediately began speaking to Overton with excited Gallic volubility. He was obviously protesting about something, but it took me a while to figure out that he was protesting about me.

Once I got the drift, I started picking up words like *"sécurité."* I gathered that Overton hadn't let him know I was coming along, and it was too early for official visiting hours, and the whole thing was seriously against regulations. (Going against regulations, I had already discovered during my brief time in France, was not something a person could expect to do without suffering for it.) The Frenchman's glasses flashed, he gestured, he said—and I understood him distinctly—"You take too much upon yourself, Monsieur!"

Overton, at least a head taller and a lot bulkier, seemed totally unmoved. "Madame uh—" he glanced at me for help.

"Maxwell."

"Madame Maxwell is here at my invitation." His French was exquisite.

"Yes, but you see—" and the man was off again, citing the intricacies of museum opening hours and unexpected visitors from the press.

Overton waited stolidly for him to finish, then said, "Madame Maxwell is here at my invitation."

I was amazed that Overton felt obliged to champion me, instead of bundling me into another taxi and sending me on my way. I stood by, peering past the Frenchman's shoulder to the dim interior of the museum, where a guard in a navy blue uniform hovered.

Overton won. The Frenchman gave way with a shrug that involved his entire upper torso. Overton turned to me and said, "Georgia Lee Maxwell, may I present Bernard Mallet, director of the Musée Bellefroide?"

Trying not to look triumphant, I shook Mallet's hand and we followed him inside. Overton had paid for the cab. I hadn't been turned away at the museum door. The day had begun to go all right.

IN THE MUSÉE BELLEFROIDE

WHEN I walked into the Musée Bellefroide, for some reason I thought of Cecilia Driscoll and her house on Rhododendron Road, which supposedly had a foyer with a "cathedral ceiling." Cathedral ceiling, pooh. Even furnished with a ticket-taker's desk and a wire rack of postcards, the Bellefroide's foyer made Cecilia's look sick. It was oval-shaped, the floor a checkerboard of black and white marble. A wide staircase with an ornate railing swept upward under a huge, unlit chandelier. Tall urns stood in niches, sconces flowered from the walls. The atmosphere was hushed, as if the rich people who lived here were still asleep upstairs, unaware of less fortunate early risers tiptoeing around below.

Mallet gestured to us to follow him, and we went down a hall paneled in sculpted wood, past a series of open doors. I got a blurred impression of paintings and tapestries, gilded furniture, sculpted busts on mar-

35

ble pedestals, twisted candelabra. Light reflected off glass-fronted display cases. Through the tall windows, I glimpsed a sun-dappled garden.

Mallet unhitched a red velvet rope barrier and we went down a staircase that was very plain-looking after the luxury we'd just passed. At the bottom was a hall with a linoleum floor. Mallet went to a closed door and pulled a ring of keys from his pocket. After he unlocked the door he pushed it open and stood back, ushering us in.

I got a brief impression of what seemed to be a storage room. An altarpiece, surely the Madonna and Child Overton had come to inspect, was standing on a table. The walls were lined with wooden cabinets and shelves, and there was a smell of paint and glue.

I had no intimations of disaster, no feelings of foreboding. My mind was on the story, on whether Overton would unbend. My overriding emotion was modest hope.

The first hint of anything extraordinary was a loud clattering on the staircase we had just descended. A moment later, three people burst violently into the room.

One of them, stumbling as if he'd been pushed, was the blue-uniformed guard I'd seen upstairs. The other two wore jeans, burgundy-colored ski masks, brown leather bomber jackets, and gloves. Both of them had stubby black guns. They looked around at us. One of them rapped out some sort of order in French.

It was the most ungodly nightmare. Here were these killers, or terrorists, or who knew what, telling us to do something, and they were telling us in French. At that moment, I couldn't have understood *Bonjour*. But the others—the guard, Mallet, Overton—were getting on the floor and lying face down, so I did the same. In a second, one of the intruders grabbed my wrists and taped them together, tight. I heard them shuffling around taping the others.

I lay with my nose pressed against the cold linoleum, wishing to God I'd never left Florida. Any indignity I'd had to put up with at the *Sun* was nothing compared to this. I was going to be killed, and all because of a story about art conservation that probably wouldn't have worked out anyway. I thought about Mama and Daddy, and about Twinkie, who was just getting adjusted to Paris. I'm happy to say I didn't give more than a passing thought to Ray Brown, the man I'd left in Bay City who wasn't worth a damn.

All of this took just seconds. I heard a drawer opening and closing. The back of my head prickled. In everything I'd read about these situations, people got shot in the back of the head. The prickling became a numbness that crawled down my neck and along my spine.

Only a moment later, the shot came. First one, then another, deafening in the quiet room. My body jerked with such force I almost thought I'd been hit. There was no sound, no cry. Then running feet, the door slamming, the key turning in the lock, where Bernard Mallet had left it.

Now Mallet was on his feet, hurling himself against the door, crying, "Stop!" in an anguished tone. Overton and I were struggling to our knees. He was so pale that his lips looked purple. All three of us, it seemed, realized at the same time that the guard wasn't moving.

His navy blue cap had fallen off. His head was a bloody mess. I remembered thinking: I was right. They *do* shoot in the back of the head. I felt as if the real me, the me who would have been horrified, was hovering somewhere out of reach. Mallet said, "Pierre!" and dropped to his knees at the guard's side.

The guard was dead. We had plenty of time to free our hands and make sure of it in the surreal interval before other members of the museum staff arrived for work, let us out, and called the police.

We didn't talk much during that time. Overton sat in a chair, half-closed eyes fixed on the floor, hands pressed between his knees, hunched as if in pain. I gnawed my lips and stared at the guard. I couldn't seem to look anywhere else. The sticky, oozing wound, the body slumped gracelessly in the blue uniform, the scuffed brown shoes pulled my eyes. I couldn't see his face. I tried to remember what it had looked like, but could only summon up his slightly bushy salt-and-pepper eyebrows. Pierre, his name had been. I swallowed. Pierre.

Bernard Mallet, meanwhile, was busy searching the storage room, opening cabinets and drawers. The altarpiece hadn't been taken. It sat on the table exactly where it had been, looking impossibly serene. When I heard Mallet give an inarticulate, shocked cry, I dragged my attention from the dead man.

Mallet's face was rigid. Behind his glasses, his dark eyes were blank. "How very bizarre," he said. "They've stolen Nostradamus's mirror."

Weirdly enough, I understood him perfectly, even though he spoke in French. I had understood everything everybody had said since the gunshots. I understood something else, too. I may never have been on the police beat, but I knew what a story was. I definitely had a story here.

NOSTRADAMUS'S MIRROR

A traveling carnival came to Cross Beach every year, and set up in a weed-grown vacant lot. Somewhere in the warren of knocked-together booths where you won teddy bears or bought candy apples, between the Loop-the-Loop and the Ferris Wheel, would be a fortune-teller's booth. "See the Future!" the weather-beaten sign out front might read. "The Wisdom of Nostradamus Reveals All!" As a child, no matter how many times I was dared to, I wouldn't go in. I felt even then it was a dangerous business.

The inspector from the Criminal Brigade who interviewed me was an older man, balding and dapper. He didn't show much reaction as I bumbled through my story, and if he made an effort to put me at ease, I missed it. What he wanted to know, several times, in French and in English, was why I just happened to show up, unexpectedly, at the Bellefroide that particular morning. Obviously, Bernard Mallet had told of his attempt to defend the museum against me. Any hope that Clive Overton would be a strong supporter of my version of events was in vain. When the police arrived, he had collapsed—taken two steps and gone down like a ton of bricks. They had to cart him away before they could gather up the guard's body, and for all I knew, Overton was dead of a heart attack by now.

"Please explain to me again, Madame . . . Mademoiselle . . ."

"Madame." There's no French equivalent of Ms. I wouldn't have been Madame Maxwell (my maiden name), but Madame Boyette, but what did it matter now? I was too old to be Mademoiselle anything.

"Yes. You say Monsieur Overton suggested that you accompany him here this morning?"

"That's right. I called him about an article I was gong to write about him, and I asked if I could see him in action—you know, on the job. And he said he was coming to the

41

Musée Bellefroide, and I could come along with him."

"When did this conversation take place?"

"Yesterday afternoon."

"So you came here very much at the last minute."

"Well—yes." Was doing something at the last minute a crime in France? I felt guilty. I started to dry my palms on my skirt, then realized how suspicious *that* looked and stopped fast, and then saw that he'd been watching the whole time.

We went through it again. If my story had begun to sound as unlikely to him as it did to me, I was in trouble. And in the meantime, what did *I* know about what had happened? Precious little.

The dead guard's name was Pierre Legrand. He was fifty years old, and had worked at the museum for several years. If he had made some attempt to stop the robbery, none of us had realized it. Nobody could figure out why he had been shot, or why the mirror—a fortune-telling mirror that supposedly had belonged to the prophet Nostradamus—had been stolen.

The inspector released me in time for Bernard Mallet's press conference, which was good because in the midst of everything I had managed to call and pitch my eyewitness account to the *International Herald Tribune*, the Paris-based English-language newspaper that was distributed all over the world. They had jumped at it, offering to pay me a pittance plus cab fare. The glory, however, would be considerable.

As I headed for the *salon* where the conference was to take place, the television lights went on and I was suddenly surrounded by microphones. Blinking, trying to rise above the thought of how dreadful I must look, I listened carefully to the questions being tossed at me but heard only gibberish. I mustered my best accent and said, in French, "I was afraid. It was horrible." When their further efforts didn't produce anything else from me, they switched off the lights and I went into the elegant, bow-windowed room and took a place in a row of gilt chairs more appropriate for an afternoon chamber-music concert than for the eager and rambunctious press.

Now it was Bernard Mallet's turn. His perspiring face was liverish in the television glare. "The mirror wasn't even on display. From the artistic point of view, it wasn't at all important," he was saying. He sounded aggrieved, as if the theft of something as unworthy as Nostradamus's mirror had been an insult to the Musée Bellefroide.

My pocket-sized tape recorder, brought along to catch all the goodies Overton never said, was winding. I put intense effort into understanding what was going on, and succeeded fairly well. Someone asked, "Could you describe the mirror for us?"

"The mirror is not the sort of glass mirror we are accustomed to today," Mallet said. He consulted a piece of paper. He held it with both hands, but it trembled even so. After clearing his throat, he read, "The mirror is made of polished obsidian, which is a black volcanic glass. It is approximately circular, fifteen centimeters in diameter, one and a half centimeters thick." (I had learned to do the conversions. About six inches in diameter, three-quarters of an inch thick.) "It is in a green, tooled-leather case which dates from much later than the mirror itself."

Another question: "It's origin?"

"Such mirrors were made by the Aztecs in Mexico. Some were brought to Europe by Cortés and his followers in the middle of the sixteenth century."

A heavyset man in the front row rose majestically to his feet. *"Monsieur le Directeur,* does this Aztec mirror have any particular interest or value, aside from being an example of an ancient handicraft?"

The questioner's smarmy tone betrayed that he knew the answer already. Mallet looked like a man about to eat an obviously spoiled mussel. "Legend claims that the mirror once belonged to the prophet Nostradamus," he said. "There is absolutely no proof that this is true."

Everyone had known, but still the words caused a stir in the room, and it was a moment or two before the heavyset man could go on. "Do you mean that Nostradamus supposedly looked into this mirror to see the future, to help him make his famous predictions?"

"So it was said," Mallet answered miserably. In the hubbub that followed he continued, in a stronger tone, "I must repeat that there is no basis for that assertion!"

Of course nobody wanted to hear that. The questions flew:

"Were other such mirrors used in divination?"

"How did the Bellefroide acquire this mirror?"

"Is it recorded that Nostradamus used a mirror?"

"I am not an expert on magic, or divination, or Nostradamus!" Mallet snapped. "Apparently, mirrors are used in fortune-telling in much the same way as crystal balls, or other reflecting surfaces. I can tell you that another mirror of this particular type, one which belonged to the British sorcerer Dr. John Dee, is on display in the British Museum. I can also tell you that the Bellefroide's mirror was acquired toward the middle of the nineteenth century by François Bellefroide, a family member with an interest in the occult. In his catalogue of purchases, he noted"—Mallet read from the paper again—" 'A divining mirror once used by the celebrated prophet Nostradamus,' and the dimensions I have just given to you. To be frank, I suspect that the seller fabricated the Nostradamus story in hopes of getting a better price."

"And who was the seller?"

"A Monsieur J. Claude, of a firm of dealers in antiquities and curios called Claude et Fils. The firm no longer exists."

"Who owned the mirror before Monsieur Claude?"

"I have no idea." Mallet looked relieved to say so.

The questions drifted back to the break-in and murder, and Mallet explained once again that the criminals had apparently forced their way past the guard, Pierre Legrand, after Overton and I had been let in. The look he shot me said it was all my fault.

The heavyset man was on his feet again, addressing Mallet with ponderous politeness: "It seems these thieves had chosen their time to strike. There were early visitors, the storage room would be unlocked. How might they have come to know this?"

Mallet's face froze. "I can't imagine."

"You can imagine no way such knowledge could be obtained?" The edge of sarcasm was obvious, even to me.

Mallet drew himself up and said, "Monsieur, if you are implicating me or my staff in this tragedy, let me point out that anyone with inside knowledge would surely have chosen an easier way to steal the mirror. The storage room is locked, yes, but the mirror was hardly our most precious holding. Taking it would have been simple enough. This cumbersome, murderous episode was completely unnecessary."

After that, things started to slow down. I paged back through my notes. Thank God Kitty had been in the office and willing to go down the hall and look up Nostradamus for me in the Worldwide Wire Service encyclopedia. I hadn't even known whether he was an actual person or a legend, but he turned out to be totally historical: "His real name was Michel de Nostredame," Kitty had said. "Dates 1503 to 1566. Born and lived most of his life in the south of France. Profession doctor—"

"Medical, you mean?"

"Yes. Did a lot of work with victims of the plague. He published a collection of obscure rhymed prophecies called *The Centuries,* and a lot of what he predicted seems to have come true. He was a favorite of Catherine de Medici, wife of King Henry II. One of his biggest coups was predicting Henry's death, but that doesn't seem to have turned Catherine off. It doesn't say whether he used mirrors."

The press conference was breaking up. My story was almost done, written at one of the Bellefroide's office desks while I waited my turn to be questioned by the police. I'd go to the *Herald Tribune* and add the press conference stuff when I entered it in the computer. It was midafternoon when I left the Bellefroide and stepped out again into the glorious weather.

All went well at the *Herald Tribune.* The familiarity of being in a newspaper office, sitting and staring at my copy on the VDT screen, was vaguely calming. They were talking page one for the story. I'd written it in third person, but it would run with an italic precede saying I'd been on the scene when it happened. Tomorrow morning, my words would be spread to all points of the globe. Odd, how numb I felt about it all.

I got a taxi on the Avenue Charles de Gaulle and headed home. Halfway there, I started to shake. By the time we pulled up at my building on the Rue Delacôte I could hardly totter inside. Fitting my key in the lock was a project, and when I finally got the door open I sat down on the floor right inside, and Twinkie came and nudged curiously at my fingers.

THE SPECULATORI

THE phone rang a couple of times that afternoon, journalists calling with follow-up questions, but my French was deserting me fast. Also, although I was sure I hadn't heard the last of the police, I had had enough of them for one day. After a final check with the *Herald Tribune*, I took the receiver off the hook and got in bed. Sunlight flooded in from the balcony, where Twinkie was crouched next to the geraniums, her tail twitching as she studied the scene below. I clasped my hands on my chest and watched the dust motes spinning in the rays of light.

Pride goeth before destruction, and a haughty spirit before a fall, the voice of one of my early Sunday school teachers whispered to me. Yes, I had been proud. Too proud to apologize to Cecilia Driscoll. Too proud to stay in my proper place and sphere, which was the Florida panhandle. Haughtily, I had flown off to an alien environment, and look what had happened. I began to sniffle, and I regret to say my tears were not for the death of my fellow human being Pierre Legrand, but for my own poor self. The mood of misery and self-recrimination continued until I was so worn out I fell asleep.

A knocking sound awakened me some time later. It was dusk. A chilly wind blew in through the half-open balcony door. The knock sounded again, louder. Quivering, I sat up, pulling the covers around me. Figures wearing ski masks and carrying guns tumbled through my mind in the couple of seconds before I heard Kitty calling, "Georgia Lee? Are you there?"

I jumped out of bed and ran to the door,

50

ready to weep with relief. She looked so beautiful and familiar, with her blazing hair and her odd clothes (today it was caramel-colored leather, with buckles at unexpected places. She got her outfits practically free, I had learned, from a friend in the *couture*). Tears did fill my eyes when I saw that she had a *baguette* in one hand and a plastic bag from the *charcuterie* across the street in the other. The scent of freshly roasted chicken came through the door with her. "I tried and tried to call," she said. "Is your phone off the hook?"

"I was being hounded by the press."

As I went to replace the receiver, she said, "How do you feel? O.K.?"

"Oh—I guess."

Kitty was glamorous, knowledgeable, younger than I was, and fluent in French. She was also warm, helpful, and kind. All this put a heavy burden on our friendship. Although I knew she had suffered, having married a Frenchman who turned out to be a dissolute ne'er-do-well, she didn't seem to suffer in the same tacky ways I did. Her Frenchman had been a member of the minor nobility. She had done her suffering in places like Cannes and Gstaad. And now, having freed herself from Monsieur de Villiers-

Marigny, she was pluckily making her way as a free-lance journalist, using her high-class connections to get fancy assignments. If she hadn't been so thoroughly likable, I'd have detested her. As it was, I stood a little in awe of her, and sometimes found it hard to talk to her about how I really felt.

We got ready for dinner. As she set the table she said, "I'll bet you're thinking about going back to Florida."

I was in my tiny kitchen heating up the creamed spinach she'd brought to go with the chicken and bread. My face burned, and I stirred with sudden energy. I didn't *have* to talk to her about how I felt. She knew without my saying anything. "Look at it this way," I said. "In all my years in Cross Beach and Bay City, nobody ever taped my hands behind me. Nobody ever shot another person in the back of the head in my presence."

"That's right." She came to the kitchen doorway, carrying the chicken in its foil bag. She said, "If you decide not to be ordinary, extraordinary things are more likely to happen to you. Some of them may be hideous. That's why so few people risk it."

Why did she have to be wise, too, on top of everything else? "What time is it? We aren't missing the news, are we?" I said grumpily.

In fact, we had almost finished eating before the television news came on at eight. Robbery and murder at the Musée Bellefroide took a back seat to several developments on the international scene, but when it came up they gave it a lot of play. The segment had: the obligatory family snapshot of Pierre Legrand, a man with salt-and-pepper hair and eyebrows, standing with a laughing, dark-haired woman identified by the commentator as his wife; a woodcut of Nostradamus; exterior shots of the Bellefroide, looking tranquil under its chestnut trees; a long excerpt from the press conference, featuring a perspiring Bernard Mallet; a policeman assuring everyone that the police were continuing their investigations; and, finally, me, saying, "I was afraid. It was horrible."

Kitty clapped me on the shoulder. "Good show, Georgia Lee. Your accent was perfect."

My hair had been sticking out in every direction, the bow on my blouse hanging half-untied. My eyes, which are gray and one of my decent features, had had an unattractive maniacal glint. My accent had been, in my estimation, only fair. "So that's that," I said, as the next story unfolded on the screen. "That and the piece in the *Herald Tribune* tomorrow."

Kitty gave me a funny look. "What do you mean, 'That's that'?"

I shrugged. "I mean that's that. It's over, thank heavens. Except I'm sure I'll have to talk to the police a few more times."

"You mean, you're not going to keep following the story?"

The thought of staying with it had occurred to me, naturally. I shrugged again, feeling uncomfortable. "Who would I write it for? The *Herald Tribune* won't have space for it, day after day." I was right about that, but I knew it sounded lame. "And besides"— I was groping—"it's unpleasant, Kitty. Pierre Legrand was killed, in cold blood. I don't want to revel in it, to keep making hay out of somebody's death."

She got up and started to clear the dishes. "I admire your delicacy, Georgia Lee."

What a liar. "Stop ridiculing me."

"No, I do. Really."

"What are you trying to say?"

She dumped the dishes in the kitchen and came back. "I'm saying, *you* didn't kill Pierre Legrand. What good will it do anybody for you to walk away from Nostradamus's mirror? It's the story of a lifetime."

"Look. The *Herald Tribune*—"

She shook her head. "You know I don't mean doing news reports every day. That'll be taken care of. I mean keep up with the investigation. Do it in depth, for a magazine. Or you could even do a book. You were *there*."

"Kitty, I'm not now and never have been a police reporter—"

She put up her hands in an "I surrender" gesture. "Do what you want. I'm just saying, it's a hell of a story."

She retreated into the kitchen and started rattling dishes and running water, leaving me sitting at the table rolling bread crumbs between my finger and thumb.

Yes, dammit. It was a hell of a story. All my newspapering instincts urged me onward, and yet I'd been badly shaken. I wanted to retreat, to write about next year's trends in panty hose, or the relative sodium content of the various mineral waters. Who was Kitty to make me feel guilty? The most dangerous thing she ever wrote about was Alpine skiing. Even though it was a good story, and I'd been there, that didn't make me obligated to stay on it, did it? I wasn't morally obliged, was I, to—

The telephone rang and automatically I

went to answer it, still chewing over the argument. The voice on the other end spoke in English, with a heavy French accent: "This is Georgia Lee Maxwell?"

"Yes."

"The incident at the Bellefroide today. Bernard Mallet is responsible." The person speaking, a man I thought, was in the grip of some strong emotion, his voice harshly burdened. The name Bernard Mallet was pronounced with such loathing that I shivered.

I wish I could report that I said something cleverer than, "What are you talking about? Who are you?" but I can't.

"Bernard Mallet is guilty." The words were like an incantation.

I grabbed the pen next to the phone pad and started taking notes. "What do you mean? He was tied up with the rest of us."

"Pierre Legrand died because of Bernard Mallet."

"You'll have to explain. Who are you?"

"Bernard Mallet knows who we are. Ask Bernard Mallet." I heard what sounded like a choked sob.

"How can I ask, if I don't know who—"

"The Speculatori. Ask him how he betrayed us, how he betrayed the mirror of Nostradamus."

"The Spec what? I can't understand you." His accent was so heavy, he might as well have been speaking French.

"The Speculatori."

"Well, listen. What do—" Click. He had hung up, in the time-honored tradition of anonymous callers. I hung up, too, and sat on the bed hugging my elbows.

Kitty had come out of the kitchen in the middle of all this and was standing there with her eyebrows approaching her hairline. When I repeated the conversation she said, "Some nut case who saw you on the tube and got your number from information?"

"I don't know. Whoever it was really believed what he was saying. He was practically crying. It wasn't a joke."

"Bernard Mallet is the museum director, right? What *about* him?"

I thought. "He's just a bureaucrat, kind of snooty—" I remembered how he hadn't wanted to let me in the museum. "Actually, he's an uptight little jerk."

After I told her how he had tried to keep me out she said, thoughtfully, "If he knew something was about to happen, he might

57

not have wanted an extra person around. Maybe that's why he go so upset."

"Yeah, but what about Overton? He knew Overton was coming."

"Well, without Overton, there would have been no excuse to unlock the storage room."

We looked at each other blankly. It didn't make the slightest bit of sense. "You're probably right. It was a crazy person who saw Mallet and me on television and worked up a fantasy," I said at last, wishing I were convinced.

Kitty nodded. "I've always heard things like that happen when there's a sensational story." After a pause that vibrated with disbelief she said, "I brought meringues for dessert. Marc-Antoine dropped some by the office."

"He's still trying to woo you back through your sweet tooth?"

"According to Marc-Antoine, his ability to create the perfect meringue and my ability to appreciate it are all that's needed for a full relationship."

As we stuffed ourselves, I was thinking. My caller had said Bernard Mallet was guilty, and he'd said it with conviction. Had Mallet's behavior in trying to keep me out of the Bellefroide been extreme? Or had it been, as

I'd thought at the time, the pathological insistence on following protocol that was typical of any French bureaucracy? I tried to fight it, but I found myself wanting to know the answer.

Kitty said, "Speculatori. Like speculate?"

"Or speculum."

"Yuk! Isn't that the thing the gynecologist—"

"Yes, it is. But doesn't it have something to do with mirrors? I'd swear it does."

"I don't know. You could look it up in the unabridged tomorrow."

"I will. I'm going to do something else, too."

"What's that?"

"I'm going to ask Bernard Mallet."

She smiled. I smiled. I was on the story.

A TALK WITH MALLET

BERNARD MALLET and I sat facing each other across his desk. His office was small but well appointed, with Japanese prints, a wall of built-in bookcases, an Oriental rug. Behind him, windows overlooked the Bellefroide garden.

Mallet, I surmised, had had a bad night.

His skin was yellowish, and his glasses magnified the bruise-colored circles under his eyes. He looked at me from under his tumble of curls like a scared animal peering from beneath a bush.

Still, he was doing his best to be rude. He spoke with exaggerated slowness, as if he thought me deficient not only in French but in intelligence, too. He received the news that I intended to keep working on the story with a further thinning of lips already pressed together. Then I mentioned the Speculatori.

He tensed. He said, "How do you know of them?"

"I got a call from one of them last night."

He seemed to be trying to smile scornfully while I recounted the conversation, but his mouth kept twisting into some other expression. When I finished, he said, "Naturally, they wouldn't ignore this opportunity to taunt me."

"Who are they?"

He didn't answer. Through the window I could see sun sifting through golden leaves, white stone urns trailing ivy, gravel walks, a wall with green treillage. At last he said, "You have told the police?"

"Not yet."

"Why not?" he flung out bitterly. "They

will surely want to know that I have been the . . . the mastermind, the one responsible for the crime?"

I was wilting under his challenge. This was a lot harder than asking for a list of the sponsors of a charity cotillion. I had marched in and repeated an accusation that Mallet was guilty of the death of Pierre Legrand. I couldn't expect him to like it. "I wanted to see what you had to say about it first," I said, preventing myself, with some difficulty, from begging his pardon.

He sat back in his chair. "What do I have to say? I will not dignify such charges with any comment."

Well. I may be a softhearted former society columnist, but I'm not a marshmallow. "Monsieur Mallet, the call I got was unexpected, but I consider it my duty as a journalist to follow it up," I said as sweetly as I could. "If you won't talk with me, I'll have to ask others."

Faced with that one, few people will refuse to have their say, and Mallet wasn't one of the few. He twitched and said, "Why should I be at the mercy of those lunatics?"

We were over the hurdle. "What lunatics?"

"The so-called Speculatori."

61

"Who are they?"

He gave an exasperated sigh. "A group of misfits who imagine themselves to be psychics, seers, I don't know what. The very simple story is this: They wanted the mirror, which they devoutly believe, upon no factual basis whatsoever, to have belonged to Nostradamus and therefore to be a sacred object. I refused to give it to them, or sell it to them. Consequently, they detest me."

I wasn't sure I'd understood. "You mean, *they* wanted the mirror, yet they're accusing *you*—"

"Ironic, isn't it? They are themselves by far the most likely suspects. And, before you ask, yes, I have informed the police."

"But what basis would they have for saying you're responsible?"

"To divert suspicion from themselves, perhaps. Or to create trouble for me, which seems to be one of their major interests. I don't know."

"But if they weren't the thieves. Would they think the mirror was stolen because you weren't taking good care of it, or something?"

His narrow face flushed. He said, vehemently, "In the Musée Bellefroide, we have silver terrines that once stood on the table of the Russian imperial court. We have a collection of exquisitely crafted gold caskets decorated with pearls and gemstones. We have Ming vases, candelabra by Francois-Thomas Germain, Savonnerie carpets. All these precious things are under my care. All of them."

"I just meant—"

"If thieves and murderers choose to attack the Bellefroide, and if they choose to steal the least interesting, the least valuable, item in the collection, how am I to be prepared for that? Do you have an answer?"

By this time, he was red down into his collar, and the cords in his neck were sticking out. His stewardship of the Bellefroide collection must be his sore spot. I backed off. "When did the Speculatori first approach you about the mirror?"

"The first time was a year or more ago. They continued to contact me over a period of about six months, until I told them categorically that they were wasting their time and mine, and we would have no further discussion."

A thought had struck me. "The mirror was kept in storage, and wasn't displayed. You say it doesn't have much artistic value."

"That's right."

"Well, then. Why not sell it to the

Speculatori? I mean, if they thought it was sacred, and really prized it—"

I'd done it again. He drew himself up, looking terribly insulted. "Even if I had so little personal concern for the integrity of the Bellefroide collection, I would be forbidden to do such a thing by the terms of the trust that created the museum. The Bellefroide collection must be kept intact. If it is not, the museum will be dissolved."

Which seemed, I had to admit, a good enough reason to hold on to the mirror.

Mallet stirred restlessly. He was obviously sick of me, and I felt the same about him. "Just one more thing," I said, and watched his eyes roll upward. "Could you tell me how to contact the Speculatori? Give me the name of the person you dealt with?"

He stared for a moment in apparent disbelief before bursting out, "Surely you're asking too much, Madame! It isn't enough that I answer your questions about people who have cursed me, accused me baselessly. Now you want me to furnish their names and addresses, so you can go to them for more false accusations!"

Fine, fine. I moved to go. If he wouldn't tell me specifics, I'd find out about the Speculatori somewhere else. As I was about to get up, he took off his glasses and pressed his hands to his eyes. His fingernails were raggedly chewed, and his hands were as small as a child's. Abruptly and unexpectedly, I felt sorry for him. "Never mind," he said in a tired voice. "Ask my secretary. She will give you their names, addresses, whatever you want."

Intentionally, or not, he'd managed to leave me feeling ashamed of myself. I thanked him hurriedly and headed for the door. He didn't get up to usher me out. When I had my hand on the knob he said, "I presume you feel it is necessary to do this?"

I wondered if I really did. Where had last night's resolve gone? "Yes," I said.

"It could be dangerous. You've thought of that? Those people yesterday—they killed senselessly."

"I've thought about that," I said. It would have sounded more convincing if my voice hadn't cracked. I left him staring down at his desk, his eyes red.

CHANTAL

MALLET'S secretary gave me a contact for the Speculatori: Bruno Blanc, with an address on the Rue Jacob. I left the museum and wandered across the street to the Ranelagh Garden. Small children, carefully tended by mothers, nannies, or *au pairs*, shrieked and played, rode the shaggy ponies being led over fallen leaves on the wide paths, or waited a turn at the old-fashioned merry-go-round. It all seemed normal, healthy, vibrant, and completely strange. That I should be here at all, walking through autumn leaves in a Paris park, was strange. I had wanted to expand my world. I hadn't wanted to have it wrenched wide open so that murder, anonymous accusations, and warnings of danger could flood in, too.

Feeling unsettled, I sat down on a slatted bench of dark green wood. My story had run in the *Herald Tribune* that morning—front page, below the fold. Seeing the words in print had helped compartmentalize the experience in a way, and distance me from it. At least I'd gotten something out of it I could be proud of.

I guessed I should try to call Bruno Blanc, of the Speculatori, but I didn't feel ready. The secretary hadn't given me his number anyway, only an address. I thought I'd go there first, see what the place was like.

Idly, I watched the playing children. They

were adorable, in their brown high-topped shoes and knitted caps. Maybe I should've had a couple of my own, settled down with Lonnie Boyette, made the best of it. Or, if things had been different with Ray. . . .

I said, "Ha!" angrily, got up, and went to look for a phone booth so I could call Kitty and see what was happening at the office.

When I got her, she said, "Whoops. You just missed Jack. He had something to tell you."

I hung on while she went down the hall to Worldwide Wire Service to get him. Jack had lived in Paris twenty years. As Worldwide's bureau chief, he heard everything. Because he had a certain sloppy, nicotine-scented charm, I had made it my business to find out his marital status, which was: married. I suspected there had been something between him and Kitty at one time, though. He had finagled the office for her at a rent so cheap that it must have been done in the heat of passion.

He came on and said, "Nice piece in the *Herald Tribune* this morning."

I felt a rush of pleasure, coupled with a need to deprecate myself. "Thanks. I'm glad you liked it. I don't think it'll win any Pulitzers, though."

"Probably not." I kicked myself for not leaving well enough alone as he continued. "I was just looking for you. Chantal Legrand, the widow of the murdered guard, has agreed to come out of seclusion and meet with the press. I thought you'd want to go."

"I sure do."

He gave me an address and said, "It's an impasse off the Rue de Charonne. The best Métro is Ledru-Rollin. Starts in forty-five minutes."

"Hope I can make it in time. I'm out in the sixteenth. I just got through at the Bellefroide."

He chuckled. "The distance you'll cover is more than just spatial. See you there."

"Wait. You're going yourself?"

"Slow news day. *Ciao.*"

I sprinted for the Métro and climbed out at the Ledru-Rollin station directly across town in the eleventh *arrondissement*, with five minutes to spare. The Rue de Charonne was a plain, unprepossessing street, and I understood what Jack meant about the distance. Here were no designer clothing boutiques, expensive *chocolatiers*, glittering jeweler's windows. Instead, you had the *tabac*, the smoky café, the hardware store. The neighborhood was by no means a slum, but it was obviously working class.

The Legrand home was located in the Cour St. Jean, which was one of many short passages that opened on the street and led to cobblestoned courtyards. In my search for the right one I investigated several, and the Cour St. Jean was much like the others—a furniture-maker's workroom on the ground floor, peeling paint, empty window boxes, a rusting drainpipe. In a dim doorway at the end of the courtyard a man stood smoking a cigarette, a couple of cameras slung around his neck. Press photographers are instantly recognizable. When I said "Legrand?" he nodded and pointed up a staircase just inside the door.

The stairs were dark and dusty, no hint reaching them of the bright sun outside. A door at the top was open and a number of people—reporters, I assumed—were milling around in an oppressively furnished living room. A sofa and two chairs, obviously a "set," were upholstered in a muddy brown fabric, and interspersed among them were tables holding china figurines and demitasse cups. A huge and ugly sideboard, with multiple drawers and a glass front revealing shelves of flower-painted dishes and a couple of trophies, dominated one wall. Lace panels hung in the windows. A plaster figurine of the Virgin Mary stood on a doily atop a large television set.

A coat closet by the door stood ajar. As I hung up my jacket I spotted Jack. He ambled over, saying, "How do, Miss Georgia Lee."

Jack had decided to make much of my being Southern, and I had been "Honeychiled" almost to death. One of these days I'd talk to him about it, but the right time hadn't come. In the meantime, I tried to hold my own. "Hi, there, Yankee boy."

His notebook was open, and a ballpoint was perched behind his ear. "You just made it. She's coming out now."

As he spoke, a woman I recognized from the televised snapshot as Chantal Legrand entered the room, accompanied by a stout woman in black. She was dressed simply, in a man-tailored white blouse, navy blue skirt, and high-heeled navy pumps. Her face was pale and her hair, despite a couple of restraining combs, was a riotous chin-length mass of black ringlets. Even in those prim clothes, with her eyes red and swollen, she was undoubtedly one of the sexiest-looking women I had ever seen. Also, she was nowhere near fifty, the age of her murdered husband.

Jack and I exchanged glances. I was glad he was too much of a gentleman for low wolf whistles or lewd comments under his breath. We crowded with the others around the couch where Chantal Legrand was now seated, sipping water from a glass handed to her by the woman in black.

The first questions were predictable, her answers nearly inaudible. How did she feel? Shocked and sad. What sort of person was her husband? A wonderful man. Did she have any comment on the reports—

Her head went up. Her jaw tightened. "Yes." she said. "It is because of those reports that I have agreed to see you today."

Evidently, I'd missed something. I'd been so interested in my own piece in the *Herald Tribune* that I hadn't slogged through the write-ups in all the French papers. "What reports?" I whispered to Jack, who made a shushing motion and didn't even glance at me.

"Some of the newspapers have been unkind enough to imply that my husband might himself have been involved in the theft at the Musée Bellefroide," she continued. "They say that the police are investigating the possibility that my husband Pierre was a partner in the crime, that he was killed to keep him silent. I must defend him. Pierre was no criminal."

Someone asked how she could be so sure. She raised her chin even higher and said, "I know because Pierre had already refused to steal the mirror. He told me he was approached some months ago by a person who offered to pay him to take it from the museum."

This caused a fair sensation, and a gabble of questions followed, from which I was able to gather that Pierre Legrand had told his wife only that someone wanted him to steal the mirror and that he had refused. He had given her no idea who it was. She assumed that the person who had approached Pierre had gone ahead with the theft and had indeed killed Pierre because he knew too much. Her husband was an honest man. Yes, they were poor, but they were honest. She had told the police her story. She didn't know if Pierre had reported any of this to the authorities at the time, but she supposed he had not. He had probably imagined that once he refused to steal the mirror that would be the end of it.

She didn't let things go on much longer

before saying "Now, please excuse me" and getting to her feet. After cooperating with the importuning photographers for a few extra shots, she turned toward the hall from which she'd entered while the reporters headed for the door. Impulsively, I approached her and said, "Madame Legrand? I'm Georgia Lee Maxwell. I'm the one who was there when your husband was shot yesterday."

She turned to me. Her dark eyes widened. I thought she swayed. After a long moment she said, "Oh, yes?"

"Yes. I'm the journalist who was with them. I just wanted to say—"

She clutched my arm, looking dazed. "But you must stay," she said.

Should I tell you I hadn't expected it, or should I be honest? I murmured something about not imposing on her grief, but my voice was so soft she probably didn't hear me. I waggled my fingers in good-bye to Jack, who gave me a dirty look as he went out the door. A few minutes later Chantal Legrand and I were sitting side by side on the couch, sipping coffee and leafing through a photograph album she had taken from the top left-hand drawer of the ugly sideboard.

In every picture, Pierre's face looked ordinary. I had seen his dead body, but if he had been revivified I wouldn't have recognized him on the street. I saw Pierre at age ten with his dog, Pierre in rugby uniform, Pierre in the army. There were also pictures of a tiny, perky-looking lady who wore, in styles that varied gradually with the years, a coat with a fur collar, orthopedic shoes and, occasionally, a hat sporting a feather.

"Pierre's mother," said Chantal. "His father died when Pierre was young."

We came to a picture showing the woman sitting on the same couch where we now sat. She looked wizened, her head sinking into the muskrat, or whatever it was, of her collar. "She lived here with you?" I asked.

"Oh, no." I heard a hint of relief in Chantal's tone. "No, Pierre and I met and married only after she died. But the apartment is much as she left it. Pierre wouldn't allow anything to be changed."

The idea of Pierre Legrand, aging mama's boy, fascinating a ripe beauty like Chantal was boggling. "How long had you and Pierre been married?"

"Four years." She turned the album pages until we reached the wedding photograph. There she was, her hair longer, her face fuller, in a snug-fitting white satin suit and hat with a short veil, holding a few lilies of the valley. She didn't look more than nineteen in the picture. I guessed her age now to be twenty-five at the outside. Pierre was beside her in a dark suit and tie, smiling. Ten or twelve people were ranged around them, from a snaggle-toothed little boy to the stout woman in black who was now puttering around in the kitchen, and who had turned out to be Chantal's mother.

I said, "These people are your family?"

"Yes." She pointed them out: "My mother, my nephew Daniel, my sister Lisette, my cousin Armand, my brother-in-law Jean-Luc—" Her finger hovered over cousin Armand, square-jawed and handsome, a cleft in his chin. She stared at the picture. "Yes, four years."

"How did you meet?"

She closed the album. "I was a waitress in a *brasserie* near the Bastille. He was alone, his mother had died. He ate there many evenings. We got to know one another. It was like that." Her mouth turned down delicately, to show that she knew it wasn't an exceptional story. "But you must tell me," she said. "You were there? At the Musée Bellefroide?"

"Yes."

"And . . . what can you tell me? What can you remember?"

I was embarrassed to feel my eyes filling with tears. "I don't remember it clearly at all. It was a blur. I barely saw your husband—Pierre—before they made us lie face-down."

"And the others? The ones who . . . did it?"

"They were disguised, you know. With ski masks and baggy jackets and gloves. It could have been anyone." I had tried and tried, hoping for a clue, some identifying mark, but there just wasn't one. "It happened very fast," I said, feeling helpless and ashamed.

In the kitchen, her mother was humming. I recognized the tune as the theme song of a television commercial for instant soup. "What do you remember about his being asked to steal the mirror?" I said.

She shrugged. "Nothing more than I told already. I knew immediately, when he came home that evening, that something had happened. He was shaken, and excited as well. He wasn't going to tell me, but I insisted."

It was easy to imagine her wheedling the story out of the doting Pierre. "Did he say how the approach was made?"

"No, not even that. He just told me, 'Imagine. Today someone asked me to steal an object from the museum.' He was shocked by it, of course, but also proud of himself. He said, 'I refused immediately and said it was out of the question.' That was the part that excited him, I think."

"Did he say it was the mirror that was to be stolen?"

"I had to beg him again to tell me. He finally said it was a mirror that had once belonged to Nostradamus. He said it was a strange thing to steal, since the museum had many objects that were more valuable. And that was all he would say, no matter how many times I asked. At last he got very serious and said he wasn't telling me because the knowledge could be dangerous. And it was, of course. It killed him."

Maybe it had. I couldn't help thinking that she hadn't convinced me Pierre was innocent. He hadn't told anyone but his wife about the approach. What was to prevent him from changing his mind? "Do you know why he didn't tell Bernard Mallet?"

"I'm not sure. I can only say my husband didn't care for Monsieur Mallet. He preferred to keep his distance from him."

I wondered if anybody liked Bernard Mallet. The Speculatori hated him, Pierre Legrand didn't care for him, and I wasn't wild about him myself. I sensed that the interview was over and got up to leave. At the door, she said, "You will be investigating? Writing something?"

"I think so."

"If you find out . . . anything . . . you must tell me. You will tell me?"

Her eyes pleaded. It was a reasonable request, but for some reason I felt uncomfortable, invaded. "Of course," I said.

As I walked across the courtyard, a brown-haired man hurried toward me. He went through the doorway and I heard his footsteps mounting the stairs. The instant I saw him, I recognized Cousin Armand, from the wedding picture. The family was rallying around Chantal Legrand. I left the Cour St. Jean and turned down the Rue de Charonne toward the Métro.

SPHINX

KITTY was out when I got back to the office, and I remembered she had been going to a gala lunch where a new fragrance was to be introduced. On my desk was a memo from

Jack, typed on the back of a press handout in his unmistakable multi-strikeover style:

To: GL
From: J
   While you were scooping us all with the grieving widow, I called B. Mallet at the Bellefroide for comment. He says Legrand never told him about possible theft of the mirror, and he is plenty pissed off about it (all could have been avoided, ta da ta da). My verdict is that Legrand looks guilty as sin, but I'm not sure of what. Mallet sounds like a bomb about to explode.
   What did the lovely Chantal have to say, hm?

I found Jack at his VDT, behind a desk piled high with newspapers, press releases, styrofoam coffee cups, printouts of stories, books, letters, photocopies of who knew what. He was also smoking like a chimney. I never went to journalism school, but I assume they give courses in Desk Messiness and Advanced Nicotine Consumption. He looked away from the green letters on the screen and said, "What say, Miz Maxwell?"
   "Just call me Scoop." I sat down in Jack's

visitor's chair, on top of some back issues of *Libération*.

He leaned back and crossed his feet on top of the pile on his desk. "So what did you get from Chantal after we ordinary mortals were ushered out?"

"Not a great deal. A look at the family photos. I gather Pierre lived with his mother in contented bachelorhood until she died. Then he recruited Chantal to take her place."

"Yes? If he won that fair lady, *Maman* must have had a wad of francs stuffed in the mattress, don't you suppose?"

I suspected he was right, but argued just to be contrary. "Don't be so cynical. Chantal *could* have married him for love. And they were hardly living in luxury there in the Cour St. Jean."

"That doesn't mean Pierre didn't come into a nest egg. The French are a thrifty breed. I'll have somebody look into the whole situation. Inheritances don't happen in a vacuum."

"So you're staying with it pretty closely."

"Hell, yes." He sat up and tugged meditatively at his drooping socks. "She's really something, that Chantal."

"Pretty, you mean?"

"Gorgeous. But I mean, why did she call that press conference this morning?"

"Well, to clear Pierre's name—"

"She sure did that, didn't she? He looks more like a crook now than he did before."

So he did. "Maybe she didn't realize how it would sound."

"Maybe. Maybe." Jack turned to his VDT. "I'll let you know if my legman comes up with anything interesting."

I walked slowly back to my office. I was grateful for Jack's willingness to share information, but it also made me uneasy. In the first place, his helpfulness made it obvious that he didn't consider me any competition. But why should he? I wasn't a wire service reporter. We would be working on two totally different kinds of stories: his reporting developments as they happened, and mine—

There was the rub, right there. My story. What story? Where would it be published, and in what form? Maybe I was wasting my time. Maybe I should be over on the Rue de Paradis, looking for good buys in porcelain for the next "Paris Patter."

I sat down and stared out the half-open window at the bank across the street. Automobile fumes drifted in, along with a cacophony of horns indicating that traffic was blocked below. Jack had resources, as he'd just tacitly made clear with his reference to the legman. If Jack decided to pour everything into it he could probably blast me off the map, even though I had been on the scene and he hadn't.

I stewed for a while before acknowledging one certainty: I was hooked on the story. No other reporter, neither Jack nor anybody else, had as much reason to be hooked on it as I did. I was going to write it, and if at the moment I didn't have an assignment from anybody but myself, that was all right. Also, I was going to be grateful for Jack's help and stop being so territorial. Filled with an uplifting sense of resolution, I turned to my notes.

I worked for several hours, stopping only to eat a cup of yoghurt at my desk, typing separate pages of observations and questions about everybody involved:

The victim, Pierre Legrand: According to his wife, he had been approached about stealing the mirror and had refused. But the thieves had shown up at a time when the museum would, unofficially, be open early and the storage room unlocked. Someone must have alerted them. Could it have been

Pierre, who was then shot so he couldn't identify his cohorts?

The widow, Chantal Legrand: We had only her word that Pierre had been approached about the mirror. Arguably, her story had made him look worse. Had she deliberately cast suspicion? Why?

Bernard Mallet: The Bellefroide director continually denigrated the mirror. His sense of responsibility to the Musée Bellefroide seemed almost maniacal. He had been extremely anxious to keep me out that morning. Had he known something was about to happen? Why would he participate in a plot to rob the Bellefroide?

Clive Overton: He had been intensely nervous on the way to the Bellefroide, which meant he could have known something. But if so, why had he invited me to come along and insisted that I be let in?

The Speculatori: All I knew about them so far was that they wanted the mirror, and they hated Bernard Mallet. Which made them excellent candidates for having committed the crime.

And, of course, there were the criminals themselves: two cruel, anonymous figures in jackets and masks. I could picture them perfectly, and yet all I could really remember was their identical anonymity. Only one of them had spoken, briefly, and his voice had made no impression on me aside from the fact that it was masculine. There had been no smells, no expressions in the eyes, no characteristic gestures. It had been almost as if they weren't human beings at all, and that made them even more frightening. And, of course, they weren't necessarily connected with any of the other people involved. They could have done what they did on their own, for reasons that weren't yet clear and might never be.

It was late afternoon when the phone rang. A woman's voice said, in French, "Is that Georgia Lee Maxwell?"

"Yes."

"My name is Madeleine Bellefroide."

I was startled. Was the name a wild coincidence, or were some of the Bellefroides still around? I could only say "Yes" again.

"I saw you on television, and today I read in the newspaper your account of the incident at the Musée Bellefroide. The museum was once my family's home."

I varied my response to "Oh, yes?"

"There is something I would like to discuss with you. Could we meet? As soon as possible?"

I was amazed, but agreed to come to her apartment. She gave me the address, in the seventh *arrondissement* off the Avenue de Suffren. An elegant part of Paris.

I had just hung up when Kitty, flushed with champagne, finally came back from lunch. "I wonder if that was a joke," I said.

"What?"

"I just got a call from a woman who said she was Madeleine Bellefroide. Is there such a person?"

Kitty was carrying a glossy-looking press kit and a sand-colored velvet bag with a gold drawstring. She put these on her desk and hung her deep lilac coat, which resembled a maternity outfit for a woman expecting triplets, on our rickety stand. "Madeleine Bellefroide? Sure. The last of the Bellefroides. She's pretty old now, and lives quietly, but you hear about her now and again."

"What's her connection to the museum? And what's that weird smell?"

"I don't think she has a connection to the museum. I seem to remember that she broke with the family years ago. She was the black sheep, or something. And the smell is Sphinx. If the Sphinx people have anything to do with it, next year we'll all be smelling like this." She reached into the velvet bag and pulled out a large bottle of eau de toilette. The cap was a gold sphinx head. "Sphinx" was written on the bottle in gold, hieroglyphic-style letters. She handed it to me. "Might as well start now."

I unscrewed the cap and smelled. "Good Lord. Is that musk? Aren't sphinxes supposed to be inscrutable? This is like being hit with a truckload of patchouli."

"You laugh. Wait till I tell you about the lunch. They picked us all up by helicopter—"

"You're kidding."

"They'd hired a fleet of them. And flew us to some place out of town where they had a huge tent set up. At the entrance were two life-size plaster sphinxes, one on either side. And inside, lots of models dressed up as sphinxes. And every table had an ice sculpture in the shape of guess what."

"But why Sphinx?"

"The only answer I can give is: why not?"

I smelled it again. My eyes watered. I coughed.

"Go ahead. Dab some on your pulse points."

"If I did, and there were camels in Paris, I'd be trampled to death in three seconds."

"That's exactly the story line of one of the commercials they showed us."

Some other time I might have tried it, but I didn't want to asphyxiate Madeleine Bellefroide. I picked up my notebook and took off. I was dying to find out what was on her mind.

MADELEINE BELLEFROIDE

MADELEINE BELLEFROIDE may have been the black sheep of the family, but she wasn't living in poverty. Her address was a handsome apartment building of pale stone on a chic street that ran between the Avenue de Suffren and the Champ de Mars. The Eiffel Tower, at the far end of the Champ de Mars, shone dully in the waning sun. I buzzed the apartment on the intercom in the marble-floored lobby, and she told me to come to the fourth floor. I rode up in one of the curlicued wrought-iron birdcages, big enough for two people if one is on a diet, that the French use for elevators.

She was standing at her open door. At first glance I thought she was in her mid-fifties. When I looked again, I realized she must be at least twenty years older. She wore her dark hair in a sleek, earlobe-length bob, with bangs to the eyebrows. It was dyed all right, but the dye job was subtle. Her thin, slightly hooked nose gave her face a fierce look. She wore a black turtleneck and loose gray slacks that looked so soft they had to be cashmere. The luminosity of the three strands of huge pearls around her neck proclaimed them to be the real thing.

She was splendid, and the apartment matched her perfectly. It was all polished dark wood, velvet upholstery, silk pillows, bronze figurines, flowing draperies framing a wall of floor-to-ceiling windows. I was impressed, and not a little cowed, and wished I'd polished my shoes before I'd come over.

She offered coffee, and when I accepted rang for a maid, who brought in an espresso pot and china cups. After the coffee was poured she said, "I'm grateful to you for coming."

I nodded. She had me tongue-tied.

"Naturally, I was interested in yesterday's tragedy. I read all the newspaper accounts, including yours. As I mentioned, I also saw you on television last night. I have the impression that you are a sympathetic person."

"Uh—I hope so."

"I wonder—do you intend to follow the case? Write more about it, perhaps?"

"Well, I had thought about it."

She nodded. "It seemed to me that under the circumstances you might. As a means of . . . exorcism? Coming to terms?"

The woman was perceptive. "Something like that."

"I see." She looked down at her coffee, which she was stirring round and round, round and round, with a tiny silver spoon. She had large, knobby-knuckled hands. "I will tell you what I want," she said. "I want the mirror."

I was nonplussed. Had she somehow misunderstood or misinterpreted so wildly that she thought I'd stolen it myself? Before I could speak, she said, "Yes, of course I know you don't have it. But I want you to help me get it."

What on earth was she getting at? I said, "I think the police—"

She made a dismissive gesture. "The police wouldn't approve of what I want to do. I want to offer a ransom—a reward for the return of the mirror. I'm willing to pay a great deal of money for it."

I still didn't understand. "Why would the police disapprove?"

"This is difficult to say," she continued slowly. "Two things happened yesterday. The mirror was stolen. And a man was killed. I am not offering a reward for bringing the murderers to justice. I am offering to ransom the mirror. Do you see the difference?"

I did see. She was saying she would pay for the mirror and let Pierre Legrand's murderers go free. I thought she was right to assume the police wouldn't approve. I wasn't sure I approved, either.

I was shaking my head when she said, "Perhaps I should explain why."

Good idea. "Please."

She smiled a melancholy smile. I was in danger of being entranced by this woman. "I hope you'll be patient. I'm afraid the story begins many years ago. I was a young girl, living with my family in the house which is now the Musée Bellefroide. At that time the mirror, which we always called 'Nostradamus's Mirror,' was displayed in a glass-fronted case in the library. It was an object of great fascination for my brother and me. Although we weren't allowed to handle it, we would stand and gaze at it. Do you have any idea what it looks like?"

"I know it's black, polished obsidian."

"Yes, it's black, a brilliant black circular

surface. We would crane our necks to try to see into it and catch glimpses of shadowy, mysterious movements. Whatever you may believe about such things, I assure you it is an object of tremendous attractive power."

I was getting chills. Up to now, I hadn't thought much about the mirror itself. It had been an element in the story, and that was all. Now, it was taking on weight and reality in my mind.

She continued, "When I was twelve or thirteen, there was a terrible influenza epidemic. Thousands of people died. I became very ill and wasn't expected to live. I lay on my bed, alternately freezing and burning, weakening daily, often delirious. Then one night, I came to consciousness. My head was perfectly clear, although my sensations seemed intensified. The smell of medicine, the feeling of the crushed lace of my nightgown around my neck, the shadow cast on the wall by a china pitcher, all seemed overwhelming to me. I realized then, with the same intensity, that in all likelihood I was going to die. I lay there, pondering this thought.

"By the light of the lamp, I could see that my nurse had fallen asleep. And the notion came to me, as clearly as if I'd been ordered to do it, that I must go downstairs and look in the mirror."

Madeleine Bellefroide's eyes were clouded. I was gripping my notebook, but hadn't written a word.

She went on. "You must understand that I was desperately ill. I was hardly able to walk two steps unassisted. Yet I got out of my bed and silently, easily, left my room and went downstairs to the library. As I said, my brother and I had never been allowed to touch the mirror, and I don't believe we were ever told where the key to the cabinet was kept. Nevertheless, I found it immediately, in the drawer of the desk. I unlocked the cabinet and took out the mirror. It was cold to the touch, and surprisingly heavy in my hands.

"No lights were burning in the library. The only illumination came from the hall. I crouched in the doorway, balanced the mirror on my knees, and bent over it.

"At first I saw nothing. Nothing at all, not even a dim reflection of my face. The mirror was empty. I felt an indescribable despair, believing this meant I would surely die. But as I continued to gaze, immobilized with horror, I saw something move in those black depths. At first it was just a flicker of white, almost indiscernible, but as I watched it grew. It was a white-clad figure walking toward me, and as she approached I saw it was myself.

"I was dressed in my white nightgown, walking through a tempestuous, relentless wind, my hair and my gown whipping violently around me. But as my image drew nearer, I was able to see that inside my chest a flame was burning, undisturbed by the gales outside. I was overcome with joy, for then I knew I would live."

The light from the windows had dimmed, and we sat in half-darkness. Madeleine Bellefroide leaned back against the pillows. "And so," she said lightly, "as you see, I survived. I replaced the mirror, went back to my bed, and told no one. I grew up, fell in love with an unsuitable man, quarreled with my family because of it. My father, the least forgiving person who ever lived, disinherited me. To make certain I never acquired any of the family possessions, he created the Musée Bellefroide. Despite my father's hateful behavior, the man I loved and I lived together happily and productively and, in time, with plenty of money as well. Ironically, I am the last of the Bellefroides. My brother is dead, and neither he nor I had children."

She put down her cup. "And now, at last, I come to the point of my long story. Once again, I am desperately ill. The doctors tell me I am dying. I am old, perhaps I should accept it, but I can't. Or, I can't without looking into the mirror once again."

I was completely at a loss. She didn't look sick, she looked wonderful. And yet, I believed what she had told me. And I could understand why she wanted the mirror.

"In a funny way, the theft makes it easier," she was saying. "At least now it is out of the museum, where I would never be allowed even to touch it."

That seemed incredible. "You mean . . . Did you ask Bernard Mallet? Surely he would have been willing to—"

"He was not. I not only asked him, I begged him. The moment I received the diagnosis, six weeks or so ago, I contacted him. He would not allow me to borrow, or even see the mirror, claiming it was prohibited under the terms of the trust. Legally, I'm sure he is correct. Morally—" She gave an eloquent shrug.

Thin lines radiated from the corners of her eyes and bracketed her mouth. Her face looked deeply sad. "What happened to the

94

man you fell in love with?" I asked. "The one you lived with all those years?"

"He's dead."

I must have looked surprised. She smiled briefly. "You're wondering what I have left to live for. Why is it so important to see my flame burning? I can't say why. But it is."

"I'm still not sure what you want me to do."

She leaned forward eagerly. "Nothing very much. I don't want to advertise the fact that I'm willing to pay for the mirror's return. But you will be talking with people, you can mention discreetly, can't you, that such a thing might be possible? And then we will see whether there is a response."

I hemmed and hawed, but I knew I was going to do it. Of course it went against my better judgment. But what was better judgment in the face of a plea from a woman of such elegance, and one who was probably dying? I have strong whims. If my decision to help Madeleine Bellefroide wasn't a whim, exactly, neither was it any more rational than my decision to come to Paris in the first place.

Besides, I don't think it could do much harm. If I got a chance to mention the ransom I would. That was all.

She saw me to the door, and gripped my hand tightly when we said good-bye. "You will call me when you have word," she said, without a hint of interrogation.

"Yes."

The light was even dimmer now. She blended with the shadows behind her, seeming to have materialized out of them. I turned away and heard the door close.

Outside, a blue-gold dusk had descended. I walked half a block to stand at the edge of the Champ de Mars. To my left, the Eiffel Tower hovered like a sentinel. Evening strollers passed, chatting in quiet voices, some linked arm in arm. Across the way, under low, spreading trees, children playing the last game of the day swarmed back and forth, screaming. Each of them sheltered a burning flame. I wondered if they could feel their flames, as I now felt mine.

MON PETIT CAFÉ

My philosophical mood was broken when I realized I was ravenous. A cup of yoghurt wasn't enough sustenance to get me through a conversation with Madeleine Bellefroide. I went back to the Avenue de Suffren and caught a number eighty-two bus.

Clinging to a pole, crammed cheek by jowl with home-going workers, my thoughts were divided approximately evenly between food and Madeleine Bellefroide's ransom. How much did she plan to offer? Should I stop for a cheese crêpe from the sidewalk stand on the Boulevard Montparnasse? I hadn't even asked her a figure. Maybe a slice of take-away pizza from La Brioche Dorée. And what, for God's sake, would be the procedure if somebody *did* bite? Or a *sachet* of *madeleines* from La Duchesse Anne. *Madeleines*. Madeleine.

By the time I got off the bus at the Place de 18 Juin 1940 I was weak from hunger, but I had reached a decision. I would stop at Mon Petit Café for a *Croque Monsieur*.

Mon Petit Café was on the corner of the Rue Delacôte and the Rue de Vaugirard. Undistinguished but cozy, it had a curving metal bar, formica tables and bentwood chairs, a "Hollywood Heat" pinball machine, and hanging lamps fringed with yellow plastic beads. The *Croques Monsieur*, the open-faced toasted ham and cheese sandwiches ubiquitous in Paris cafés, were pretty good there. I was getting to be a regular and had struck up an acquaintance with Monsieur Franceschi, the effusive owner, and his dog, a haughty and refined German shepherd named César.

This evening, César barely woke from his nap under the pinball machine to acknowledge my arrival, but Monsieur Franceschi, who was bald, mustachioed, dimpled, and adorable, made up for his dog's indifference by bustling around me with even more fervor than usual. It turned out that he'd seen me on television the night before. "Right there!" he said, gesturing at the set above the bar. "It was only a split second, but I recognized you, Madame. I said, 'My God, how dreadful she looks. She must have been terribly frightened, to look as bad as that.'"

I thanked him so much for his comment, but I don't think he caught the sarcasm. Eventually, he went off to shower attention on other customers, and I settled down to my food, trying to digest the events of the day.

I had been deeply affected by my meeting with Madeleine Bellefroide. Something she had said about the mirror kept running through my mind: *I assure you it is an object of tremendous attractive power.* The record proved her right. The Speculatori wanted the mirror; Madeleine Bellefroide wanted the mirror; the thieves, whoever they were, wanted the mirror; the person who asked Pierre Legrand to steal it wanted the mirror. No matter how many overlaps there were in the group, it still added up to a lot of coveting.

Combined with that was Bernard Mallet's almost frenzied protectiveness of an object he claimed had little value. I could understand why he wouldn't sell the mirror to the Speculatori, but his refusal to let Madeleine Bellefroide see it struck me as almost sadistic. Maybe he had to toe the line for some board of trustees, but I couldn't believe that even the most stringent overseers would have begrudged her that favor.

Actually, I was beginning to feel extremely interested in the mirror myself and excited by the possibility, admittedly slight, that I could be instrumental in getting it back. I could almost see it in my mind, as Madeleine Bellefroide had described it: a cold, brilliant black surface with shadowy movements in its depths. I didn't want to look into it,, certainly not. I had always been terrified to have my fortune told. Yet, if the mirror were available to me, could I resist? I wasn't sure I could.

I wondered if Madeleine Bellefroide had really looked into the mirror and seen the vision she described. She had been a sick, delirious child. The episode could have been a hallucination, or a dream.

Or, if you wanted to look at it that way, the episode could have been a lie, and Madeleine Bellefroide was in some way making use of me. I hated the thought but felt more worldly for having had it.

Monsieur Franceschi insisted I have dessert, so, over a cassis *sorbet*, I thought about my next move. I had to contact the Speculatori. I wanted to find out, if I could, which of them had called me and bad-mouthed Bernard Mallet. And the Speculatori would be fertile ground for a mention of Madeleine Bellefroide's ransom offer.

I dug out the paper Mallet's secretary had given me: Bruno Blanc, with an address on the Rue Jacob. I was still disinclined to call and make an appointment, since that struck me as a perfect way to get turned down flat. I would follow journalistic tradition and show up unexpectedly, making sure I got my foot inside when the door opened.

With that settled, the last of the sherbet eaten, and Monsieur Franceschi's urgings about coffee fended off, I left Mon Petit Café and walked the half-block home. I buzzed myself into the building and crossed the lobby, past the deserted apartment of the concierge, who was a member of the laissez-faire school of caretaking. In the months I had lived there I'd barely seen her and wasn't even sure of her name. Since the elevator had been known to stop between floors for long and nerve-racking intervals, I had gotten into the habit of climbing the three flights to my apartment. I arrived puffing, as always, and was so involved in greeting and feeding Twinkie that it was probably ten minutes before I noticed the envelope, which had apparently been slipped under the door with enough force to sail it beneath the coat stand.

I wasn't especially curious. "Georgia Lee Maxwell" was typed on the outside. I thought it was a notice about the rent, or a hand-delivered invitation. But the typed note inside was in English:

Georgia Lee Maxwell—
  The mirror of Nostradamus destroyed Pierre Legrand. Stay away from the mirror of Nostradamus.
  You are warned.

I picked up Twinkie, and the two of us sat at my dining table, with the note on the table in front of us. Twinkie eventually got tired of looking at it and purred herself to sleep. I knew I would have to go down and see if the concierge had returned, although surely she hadn't, and even if I did find her she wouldn't have seen anybody coming up to shove threatening notes under my door. I knew I would have to tell the police, too, although no doubt this was nothing but the work of some nut who, like Madeleine Bellefroide, Monsieur Franceschi, and countless other people, was impressed because I had said a few words on television.

So I'd been warned. What was I supposed to do? Fold? The more I thought about it, the more ticked off I got. I thought about Daddy. Daddy was not the sort of father who gave out a lot of sage advice, since he always had better things to do with his time. He did give me one maxim to live by, though: Don't come back without the story.

To me, that meant if you go out after a story, get the story. Don't come back whining that the car broke down, or the person wouldn't talk to you, or they moved it up an hour and you missed it, or somebody sent you a note warning you off.

What counted was getting the story. And that's what I was going to do.

LONG DISTANCE

THE same dapper Criminal Brigade inspector who had interrogated me at the Bellefroide appeared soon after I'd called to report the letter. He was exactly as he'd been at our first encounter—just as well dressed, and not a bit chummier. When his eyes scanned the room, I was as uncomfortable as if I'd hidden the mirror in a kitchen cupboard. He looked at the letter and said, "English," making me wonder whether its being written in my native tongue was damning evidence against me.

Reluctantly, I invited him to sit down. He settled on my mustard brocade sofa. "Do you have a typewriter?"

"A . . . yes, I do. But it's at my office." Kitty and I were talking word processor, but neither of us had the money.

"I see. But might you have something here that was typed on it?"

Really! Annoyed at this blatant suggestion

103

that I'd written the damn letter to myself, I unearthed half a page of an abortive "Paris Patter" on the Sunday afternoon organ concerts at Notre Dame.

He glanced at it, then at the letter, and said, "We took your fingerprints yesterday, at the museum, didn't we?"

"What—Yes. Yes, you did."

"Good. We have them on file, then, to compare with any we find on the letter."

"Look. *I* didn't write the letter, and I resent—"

He cut me off, his expression bland. "Please understand, Madame. We must consider all possibilities. If the letter had been typed on your machine—and after my superficial comparison I would guess it was not—that doesn't mean you typed it yourself. And as for the fingerprints, surely you touched the letter when you opened it. We must know your prints to distinguish them from others that may be on it."

"I see," I muttered. I was blushing like a chastised schoolgirl.

He leaned back, hands folded on the vest of his perfect blue suit. Although it was late in the day, the knot of his tie snuggled in the V of his collar as if it were sewn there. I kept wanting to blurt out a confession, even though I wasn't guilty of anything. Or at least, not guilty of much. I *was* guilty of not mentioning Madeleine Bellefroide and her offer to ransom the mirror, and that's what was throwing me off.

He asked a few more questions—the circumstances of finding the letter, whether I had any suspicions of my own—and left. I tottered into the kitchen, hunted up a bottle of calvados I'd been thinking I might give somebody for Christmas, and opened it. Fortunately, I'd had several sips by the time the phone rang.

I was tempted to let it go. I didn't want any more anonymous information or advice. I eyed it warily through a couple of rings before picking up the receiver and answering.

"Georgia?"

Only one person calls me Georgia instead of Georgia Lee. It sounded like he was across the street, and I prayed that was owing to a good connection and not actual proximity. "Hi, Ray." I sat down on the bed, glad I'd brought my glass with me.

"What's happening over there, girl? Today's paper says you were someplace where somebody got killed."

So the *Sun* had picked up my name from

the wire service stories about the incident at the Bellefroide. They'd probably been trying to reach me. "Yes, that's right. It was just— bad luck."

"I called your Mama to get your phone number. She's having a fit."

"I talked to her last night." She *was* having a fit. Hearing from Ray, who she'd spent years hoping would be her second son-in-law, wouldn't have helped, either.

"So listen, Georgia. Are you all right?"

Ray owns a Bay City drugstore chain. He does his own Ray's Drugs television commercials. When he wants to sound sincere and concerned, he knows how to do it, and it's amazing how he can make you believe him. "I'm fine. There's really nothing to worry about." I sounded so quavery it was embarrassing.

"Aw, honey. I hope you don't mind that I called. You don't, do you?"

Of course I did, and he knew it, but I wasn't going to writhe for his edification this time. "No. Not at all."

"And you're O.K.?"

"Fine."

"Fine as frog hair?"

"Fine as frog hair."

"Good. I'm glad to hear that." When I

didn't reply, he went on, "Do you mind if I ask you something?"

"Ask." I knew what was coming. I could've written it out before he said a word.

"Why don't you come on back, now? You've made your point. You could've gotten hurt bad over there."

"Ray—"

"The beach house is on the market, Georgia. There won't be any more of that."

"That" being the women—once it was actually a high school cheerleader, and he's lucky he wasn't arrested—he used to take out there when I was otherwise engaged. Thinking about it got me mad, in spite of myself. "What difference does the beach house make? A tomcat can do it in one backyard as well as another."

He laughed. "That's why I miss you. You could always see right through me."

Always. So why had I wasted the crucial years between thirty and thirty-five letting him twist me, turn me, string me along, and string me out? Was it for his sun-streaked, chestnut hair, green eyes, and the best tan north of Key West? For his five shopping mall drugstores? Or just—and this was the explanation I hated the most—that I was so desperate to have a presentable man around

107

that I didn't care how shabbily he treated me? Tears started to my eyes. I blotted them with the back of my hand and said, "I live in Paris now, Ray."

"But look what happened to you there. It's dangerous."

"What happened was unfortunate. But I live here now."

"Becky misses you, too."

This was dirty pool. Becky was Ray's teen-aged daughter, a gawky, withdrawn girl who had liked me a lot.

I steeled myself. "Give Becky my best. Tell her I'm doing fine. But—"

"I mean it, Georgia."

"So do I."

Silence. Then he said, "Hey. It's almost two-thirty in the afternoon here. What time is it over there?"

"Almost eight-thirty at night."

"I'll call you again sometime. O.K.?"

"I don't think—"

"Your old friends have a right to know what's going on, if you're going to mess around and get yourself in trouble."

"All right, then." I was too exhausted to argue.

"You take care of yourself. I mean that."

"I will."

His "Bye, honey" was almost a whisper, and then the connection was broken. I hung up and swallowed the rest of my calvados in one burning gulp.

He had managed, in his customary style, to wipe me out completely. The thing about Ray was, he couldn't stand to have anything he could actually get. When he could have me, which in the past years had been pretty much whenever he crooked his finger, I was lower than dirt. But let me pick up and go to Paris, and I was worth a transatlantic phone call and a lot of sweet talk. This time he may have wiped me out, but he hadn't fooled me, and I wasn't fooling myself, either. Let him go exercise his charm on somebody with fewer troubles than I had.

I had an explosive little cry, but it didn't last too long. Yes, let's face it, part of the reason I came to Paris was to get away from Ray, although I'd broken up with him—for the umpteenth time—before the Cecilia Driscoll crisis arose. What I'd told him was true, though. I lived here now. And God knows I had enough to think about without brooding about him. I blew my nose. Tomorrow I had to tackle the Speculatori.

ON THE RUE JACOB

THE next morning, I felt better than I'd expected, with neither an emotional hangover from the phone call nor a brandy hangover from the calvados. The weather was crisp and beautiful for the third day in a row, a circumstance unprecedented in my Paris experience. I set out fairly early after breakfast, taking the Métro to St. Germain des Prés and emerging next to the Place St. Germain. Sun spilled into the square. Across from the ancient church, the Deux Magots café had set up outside tables and was doing a brisk midmorning coffee trade. I marched righteously past the lolling customers. I had better things to do than stretch my legs out, smoke, drink cappuccino, and read the latest political scandal in the newspapers. I crossed the Place and plunged down the traffic-choked Rue Bonaparte to the Rue Jacob.

This was a fashionable, albeit semi-bohemian, part of town. The Rue Jacob was a street of bookstores, galleries, antique shops, and boutiques of various sorts. The address Mallet's secretary had given me turned out to be a quaint-looking bookstore called Le Jardin Métaphysique. Several decks of tarot cards were fanned out in the front window, which also contained a crystal ball, a poster showing acupuncture points, and a few books, including a treatise on alchemy and, I was interested to see, a volume titled *Centuries: The Prophecies of Nostradamus.* Above this display, prisms hung from strings. All of it looked as if it had been there a while. The cards and poster were fading, the covers of the books were curling, and I could see dust on the crystal ball.

I was searching for someone named Bruno Blanc, but I didn't know if he owned the shop, or worked here, or just used it as a mail drop. As I strained to see into the interior, I suddenly got jumpy. Feeling vulnerable and conspicuous, I glanced around, but the street was placid in the sun. A couple of elderly women carrying string bags went by, chatting; a blond man leaned in a doorway across the street, eating french fries out of a cardboard tub; a young woman pushed a stroller carrying a tiny boy and an enormous white teddy bear.

Still, I wasn't ready to go in. I had a

feeling that my visit to Le Jardin Méta-physique would be significant, and I wanted to be sure I was prepared. I turned away.

Nearby I found a small café. Its two side-walk tables were decorated with black-eyed Susans in blue bottles. I took a seat and had cappuccino after all.

As I sipped, I told myself to stop wasting time. I would go into the store, browse around, get the lay of the land. Then I'd ask for Bruno Blanc. Totally straightforward. I paid the check and started off again.

The blond man who'd been eating the fries was now, I noticed, studying the post-cards on a rack outside a *papeterie*. It oc-curred to me that he must be waiting for somebody, and then I pushed open the door of Le Jardin Métaphysique and forgot all about him.

A bell above the door jangled as I entered, scaring the wits out of me. It summoned a languorous girl who asked, without particu-lar enthusiasm, if she could help me. When I said I wanted to look around she didn't press the issue but subsided behind a counter. I took off my coat and wandered through the cramped, musty-smelling aisles, inspecting volumes on witchcraft, astrology, and ESP. It was so quiet that every time I leafed through a book the sound of the pages turning seemed deafening. None of this lowered my tension level.

If I continued this course of action I might unearth tips on how to read tarot cards, but I was unlikely to find Bruno Blanc. I kicked the next phase of the plan into gear by asking the languorous clerk where I might find him. Indicating a vague direction with her head she said, "Upstairs. Second floor."

The stairs were behind a curtain at the rear of the shop. I climbed to the second-floor landing, where I found a door of dark wood. There was no name on the bell, no brass plaque saying Speculatori National Headquarters. I rang. When that didn't raise anybody I leaned on the bell, and a few seconds later the door opened.

The woman who stood there had pure white hair that trailed over her shoulders in wispy split ends that made me long to wield a pair of scissors. Her eyes were wide and blue, her face pale and devoid of makeup. It was hard to guess her age, but she was certainly no ingenue, although she wasn't as old as the color of her hair indicated, either. She was dressed in white—if she were Mrs. Blanc, the French word for "white," she was presenting herself appropriately—in a floor-length shift with wide sleeves. A blue shawl was pulled around her shoulders. I guessed the effect was meant to be ethereal, although I didn't think it quite came off. Behind her, I could see a book-lined room, a desk with a green-shaded lamp, a threadbare rug.

I said, "Is Bruno Blanc here?"

She shook her head, the split ends brushing her shoulders.

I tried to see if anyone else was in the room. "Is this the headquarters of the Speculatori?"

She shook her head again. She looked agitated, the blue eyes widening.

God, maybe she was a deaf mute. I spoke louder. "Bernard Mallet at the Musée Bellefroide gave me Monsieur Blanc's name, and this address. He said Monsieur Blanc was the head of an organization called the Speculatori, and—"

By now, she seemed truly anguished. She broke in and said, in stumbling French, "I don't speak French. I'm an American."

I stared at her. I switched to English and said, "No kidding."

Her face lit up. "You speak English?"

"I'm American."

I thought she was going to hug me. "Oh, that's *great*. I thought you were French."

I have to tell you that being mistaken for a French person after all my struggles with the language, even if it was by a strange-looking American woman who spoke no French at all, did me a lot of good. I said, "I'm looking for Bruno Blanc. My name is Georgia Lee Maxwell."

Her stunned face told me that the favorable impression I'd made by speaking English had just been enhanced. "*Wow*," she said. "You're Georgia Lee Maxwell? You wrote that story in the *Herald Tribune* yesterday?"

I do love a person who notices bylines. "Yes," I said.

"*Far out*. Great to meet you." She stuck out her hand and gave mine a good pumping while I tried to cope with "Far out." "Come in, come in," she said, standing back.

There was no furniture aside from the desk and its chair and the bookcases. Two partially burned candles in brass candlesticks stood on the floor, which was also piled with pillows in Indian prints. She plopped down cross-legged on a pillow and said, "Bruno's not here right now. Would you like some herb tea while you wait?"

I was having trouble getting a grip. I had come expecting a den of mystics and seers and instead I had stumbled on Berkeley in the sixties. I declined the tea. Since I hadn't really liked sitting on the floor on Indian-print pillows even when it was in style, I sat in the desk chair.

My companion beamed at me. "It is so great to run into somebody who speaks English."

"Bruno Blanc—"

"Sure, Bruno does. But all his friends are French, and that's all they speak."

I hadn't gotten a fix on this woman at all. "You haven't told me your name."

She clasped her hands. "I've had so many, I hardly know what to say. Let's see. There was Janie Rainbow and Jane Marysdaughter. Then when I went to India I was Padma. The Ouija board gave me Marana. Some-times Bruno calls me Janine."

I figured that speech was a set piece. It was way too cute for me. "Well, never mind," I said.

She laughed, a sound that could have etched glass. "You can call me Jane," she bubbled as if it were the best joke in the world.

I was beginning to wish I'd waited for Bruno downstairs and left this aging hippie to burn her incense, which is what it smelled like she'd been doing when I arrived. I doubted I could get any pertinent information out of her.

She cocked her head to one side and looked at me. "I guess you'd like to talk with Bruno about the mirror," she said.

Hm. No need to condemn aging hippies prematurely. "I understand he—or the Speculatori—wanted it."

She looked thoughtful. "I don't think he'd put it that way. According to Bruno, the mirror can't be possessed. On the contrary, it possesses. What he wanted to do was free it, let it fulfill its purpose in the world, instead of being kept prisoner by the uninitiated."

Since we were this close to the subject, it seemed appropriate to ask, "Could he have stolen it?"

She shrugged. "Maybe. He was pretty passionate about it. But I don't think he did, because when it happened he was plenty upset. And of course that guy got killed, and Bruno considers life to be sacred, you know?"

"What about other people, other members of the Speculatori who—"

She was shaking her head. "I don't know. I'm not one of the Speculatori or anything, I'm just a friend passing through town. I've been on a meditation retreat in India, and now I'm heading back to Oregon. And Bruno doesn't talk much about the Speculatori, anyway."

"You don't know anybody else who's involved?"

"Nope. Bruno is the sort of secretary."

After a pause, with an avid look I'd seen on many faces before, she said, "Are you going to write this up for the paper?"

I used her eagerness as leverage. "Possibly. If I can get enough hard information, that is."

"Gosh, I'm sure Bruno would be glad—"

A phone rang, somewhere in the back of the apartment, and she excused herself to answer. That was good luck. I'd been afraid I was going to have to change my mind about the herb tea, and I detest herb tea. Keeping an ear out for her, I slid out the lower right-hand drawer of the desk. The idea of doing this had come into my head in the last couple of minutes. Either you'll approve or you won't, so I won't waste time defending myself.

With Jane trilling, "Hi!" and "Oh, yeah?" in the background, I looked in the drawer. It was empty except for a bundle swathed in black cloth. In a slightly disconnected state,

I watched my hand move toward the cloth, touch it. The cloth was soft and slippery, and whatever it concealed was cold and hard. Holding my breath, I pulled the cloth away.

Staring at me, like a giant, disembodied eye, was a crystal ball on a black stand. I gasped and dropped the cloth back over it. Shakily, I closed the drawer. Would the ball show my intruding face the next time Bruno Blanc gazed into it?

I tried another drawer. Jane's voice had lowered, but she was still talking. The contents here were less exotic, more in the check stub and bill receipt line.

I surely didn't have much more time. The middle drawer had ballpoints, unused paper and envelopes, paper clips. The top left . . .

In the top left drawer was a document holder, one of the folding cardboard ones the French love. It was stamped with ancient-looking images of the sun and moon in gold and black, and neatly tied with a black grosgrain ribbon. If I owned such a thing, I'd certainly keep my important papers in it.

I gave an end of the ribbon a tug, and it untied cooperatively. A peek inside the folder and a quick riffle through the sheets in it confirmed that these were papers relating to the Speculatori. I spotted at least one letter to Bernard Mallet at the Bellefroide.

I'd have loved to take a leisurely look, but time was running out. Jane's tone, now barely audible, sounded valedictory.

Damn. When I shuffled the papers back together, preparing to close the folder, I passed a sheet I hadn't noticed before. It was a scribbled list of names, seven or eight of them. All were French except one. All were unfamiliar to me except the same one: Clive Overton.

I closed the folder and was retying the ribbon into a semblance of the way it had been when Jane said, "Bye." I closed the drawer, wondering what the name of Clive Overton, the art conservator who'd collapsed at the Bellefroide, was doing on Bruno Blanc's list. It could have been a list of members of the Speculatori. Or it could have been a list of enemies of the Speculatori. Why hadn't it occurred to me before now to check up on what had happened to Overton? I had to think more about this, but I didn't get a chance right then because Jane returned.

Her manner was considerably subdued. She said, "Listen. I'm sorry, but I've got to go out. You'll have to catch Bruno later, I guess."

She was running her fingers nervously through her hair. I said, fishing, "It's not an emergency, I hope?"

"Nope, nope, nothing like that. Just—unexpected. Sorry."

I could hardly do anything but leave, but as I was going I remembered Madeleine Bellefroide's ransom and said, "Would you tell Bruno something for me? Tell him a ransom is being offered for the mirror's return. A lot of money, If he wants to know more, he can contact me." I scribbled my name and office address on a page from my notebook and gave it to her.

I wasn't sure she was listening. I said, "O.K.? You'll tell him?"

"Sure," she said. "So long."

I was disappointed that I hadn't seen Bruno, but more than that I was interested in the call that had transformed Jane from extrovert to introvert in such a short time. It might have been from a dentist, saying he'd had a cancellation and she should come over for a root canal, but I didn't think so. I thought the call had been from Bruno. And I really wanted to know where she had to go all of a sudden.

It was only a short step from mad curiosity to the idea that I should follow her.

I was back out on the Rue Jacob by this time. I could follow her, but she'd catch me doing it. She'd just seen me, seen what I was wearing, everything.

So I'd disguise myself.

I had a little time. She'd have to change. I didn't think she'd glide around the streets of Paris in a long white shift. I glanced up and down the street, and my eye fell on a boutique with a window display of the three wise monkeys, each of whom was wearing a fetching knitted hat and matching scarf. A hat would cover my hair. Since the weather was good, I had my sunglasses. And I hadn't been wearing my coat when she saw me, because I'd taken it off in the bookstore and had carried it over my arm.

I rushed into the store and, glancing every other second at Le Jardin Métaphysique, purchased the cheapest hat, brown-and-gold plaid with a gold pom-pom on top. It covered my head to the eyebrows and looked a bit odd with the sunglasses, but it certainly altered my appearance. I was just stuffing my change into my wallet when Jane emerged. She had indeed put on street clothes: tight jeans, black leather jacket, high-topped sneakers, black beret with her hair tucked up under it.

She started off purposefully down the street. I slipped out of the boutique and started off, just as purposefully, after her.

SURVEILLANCE

I stayed across the street and sauntered down the Rue Jacob in Jane's wake, keeping her bobbing black beret in view. I was disconcerted when she turned left on the Rue Bonaparte and disappeared from view, but I crossed over, quickened my pace and relocated her. We soon reached the Place St. Germain, where the coffee-drinkers and a circle of others were watching an itinerant juggler. In the midst of the activity I felt safe in my makeshift disguise, although the new hat was too hot and my scalp was sweating.

I was getting quite cocky by the time we had crossed the square, and then Jane threw me completely by descending into the Métro at the stop on the corner.

I halted at the top of the steps. How the hell would I follow her on the Métro? My disguise wasn't exactly impenetrable. If she got in a crowded car I might get away with it, providing she didn't spot me on the platform before the train arrived. On the other hand, what if she did? Wearing sunglasses and a hat in the St. Germain des Prés station might be inappropriate, but it wasn't proof of nefarious intent. I'd keep on, play it by ear. I hurried down, digging in my purse for my Carte Orange monthly Métro pass, hoping she hadn't already passed the barrier and disappeared in the corridors.

She hadn't. I spotted her in the ticket line and stood at the newsstand leafing through the French equivalent of *TV Guide* until she headed for the barrier and put her ticket through. She was following the signs for the Porte de Clignancourt–Porte d'Orleans line and, naturally, so did I. There were lots of people in the white tile corridor, and I didn't feel in danger of being spotted. We passed a young woman violinist playing something fast and fiery, maybe a mazurka—lively background music for my private chase scene—and emerged on the platform for the trains going toward the Porte de Clignancourt. Jane seemed to lose herself in contemplation of the posters on the walls, blown-up woodcuts of the old Abbaye St. Germain. I studied the mounted Métro map and kept the corner of my eye on her.

Moments later the train arrived, already well filled with passengers. Jane pushed her way into a car. I got in the same one but entered the door at the opposite end. All the seats were taken, and many people were standing. I got my hand around a pole and searched for the black beret. As the train started off I found it, among many other heads, blotting out part of an advertisement for winter underwear posted at the far end of the car.

I stared determinedly at the black spot, anxious not to lose her when she got off. I was so consumed with my pursuit that the purpose of it had become almost secondary. We stopped at Odéon, St. Michel, Cité. The beret stayed put. At Châtelet, a big transfer point, there was considerable flux as passengers got off and on. I lost sight of her for a moment or two, but then I saw the beret again. She seemed to have gotten a seat, one of the fold-down ones next to the doors, and was sitting with her back to me. I relaxed somewhat. That probably meant we were staying on a while.

The stops slid by: Étienne Marcel, Reaumur Sebastopol, Strasbourg St. Denis. The beret didn't move until the Gare du Nord, when it stirred and turned and I saw to my horror that its wearer wasn't Jane at all, but a bent-over man old enough to have fought in the trenches during World War I. As he shuffled out the door I cursed: myself, for trying to keep my eye on somebody while wearing sunglasses in a Métro car, and the French, for having an item of headgear as common as the black beret.

Then I saw Jane. She had found a seat all right—practically underneath my elbow. While my attention was fixed on the old codger, she had somehow worked her way to my end of the car. I backed away carefully and by the next stop had gotten a seat myself, in the corner.

The car had emptied considerably. I began to worry about her seeing me, but she wasn't really looking. She nibbled a fingernail, studied her reflection in the window, and showed no inclination to get out. We had almost reached the Porte de Clignancourt, which was the end of the line. Paranoia set in, and I began to wonder if she were part of an elaborate ruse to draw me away from the Rue Jacob, where even now Bruno Blanc and the Speculatori were bent over the mirror in mystic consultation.

Soon, we pulled into the Porte de Clignancourt station. Jane left the car without a glance at me and walked toward the exit. Taken by surprise, even though this was what I'd been waiting for, I rushed after her.

We emerged on a busy intersection where several streets came together. Buses lumbered by, horns hooted, and the pavements were filled with people, most of whom were moving in the same direction. Jane joined the crowd, and I followed Jane and everybody else across the intersection.

The opposite sidewalk was lined on both sides with tables and stalls selling God knows what: canvas carryalls, stuffed animals, aluminum saucepans, boots with flower appliqués, plastic earrings. It dawned on me that today was Saturday, and that the largest and most famous flea market in Paris was in this neighborhood. We must be on the outer fringes of it now.

Jane pushed along, not stopping to check out the cut-rate batteries, cow-shaped milk pitchers, and racks of leather pants. I elbowed my way behind her, jostled by bargain-seekers. It was too bad I didn't have time to check this out for "Paris Patter." I'd planned to get out here for that purpose sometime. The most famous part of the flea market wasn't the modern stuff we were passing now, but the thousands of dealers in antiques, curios, and secondhand wares of all sorts. As people always say about everything, people said the flea market wasn't what it used to be, that the fabulous bargains in antiques once found there were found no more, that the prices were as high as in shops, and so forth. Right now, the price level wasn't my concern; keeping up with Jane was.

We had reached a wide pedestrian precinct filled with booths. Jane's steps slowed. She paused beside a table piled high with rolled-up Ace bandages and glanced around uncertainly. I hoped she wouldn't catch sight of me hovering and approach to ask directions, but in fact she snagged a boy of about twelve who must have spoken English, because in a minute he was pointing and she was nodding vigorously. We set off with renewed confidence.

The nature of the merchandise began to change from modern junk to older things which may have been junk as well but were quainter. We traversed an open passage where gilt-framed mirrors reflected chairs with sprung seats, and rusted metal picnic tables shared space with life-size statues of torch-bearing Nubians.

At last we entered a building like a vast shed which had aisles lined with numbered stalls. A few of the stalls were closed, their contents hidden by pull-down shutters of corrugated metal, but most were open. Jane threaded her way slowly through the shoppers, looking from side to side at the vendors of ship's figureheads, duck decoys, jet necklaces, cherrywood barometers, and old sheet music. By now, I was definitely too warm. A trickle of perspiration slid down the back of my neck from underneath my hat, and my sunglasses were slipping on my nose.

Jane stopped, looking lost, and turned all the way around toward me. I tried to lose myself in a display of mounted antlers and disgusting stuffed animals. Then a male voice with a French accent called, in English, "Jane! Over here!" and she waved and crossed diagonally to a stall where two men were standing.

I slipped over as close to them as I dared. Both men were tall. One, who had a beaked nose and frizzy, shoulder-length gray hair, was almost cadaverously thin. The other was breathtaking. He was very French-looking, on the order of Louis Jourdan in *Gigi*, with dark hair and eyes. He was wearing a jacket in a muted blue-gray tweed and a blue turtleneck. If this looker were Bruno Blanc, I was damned envious of Jane.

It seemed that he wasn't. As best I could tell, the frizzy-haired one was performing introductions. The Louis look-alike took Jane's hand and inclined his head over it slightly, as if he longed to bury his face in her palm and lick it until she swooned. For the moment the only sure identification was the frizzy-haired man, whom I heard Jane refer to as "Bruno."

The three of them moved toward the back of the stall, even farther out of earshot. The handsome man, whom I guessed to be the proprietor, was apparently a specialist in scientific instruments. Several brass telescopes on wooden tripods stood in the boxlike space, and glass-fronted cabinets held old cameras, microscopes, a sextant or two, various weighing scales, retorts, and beakers. I slipped closer. In a bowl on a table was a supply of cards. I picked one up: Lucien Claude, Scientific Instruments, and a phone number. I put the card in my purse.

As Jane, Bruno, and the handsome man—Lucien Claude?—conversed, I realized that I had successfully completed my operation. I had followed Jane and found Bruno. Now what? Did I expect Bruno to walk out of here with the mirror under his arm? Should I wait until Jane and Bruno left and then strike up an acquaintance with the devastating Monsieur Claude? This plan had strong appeal, and I had all but decided to follow it when something happened to change my mind.

For no particular reason, I glanced over my shoulder. Across the way, where I had stood among the antlers and stuffed animals, was a stocky blond man. He was watching me. I knew immediately that he was the same blond man I'd seen eating french fries, and later looking at post cards, across the street from Le Jardin Métaphysique on the Rue Jacob. It was obvious that while I'd been so single-mindedly following Jane, the blond man had been following me.

A hollow place yawned in my gut. This man had seen me go into Le Jardin Métaphysique. He had seen me emerge and had seen me disguise myself and go off after Jane. I had been so focused on my own pursuit he could've been, and probably was, in the same Métro car with us.

We stared at each other, eyes locked. He started toward me. I backed up a few steps as he came forward. Then I turned and started off down the aisle at a brisk pace, dodging browsers and bulky items of merchandise like a huge rattan baby stroller and a juke box.

I knew I didn't like the man's looks, hadn't liked them since I first saw him stuffing his broad, unpleasant face with fried potatoes. I didn't like his short blond hair, brushed forward over his low, Neanderthal forehead, and I didn't like his bulky shoulders, which seemed about to burst the seams of his trench coat. Who would wear a trench coat when following somebody, anyway? It was such a cliché.

I speeded up, intent on the rectangle of light at the far end that led to the outside. When I glanced behind me I saw him barging determinedly forward, not even trying to be casual about it.

I thought about yelling for help, but for the moment had forgotten how to yell for help in French. Besides, I wasn't sure how to explain what the man had done to me, which so far was really nothing.

At this point, when to all intents and purposes I was running rather than walking, a precious little long-haired white dog crossed my path. I mean she literally crossed my path, and unfortunately her leash was tied to a rolling tea cart piled with an assortment of china. None of it was Limoges, or Sévres, or anything terribly valuable, which was lucky since several pieces fell off and broke when the cart jerked as I tripped over the leash.

I landed on my knees, my sunglasses flew off, and two anguished howls went up, neither of them from me or the dog. The cart's owner was bemoaning the loss of her china, while the dog's owner, shrieking, "Mimi!" was rushing to banish any shame or discomfort her pet might be feeling. I hauled myself to my feet unaided, but in the next instant my trench-coated friend was at my side. He hovered in the background while I paid for two teacups and a dessert plate and then slid his hand firmly under my elbow and steered me away.

I was caught. I wondered if I were going to be shot, like poor Pierre Legrand. Or tortured, pumped for my information about the mirror, such as it was. Maybe if I mentioned Madeleine Bellefroide's ransom—

"Perhaps I may buy you a cup of coffee, Madame?" he murmured in my ear. "I have some questions to ask you. I am Inspector Gilles Perret, of the Criminal Brigade."

JOSEF'S STORY

IT was lunchtime, so Inspector Perret and I found a nearby *brasserie* where he interrogated me over *choucroûte garnie*, huge plates of steaming sauerkraut laced with juniper berries and topped with plump sausages and hefty slabs of smoked pork, a delicious if near-lethal dose of cholesterol and salt. The questions he asked were the ones you'd expect, having to do with why on earth I was acting so suspiciously. The police, too, had discovered Bruno Blanc's interest in the mirror, and the inspector had been assigned to keep an eye on the comings and goings at Le Jardin Métaphysique. I had provided the most interesting activity so far, so he seemed let down by my claim that I was merely a witness and journalist, not a thief and possible murderer.

"You see, Madame," he scolded, cutting a bite of sausage and dipping it into mustard of eye-watering strength, "I understand that you must do your job. But these diversions make it more difficult for me to do mine."

I tried not to think about Madeleine Bellefroide's ransom, and what effect *that* might have on his job. "If I hadn't come along and aroused your suspicions, you might not have followed Jane yourself," I pointed out. "This way, you got a new lead—Lucien Claude, the scientific instruments dealer."

I took out Claude's card and Perret copied down the information. Then he picked up his knife and fork again and shook the greasy knife admonishingly. "I urge you to be careful. This is a murder case. It isn't like going to Monte Carlo to write stories about movie stars."

I had never thought of going to Monte Carlo to write about movie stars, but it wasn't a bad idea for later when this was wrapped up. In the meantime, I reminded him, "I know it's serious. I was there when Legrand was killed." Perret, I had decided, wasn't nearly as awful-looking as I'd first thought, although he was no Adonis like Lucien Claude. Blond and burly, he had bright blue eyes with a slight downward slant and ears that stuck out rather fetchingly—the kind of man the expression "you big lug" was invented for. And his concern for my welfare was touching, after the chilly and distrustful treatment I'd gotten from his dapper colleague.

We finished lunch pleasantly, and after the bill was paid he excused himself to go, I presumed, back to his post on the rue Jacob. I was gathering together my things preparatory to a visit to the ladies' room when, picking up Lucien Claude's card, I had a thought.

The thought was: The Bellefroide family acquired Nostradamus's mirror from a dealer named Claude.

I was just about positive, but I checked my notebook to be sure. Garbled as my notes of Bernard Mallet's press conference were, on this point they were clear: "Mirror bought, mid-nineteenth century, François Bellefroide, from J. Claude et Fils, dealer." I also remembered Mallet's saying the firm was no longer in business.

The likelihood of its being the same family was slim to none. Claude was a common French name, and probably dozens of Claudes were antique dealers. But how many of those dozens had been talking this morning to Bruno Blanc, who on his own admission wanted to own, or rather to liberate, the mirror? Even if the connection *was* thin, it was a good enough excuse to see what Lucien Claude looked like up close.

Back at the flea market I found Lucien Claude alone in his stall. Half-sitting on the edge of a table, arms folded, one leg bent and foot dangling, he looked like an ad for champagne, fancy cars, silk underwear, or whatever denotes the good life.

I had taken off my knitted hat and done the best I could with my traumatized hair. I thought the best tactic was to be as straightforward as possible, while not betraying that I knew of his connection with Bruno Blanc. Accordingly, I introduced myself as Georgia Lee Maxwell, journalist.

"Lucien Claude," he said, and gave me the same soulful handshake he'd given Jane. His eyebrows arched when I said I'd been on the scene at the Bellefroide and was doing a story about the theft of Nostradamus's mirror, but he didn't betray shock or surprise. He seemed urbane and decidedly unflappable.

"What brings you to me?" he asked.

I had worked this out beforehand. "Your name. I know that a dealer named Claude sold the mirror to the Bellefroides in the first place. I thought perhaps there was a connection."

He smiled a perfect, crinkly-eyed smile and said, "Out of all antiques dealers named Claude, I have been chosen as the possible heir?"

"Well—I haven't investigated all of them." I was getting flustered. "I thought scientific instruments might be more likely—"

"Of course. Fortune-telling mirrors could almost be considered scientific instruments, couldn't they?" He was a smoothie, obviously accustomed to making an impression, his manner just this side of teasing.

"I took a chance . . ."

His smile deepened. "Telescopes contain mirrors, after all, and astronomers study the heavens just as astrologers do."

He had rendered me speechless, but that was all right because he went on, "You are very clever, and the first journalist to find me. Josef Claude, of J. Claude et Fils, was an ancestor of mine. He sold the mirror to François Bellefroide. It's quite a family legend."

I was amazed to have struck this mother lode. "But at his press conference Bernard Mallet said the firm was out of business, and he didn't know anything about the provenance of the mirror," I stammered.

Claude's lip curled. "Bernard Mallet knows

nothing because he wants to know nothing," he said contemptuously. "The information was there if he cared to find it."

"And he also implied that your ancestor—Josef Claude—made up the Nostradamus story so he could get a better price for the mirror."

He snorted with laughter. "Josef would surely have been capable of doing such a thing," he said. "In this case he didn't. According to the family story, he was completely convinced that the mirror had magical powers and had belonged to Nostradamus. The mirror changed his life."

Chill bumps popped out on my arms, the way they always did when the mirror was mentioned, but also because this was a scoop. I pulled out my notebook. "Would you be willing to tell me about it?"

He glanced around. The stall was still empty. "Why not? Business is terrible."

I uncapped my pen. "You say the mirror changed Josef's life?"

He clasped his hands around one knee and rocked back a little. Storytelling posture. "Decisively," he said. "You see, Josef, my revered great-great-great-uncle, began as a tramp and something of a madman. He had fits and babbled in unknown tongues. He married an unfortunate woman and fathered a child, but then refused to stay home or settle down, and traveled through the countryside with a horse and wagon, sleeping in ditches. I think he did a small business in buying and selling junk. My family, I tell you willingly, were not very grand, but even so he was a shame and embarrassment to them.

"Josef often stayed away for months on end, covering great distances. According to the story he told later, on this most important trip he went as far as Provence, in the south of France. Toward nightfall one evening, he was in the vicinity of a town called Salon. Have you heard of Salon?"

"No."

"It is the town where Michel de Nostredame, or Nostradamus, lived for much of his life, where he died in 1566, and where he is buried." Lucien Claude smiled his heartthrob smile. "The story becomes intriguing, doesn't it?"

"It sure does."

"The weather was dreadful. A torrential rain was falling, the wind was blowing, and Josef's horse went lame on the rocky path. Such conditions weren't unknown to Josef, of course. He began to search for shelter, but no snug farmhouses or warm barns turned up as the storm worsened and his horse's limp became more pronounced. At last he saw, some distance off the road, a tumbledown stone cottage and shed. The place was dark and looked deserted. Josef settled the horse in the shed and, with his lantern, went into the cottage to take shelter for the night.

"As soon as he entered, he heard hoarse, rattling breathing. He held up his lantern and saw an old man lying on a filthy bed. The man was ill, surely dying. He begged Josef for water, which Josef gave him. Josef sat by the old man through the night, and during that time the old man told Josef about the mirror of Nostradamus.

"Some of his ancestors, he said, had been servants in Nostradamus's home. The old man claimed the prophet had given his forebears the mirror out of gratitude for their services, but Josef thought it more likely that they stole it when he died. In any case, the treasure had never been harmed or lost, and this old peasant was its guardian. As he felt death overtaking him, he gave it to Josef."

At this critical moment, a couple of people approached to ask Lucien Claude about prices, and I came back to the flea market, its babble of commerce the reminder that life could be normal instead of an imitation of fairy stories. When Claude had finished he returned and said, "That was Josef's story, at least. It's possible that he battered the old man to death and stole the mirror, but there's no way to prove it now."

"And the mirror had a profound effect on Josef?"

"The peasant kept the mirror, wrapped in cloth, under one of the stones of his hearth. After the old man died, Josef found it and unwrapped it. He spoke of its heaviness, its coldness, the glossy black of its surface. Naturally, he looked into it.

"At first he saw nothing. Then came a slight movement in its depths, like a twitching of something coming awake, and a scene emerged.

"It was a terrible struggle between a man and a monstrous black bird. The bird tore at the man with its beak, slashed with its claws, while the man pounded the bird. The battle was so savage that at first Josef did not recognize the man as himself. When he did, tears started to his eyes, because the man and the bird would surely kill one another. As he watched, however, his image put his arms around the bird, enfolding it lovingly, the bird settled against his chest, and the two melted into one. Then the mirror was black again.

"The next morning, Josef buried the peasant and started for Paris. When he arrived weeks later, he went to his wife and son and humbly begged them to forgive him for the pain he had caused. With the little he had, and help from his family, he became a junk dealer, and in time he founded a respectable business in secondhand goods, J. Claude et Fils. Eventually, he sold the mirror to François Bellefroide. The firm continued until his direct descendants died out."

I'd been holding my breath. I could see the struggle between man and bird, and their reconciliation. I exhaled slowly and said, "There's something I don't understand."

"What?"

"The mirror had been so important to Josef, changed his life, shown him this . . . vision, or whatever. Why would he sell it?"

Lucien Claude rubbed the tip of his finger over the table top. "Oh, you may imagine he got an outstanding price."

"But still, it doesn't seem right."

He shook his head. "No, it doesn't, unless you know one further thing. Josef kept the mirror for years. When he needed guidance, he gazed into it. He never saw another vision."

SCRYING

I must have looked as overcome as I felt, because Lucien Claude threw back his head and laughed. "It's a wonderful story, isn't it?" he said. "God knows if it is true."

I had the awful feeling he might have made it up for the occasion. "You weren't kidding? About the family legend?"

"Absolutely not. The version I just told you is exactly the one my parents told me. But to believe it we must trust Josef, who has been dead a long time and who, as I mentioned to you, went through a period when he wasn't in his right mind."

"It was awfully convincing," I said, almost belligerently, and then asked myself when I had acquired a stake in the mirror's authenticity. Another thought occurred to me: "Josef's story—is it common knowledge? I mean, did the Bellefroides know it?"

He shrugged. "If Josef thought it would enhance the price of the mirror, he may well have told François Bellefroide at the time of the sale. It isn't a secret, but it's hardly the kind of tale a businessman wants widely circulated about himself."

I nodded. If Madeleine Bellefroide had heard about Josef Claude, even if she hadn't remembered consciously, that might account for the similarity between their stories. Both said they had seen symbolic images of themselves. Madeleine's had shown her the steadily burning flame of her life. What had Josef's bird signified to him? His madness? His restlessness? Whatever it was, he had made his peace with it and gone on to a different kind of existence.

"And the people at the Musée Bellefroide? Do they know?" I asked.

"Possibly the former director did. Bernard Mallet is too busy keeping dust off his Sèvres table services to concern himself with Nostradamus's mirror."

Claude stood. People were drifting into the stall, and I knew I'd have to leave soon. "I don't suppose you've heard anything about the mirror since it was stolen," I said.

"The police have asked all of us to be on the alert for it," he said, which I noticed wasn't really an answer.

I took a breath. "I've heard that a ransom may be offered. A lot of money."

"Oh, yes? Offered by the museum?" His

tone was perfectly casual, and the tension I sensed may have come from me.

"No, by an individual."

"But that would be stealing, surely? The mirror is the museum's property."

"The person offering the ransom would give it back to the museum," I said, although I didn't remember Madeleine Bellefroide saying so.

"That's very generous and very strange. Who is this person?"

Although he still betrayed no more than normal interest, I was sure now I could feel an intense curiosity radiating toward me. I dropped my eyes, as if he might read Madeleine Bellefroide's name in them, and said, "The person wants to be anonymous for now."

"But he—or she—would be willing to pay well?"

"That's my impression."

"I see." A hunger in the question gave me a clue to Lucien Claude. Money turned him on.

I told him to call me if he heard anything, gave him my address and phone number, and moved to go. I had only one question left. "Have you ever heard of a group called the Speculatori?"

He gave me a look of comic exasperation. "Bruno Blanc and his colleagues? My God, yes. Bruno ferreted me out long ago. I told him Josef's story—why not?—and since then he has plagued my life, asking for more details. Now that the mirror has been stolen he's like a wild man."

"Do you think he stole it himself?"

"I almost wish he had. Then he might go into hiding with it and leave me alone. And now—" He made a gesture toward the several people who were hanging around looking like potential customers, and I thanked him and left.

On the long Métro ride back, I thought about Lucien Claude. He was achingly handsome, the soul of charm, a polished *raconteur*. The major emotion he had shown was amusement. He seemed almost as cold and glossy as the mirror itself.

I climbed out of the Opéra Métro station to find that the weather had changed. The golden Apollo on top of the opera house hovered against a background of scudding clouds. The wind had picked up, and there was a touch of chill in it. Before long my hat, which had been superfluous this morning, would be welcome.

The office door was standing open, as

usual, and as I approached I caught sight of Kitty sitting at her desk. She must have heard my footsteps, because she looked up and, seeing me, rolled her eyes wildly. I walked in without taking the hint, where-upon Bruno Blanc, who had been sitting at my desk, unfolded himself and stood up full length to glower at me.

"So," he said.

I glanced at Kitty. Her eyes were cast upward, and her expression conveyed that she had tried to warn me, but since I'd been too obtuse to catch on I would now have to suffer as she had been suffering. I turned to Bruno Blanc, remembered that I wasn't sup-posed to know who he was, and said, "Hello."

"So. You intrude in my business. You had better be careful," he said, shaking his wealth of gray frizzy hair at me. His face radiated fury. Jane must have told him about my visit to the Rue Jacob this morning. I had given her, I recalled, my office address and phone.

"Georgia Lee, let me present Bruno Blanc," said Kitty in an artificially bright tone. "Monsieur Blanc has been anxious to talk with you."

"You're like a vulture, picking through

the pain of others," Bruno hissed. "You arrive in secret, insinuate yourself, pry."

I had to admit the accuracy of his accusations. I had arrived in secret, insinuated myself, and pried. I had also, and thank heavens he didn't know it, snooped in his desk, tracked his girlfriend to the Porte de Clignancourt, and watched Bruno himself talking with Lucien Claude. "I was hoping to find out—"

"Hoping to find out! You were hoping to find out what you have no business to know!"

Justified as his anger might be, I wasn't going to be his punching bag. I planted my feet and said, "Monsieur Blanc! What are you so afraid of?"

To my surprise, it stopped him cold. He made chewing motions with his mouth a couple of times and sank down into my chair. "I'm so afraid," he whispered harshly. "I'm so afraid the mirror is gone forever."

Kitty and I exchanged looks. I replied to her unspoken question with the unspoken answer that she should leave Bruno and me alone. She got up and slipped out, and I perched on the edge of the desk.

I wasn't sure how to proceed. Bruno rasped, "All my work, all my study. And now it's gone."

He was carrying on like the mirror had been stolen from him personally. "But . . . you didn't have access to it in the museum, did you?"

He shot me a resentful glance. "Access! That fool Mallet didn't give anyone access. No, the mirror chooses when it will be quiescent, when it will be free. I am only afraid that it has removed itself from my sphere."

He was talking about the mirror as if it were alive, and that made me nervous. "What would you do with the mirror if you had it?"

"Do with it?" He looked at me incredulously. "What did Nostradamus do with it? I would look into it and see the future. Do you know all the things he predicted? The French Revolution, the first and second world wars, the coming of nuclear weapons. . . ."

I wondered if it had made Nostradamus happy to know how many disasters were on the way. "Are you sure it would work for you?"

He looked stronger, more confident. "I know it would, for two reasons. First, because I am naturally gifted in the art of scrying, which is divination by gazing into a reflecting surface. Second, because I have devoted my life to improving my gift through study and practice.''

I probably looked sceptical because he said, "I can demonstrate, if you like.''

That was the last thing I wanted. "Oh, no. I mean, I'm sure you could, but you probably have to have the right conditions, and—''

"The right conditions have nothing to do with external matters. They are inside me. Now. Do you have a cup or a bowl?''

I could've said no, and I would've, but Kitty's teacup, a wide-mouthed piece of delicate white bone china with roses around the rim, was sitting on her desk next to the bottle of Sphinx perfume, and he spied it. He picked it up, held it cradled in his hands a moment, and handed it to me. "Rinse it, please, and fill it with water.''

I took it to the ladies' room, feeling two conflicting emotions: abject fear and utter scorn. I rinsed out the dregs of Kitty's tea and filled the cup almost to the brim. I looked into it. On the surface of the water I saw a quivery image of my face. No flames, no birds.

When I got back to the office, Bruno had turned off the overhead light and was sitting in my chair with his hands resting loosely on

151

the desk. The cold illumination from the window emphasized his ravaged look. Without turning his head he said, "Please put the cup between my hands."

I put the cup down, glancing at his face as I did so. His eyes were shadowed, but there was no particular intensity in his expression. I went and stood next to the half-open door, so I could get away if anything unexpected started to happen.

He sat silently, gazing ahead of him, hands on the desk. My scalp prickled. I wished Kitty would come back and break this up, but obviously she'd had enough of Bruno already.

Bruno gave a faint sigh, sat up straighter, and inclined his head over the cup. In a few moments he said, in a conversational tone, "I feel the ocean."

I wondered if I were supposed to say anything. He hadn't given me instructions. I thought I'd better keep quiet.

"I feel the ocean, strong surges, strong currents," he said.

Of course I thought about Cross Beach. I grew up with the ocean, saw it every day.

"Exile," he said suddenly, in a tone of pained shock. "Exile, exile."

It sounded like the saddest word in the

language. I pressed my hand to my mouth. I was an exile. I had exiled myself.

His pace picked up, his voice breathless. "You are standing in a dark place, holding a light. You refuse to look where the light falls but persist in searching the shadows."

I refuse to look where the light falls. I'd have to remember . . .

"What have you done, that you should be so hounded, so pursued?"

I didn't like the sound of this. I also wondered if Bruno were trying to scare the socks off me.

"Go back!" Bruno sounded really alarmed. "Go back! You must go back!"

Enough was enough. I snapped on the light and said, "O.K. O.K. I believe you."

Bruno sat quietly for a moment. Then he blinked a couple of times and stood up. "You must be careful, Madame."

"Right," I said. "Thanks for telling me." I was ashamed to notice that I was breathing hard.

"I'm sorry," he said, moving to touch my arm.

I shied away. The ocean. Exile. Standing in a dark place, holding a light, but looking in the shadows. I'd always known I didn't want my fortune told.

153

We stood there without speaking. Then, in an abashed way, he said, "Jane told me something. She said a reward is being offered for the return of the mirror."

"That's right."

"Can you tell me . . . how much? By whom?"

I was in no mood to discuss it. "I can't say unless we have reason to believe we can get the mirror back."

"I see."

He didn't stay around much longer. After he left, I sat down at my desk. I bent over Kitty's teacup. I saw a quivery image of my face.

DISAPPEARANCE

"I wish I'd stayed. Maybe he would've given me a reading, too," Kitty said.

Kitty was drinking tea out of Bruno Blanc's erstwhile magic mirror. I was drinking out of a mug with the legend, "Bay City—Sand, Surf 'n' Sun." "I think you've missed the point," I said. "Didn't you hear the part about how I was fiercely pursued and should go back because I was in danger?"

She waved it off. "He wanted to scare

you. He was ticked off that you came to his place and pumped Jane. But the ocean and exile business was perceptive, wasn't it?"

"He also said I was in the dark holding a light, but looking in the shadows."

She thought for a minute. "You *are* in a dark place holding a light. By doing this story you're trying to illuminate events that were dark before."

"According to him I'm not doing a very good job of it, since I'm looking in the shadows instead of where the light falls."

"Hm." She sipped, then said, "Maybe he means you're ignoring the obvious." She looked triumphant. "Hey! Not a bad interpretation."

"Lovely." I was in a foul mood. I agreed with Kitty that Bruno had probably used his reading to scare me. The problem was, he had succeeded. There had been those pertinent allusions in what he'd said, and the episode had left me feeling exposed.

"You know what's weird?" I said.

"Yes. The way Bruno Blanc wears his hair."

"I mean really."

"What?"

"The way Bruno Blanc talks about the mirror as if it's alive and running the show.

He said it chooses whether to be quiescent or free, it isn't possessed it possesses, stuff like that. Which reminds me of that letter I got. It said, 'The mirror of Nostradamus destroyed Pierre Legrand.' Like the mirror could act on its own."

"So maybe Bruno wrote it? First the note, to get you scared; then the fortune-telling, to get you terrified."

"Could be." I wasn't positive.

While Bruno was telling my fortune, Kitty had gone to an English-language bookstore on the Rue de Rivoli and found an abridged paperback edition of the prophecies of Nostradamus. She'd been perusing it since her return, and now she picked it up again. A wild-eyed picture of Nostradamus glared at me from the cover as she said, "Here's the part that tells how he prophesies. Get this: 'Sitting alone at night in secret study, it is placed on the brass tripod. A slight flame comes out of the emptiness and makes successful that which should not be believed in vain.'"

"That clears everything up, all right."

She was silent a minute, reading. Then she said, "It goes on about the tripod, and water, and trembling when the god approaches. According to the explanation—"

"I'm glad to know there *is* one."

"The commentary says there are lots of interpretations of this passage, but one is that he's sitting in his study gazing into a bowl of water that was placed on the brass tripod. I mean, it's close, isn't it? What was it Bruno called fortune-telling by looking into a reflecting surface?"

"Scrying."

"Yeah. So here, maybe Nostradamus is scrying, right? And a bowl of water on a tripod isn't too different from a mirror."

"And believing any of this crap isn't too different from being completely nuts." I was irritated with Nostradamus. If he saw visions when he looked into a bowl of water why didn't he just say so?

Kitty put the book down. "You're starting to sound cranky. You must need food."

Food was Kitty's panacea for every discomfort. In her book broken hearts, career setbacks, and mid-life crises could be alleviated, or even banished, by ample nourishment. Although I sometimes scoffed at this approach, the truth was that it nearly always helped. She had a big green apple and a hunk of Gruyère in her desk, and we split them and ate them with the rest of our tea.

As I threw my half of the core in the trash can I said, "At least the next move is clear."

"It is?"

"Sure. I've got to see if Clive Overton, the art restorer, is able to talk. I found his name on a list in Bruno's desk, and I want to know what the connection is between them. I haven't heard a word about Overton since he keeled over at the museum."

"Better check him out," said Kitty absently. She'd picked up the Nostradamus book again.

I didn't know if Overton was in a hospital or not. The obvious place to begin looking was his hotel, the Relais Christine. But when I called and asked for him, a sweet-voiced woman informed me, sounding genuinely regretful, that he had checked out and left yesterday.

"You mean, checked out personally? I have to reach him. I'm a friend of his." (Well, I *could* have been his friend, if we'd had time to get better acquainted.)

"Oh, yes, Madame. He returned to pick up his things."

"But this is terrible."

"He didn't tell us where he could be reached. He only apologized for leaving sooner than he had planned."

158

Continued energetic probing produced nothing more. Overton had made no further reservations at the Christine, and she had no idea when or whether he might be returning. She was sorry that regulations prevented her from giving out his home address or telephone number.

I hung up and grumbled to Kitty. "What the hell do the police think they're doing? He may have left town."

"They haven't told *you* not to leave town, have they?"

"No."

"So you and Overton are in the same boat, right? Witnesses. Besides, why do you think he's left town? He just checked out of the hotel."

"All right, *all right.*"

"And maybe they know there's a connection between Overton and Bruno and they don't think it's important."

"I didn't say *I* didn't think it was important. I said maybe the police . . ."

And so on. We wrangled until we both got tired of it, and then I called London information and, easy as pie, got Clive Overton's phone number. Which did me no good at all, because when I called and let the phone ring twenty-five times, and then redialed for twenty-five more, nobody answered. "Wouldn't you think one of the world's greatest art conservators would have an answering machine, or a service?" I said.

"Not necessarily. It could be that—"

"Kitty, if you don't stop arguing with everything I say I'm going to scream."

"I just wanted to—"

"I'm warning you."

"Georgia Lee—"

"Shh."

She bit her lip and looked down at her desk. On it, in addition to the bottle of Sphinx and the prophecies of Nostradamus, were scattered swatches of material for a story she was doing on the slipcover craftsman who slipcovered the furniture of all the French movie stars. On each swatch she had pinned a piece of paper with the name of the star whose furniture was covered in that pattern.

In silence, I got out my notebook. Since I couldn't reach Overton right now, maybe I'd type up some notes.

Suddenly, Kitty pushed her chair back, jumped up, and ran to the door. She said, in a rush, *"He might not have a machine at home if he had an office somewhere else."* She disappeared, and I heard her rapid footsteps going down the hall.

Well, hell. I opened my desk drawer and took out Overton's bio. On it was the name of his business: Art Services, Ltd., and a telephone number that wasn't the one I'd just called. I made excuses for this bush-league performance by telling myself I'd been upset, but I was blushing as I dialed.

Kitty peered hesitantly around the door as I was finishing a brief conversation with Clive Overton's secretary at Art Services, Ltd. "Wait till I tell you," I said as I hung up.

She had the grace not to gloat, but simply said, "What? Did you find him?"

"I sure didn't. He isn't expected back in London until next week. His secretary says he's in Paris, staying at the Relais Christine."

NEGOTIATIONS

I kept trying Clive Overton's number throughout the evening, just in case he'd gone home and neglected to notify his office, but there was no answer. "Do you think the man has taken the mirror and skedaddled?" I asked Twinkie at ten o'clock that night, after the fifteenth call.

Twinkie was crouched in a corner, staring at a dust bunny. Dust bunnies were her Paris discovery. In Florida, I'd had a cleaning lady. "His name was on a list in Bruno Blanc's Speculatori file," I continued. "Maybe they're in this together, and Bruno's anxiety about the mirror is an act."

A draft rocked the dust bunny. Twinkie's ears went forward and her body tensed.

"Or say Overton was on the scene to divert suspicion from himself while his confederates took the mirror, and then he faked a collapse. Or maybe the collapse was genuine, because he hadn't known they would shoot Pierre Legrand."

She wisely decided not to pounce. Stalking a dust bunny was probably more fun that catching one.

"And now he's slipped clean away, leaving not even a dust bunny behind."

In that case, Twinkie wasn't interested. She jumped on the bed and began attending to her toilette. I lay back and tried to figure out a way I might track Overton down, but nothing occurred to me, so eventually I fell asleep.

I drifted through nightmares. I was on the beach in Bay City. A cadaverous, frizzy-haired figure in black approached me. When he got close enough I saw it was Ray, with Bruno Blanc's hair blowing around his face. I gasped, awoke, and lay there trembling until I dozed off for the next round.

After a night of that, I overslept the next morning and got up with a headache. I had a hard time getting started and was still pottering around my place, drinking coffee and trying to decide what to wear, when the phone rang about noon.

It was Lucien Claude. He sounded breathless, much less in control than he'd been yesterday. "Madame Maxwell? Madame Maxwell, I've been approached about the mirror."

"You what?"

"The mirror. The ransom. Someone has approached me."

I gripped the phone. Could the word have spread that rapidly? I supposed antiques dealers had the sort of jungle-drum method of getting news out that most professions have. "How? What happened?"

"After we talked yesterday, I discussed the ransom possibility with several of my friends who are also dealers here. You didn't say to keep it a secret, so . . ."

"No, it wasn't a secret."

"I didn't mention your name but said only

that this was the report I'd heard. My friends must have told others. And this morning, just a few minutes ago, I received a telephone call. It was a man. He asked if I were the person who was willing to pay for the mirror. I said . . . I didn't know what to say, so I said no, but I could contact those who would pay."

"And what did he say?"

"He said, 'I have it. I will call you back in one hour.' And he hung up."

Now I realized how little I'd expected any response to Madeleine Bellefroide's offer, and how ill-prepared I was to handle it. How did I know Lucien Claude's caller was telling the truth? Or that Lucien himself was telling the truth? I had to have time to assimilate this. "Listen, I'd better call the person who's offering the money and get right back to you."

He gave me his number again and got off the phone. I sat and tried to order my thoughts, but it was useless. I turned back to the phone and dialed Madeleine Bellefroide.

When I told her we might have a taker, I heard a sound like a hiss. In a moment she said, "So it has happened."

"Yes. Or . . . it seems so. If the caller is genuine."

She was silent again. Then she said, "I

will pay one hundred fifty thousand francs. But I must have proof."

Allowing for fluctuation in the exchange rate, a hundred and fifty thousand francs was in the neighborhood of twenty-five thousand dollars. It seemed a decent sum for an artifact Bernard Mallet considered worthless. "I'll tell him," I said.

"My name can't be mentioned. The entire matter will be in your hands."

I had a thought. "What about Lucien Claude?"

"What about him?"

"Well, he's the one who got the call. He may want to be involved, somehow."

She gave an impatient-sounding snort. "He'll want to be paid for his trouble, I believe you mean."

"Yes." I was pretty sure Lucien wasn't in this for humanitarian purposes.

"Make whatever arrangement seems fair. I said I'm willing to pay. But I will not pay without proof." Madeleine Bellefroide's privileged upbringing was evident in the ease with which she gave orders. It was hard to remember that she was sick, dying, desperate, but I did remember. I'd promised to help, and I wouldn't go back on my word.

"One more thing," she said.

"Yes?"

"I am inexpressibly grateful to you."

When I got off the phone I was sweating. I pushed the hair off my slick forehead and called Lucien, wondering how he'd react to Madeleine's conditions.

Somewhat to my surprise, he was agreeable about turning the negotiations over to me. He said, "Of course. When he calls back, I will refer him to you." I didn't mention a cut for him, and neither did he. We said good-bye, and I settled down to wait for the call.

Actually "settled down" is inaccurate. If I'd had trouble getting myself together before, now I was hopeless. My earlier indecision about what to wear deteriorated into near-immobility. I had to get dressed. Suppose the caller wanted me to rush out somewhere and do something? Yet none of my clothes seemed remotely right for mirror-ransoming. I stood in front of my towering armoire in my underwear, my breath coming in constricted wheezes. I had just, at long last, selected and put on a red turtleneck sweater-dress when the phone rang, fifteen minutes early.

I threw myself across the bed, fumbled

the receiver from the hook, and squawked, "Hello? Hello?"

"Hi, Georgia Lee, it's Kitty."

"Kitty."

"I was wondering why you hadn't come in today. Is everything O.K.?"

"Oh, *God.*"

"Georgia Lee! What's—"

I told her everything was fine, fine, fine, but that I'd have to get in touch with her later. I hung up and waited for every hair on my body to subside. Then I did settle down, sort of, to wait for the call.

A buffeting breeze rattled the doors to the balcony. Twinkie snoozed on one of the dining chairs. The phone did not ring. I've never been much of a one for pacing up and down, but I tried it just to pass the time. The appointed hour for the call came and went. Maybe I'd broken the phone, somehow, when I'd answered it before. I checked again to make sure it was on the hook, picked it up very fast to see if there was a dial tone, put it down and checked to make sure it was on the hook.

The phone rang only half an hour after it was supposed to. By this time, I was so short-circuited that I picked up the receiver slowly and delicately and answered with complete calm.

It was Lucien Claude.

I could have screamed. He said, "I'm terribly sorry. This is embarrassing, but . . . he just called me back."

What was embarrassing? "What did he say?"

He cleared his throat. "He refuses to call you. He says he will deal only through me."

He was trying to sound distressed, but I could hear the satisfaction oozing through. "I see."

"I tried to convince him, but he's jumpy, you know?"

"So what's the situation now?"

"I told him I had to check with my contact. He will call me back in fifteen minutes."

I thought it possible that Madeleine Bellefroide and I were being jerked around by the dashing Monsieur Claude. For the moment, I'd go along with him. "Tell him this. We will pay one hundred fifty thousand francs for the safe return of the mirror. As a first step, we must have proof that he actually has the mirror and that it is intact." I was rather proud of this speech. Lucien said he'd call me back when he heard from the man again.

My determined stance had made me feel better. I wasn't a complete rube, and Lucien Claude wasn't going to prance off with the ransom money without delivering the mirror.

He called back in twenty-two minutes, sounding credibly excited. "He agreed to the terms. I'll have the proof tonight."

"Tonight? How will you get it?"

"Oh"—he laughed awkwardly—"I had to promise him not to tell anyone about the arrangements."

Naturally. "Before any agreement is made, we have to see and accept the proof."

"Of course, of course. I'll be back in touch with you."

I drummed my fingers on the table next to the phone. I didn't trust Lucien Claude. I thought he was treating me like a patsy, and I hate that feeling.

All I could do, though, was wait for the next development. I combed my hair, put on my coat, and left for the office.

LUCIEN

I spent the afternoon abstractedly going over my notes, stopping occasionally to try calling

169

Clive Overton again. I seemed to have nothing but more questions to add to my original questions: Where is Clive Overton? What is Overton's relationship to Bruno Blanc? Did Lucien Claude really get a phone call or is he pulling a scam? I stared blankly at my stack of papers, half-listening as Kitty discussed slipcovers in numerous telephone calls.

At one point Jack wandered in. "There you are," he said to me. "Just wanted to tell you the result of my guy's foray into Pierre Legrand's background."

"What did you find out?"

He took his usual perch on the windowsill and lit his usual cigarette. "Nothing earthshaking. My hunch about Pierre having some money was right. The family owned a piece of property in Normandy, and his mother eventually sold it for a decent amount. We're not talking vast sums, you understand."

"But that apartment! And the man worked as a museum guard, for heaven's sake."

"I guess he believed in being thrifty. And maybe he liked the work—quiet, pleasant surroundings, not too taxing . . ."

"Unless you're getting shot in the head."

"Unless you're getting shot in the head. Right."

I thought about Pierre working as a guard, refusing to alter his mother's apartment, all the while sitting on a respectable nest egg. "This is interesting. Thanks for telling me."

"Anything to please." He leaned over to glance at my notes, a maddening habit he had. After a minute he said, "Who's Lucien Claude?"

Despite my best intentions, I felt my territorial hackles rising. "Somebody I uncovered who has a peripheral connection to the case."

"Ah *ha*. Playing your cards close to your pretty little chest, eh?"

"Jack, considering the source, I'll let you get away with 'pretty.' But 'little'—"

"O.K., don't tell me who he is. It was just idle curiosity. We won't be back on it seriously until they arrest somebody."

"Since you put it that way, I won't."

"Sure. Let Uncle Jack find out about Pierre and mom, but when it comes to giving him anything—"

"Jack—"

I told him who Lucien Claude was, omitting any mention of the ransom. Just for spite, I ended up with, "And he's absolutely the most gorgeous man I've ever seen."

"Probably gay," he said and left the room.

It was early evening, and we were winding

up at the office, when the phone rang. Kitty answered, thinking it was a slipcover call-back, but it was for me. When she said, with her hand over the receiver, "It's a Frenchman. He sounds like he's under pressure," I jumped to the correct conclusion that it was Lucien Claude.

He skipped the amenities and got right to the point. "I'm very sorry, Madame Maxwell, but I cannot do what you want."

A bubble of anger popped in my head, but I kept my voice calm. "What do you mean?"

"The ransom. The proof. I can't help you." He sounded shaky.

"Why not? What happened?"

"I just . . . something else has come up."

I wondered if he were trying to shake me down, panic me into offering him money by threatening to pull out. "All right. Tell me where to get the proof, and I'll handle it myself."

"I can't do that. I don't yet know myself."

I *was* mad by now. My tone was icy as I said, "Look, Monsieur Claude. You insisted on being involved, and I was counting on you."

"I know. I'm terribly sorry."

"If it's money you want, that can be arranged."

"Madame! I never thought of that."

Like hell. "Of course you should be recompensed. It's only fair."

The conversation lapsed while he thought this over. In the background, I could hear the hubbub of the flea market. I pictured him standing in his stall, licking his gorgeous chops. I said, to turn the screws a little, "My contact is anxious to have the mirror. I'm sure any reasonable figure you named would be acceptable."

He said, "You're very persuasive."

"We're relying on you."

More hesitation—window dressing, I assumed—and then, not at all to my surprise, he came around. "All right, then."

"I'm deeply grateful."

If he caught my sarcasm he didn't let on. His voice shook again as he said, "In that case, I must say good-bye immediately. I should be at home, waiting for a telephone call."

"At home?"

"Yes. I live in Montparnasse. It will take me half an hour or more to get there."

So Lucien and I were neighbors. He said, "I will be in touch with you," and hung up.

I got up and put on my coat, thinking hard. Lucien wanted the money, obviously. I was grateful that he'd consented to go ahead without haggling over the amount. But I thought he had sounded genuinely frightened, too. I unearthed the Paris phone book and skimmed the listings for "Claude." The only Lucien was on the Rue Vavin, which was ten minutes' walk, at most, from my place on the Rue Delacôte.

I hadn't really formulated a plan, but when I climbed out of the Montparnasse Métro station twenty minutes later, I didn't walk toward the Rue de Rennes and home but went in the opposite direction—down the Boulevard Montparnasse in the direction of the Rue Vavin.

It was about six-thirty, almost completely dark, a blustery evening. The Boulevard, glowing with neon and choked with traffic, was bright and gaudy. I passed the movie theater, the Notre-Dame-des-Champs church, the travel agency. Now I was on the section of the boulevard where the famous café hangouts of the twenties were located. La Coupole, still a fashionable place to go, was across the street, and a little farther on was Le Dôme. La Rotonde, which I was approaching, was on the corner of the Rue

Vavin. As I turned left I glimpsed people inside having aperitifs, chatting, reading. What would Parisians do with themselves, I wondered, if all the cafés closed? The streets would be clogged with lost souls longing for an espresso or a glass of beer to linger over for hours, and a little round table to rest their elbows on.

I hadn't written down Lucien Claude's address, but it stuck in my mind. I continued along the Rue Vavin, which was narrower and darker than the boulevard. After crossing the Boulevard Raspail I discovered that Lucien Claude lived in a striking, multi-balconied structure of white ceramic brick I had often passed and admired. It was on my route to the Luxembourg Gardens, one of my favorite places to stroll and, in my opinion, the most wonderful park in Paris. I didn't think Lucien had had time to get here from the Porte de Clignancourt, and I wasn't sure what I planned to do anyway, so I went into the grocery store across the street and bought half a kilo of green beans and a small goat cheese. At a newsstand, I bought that evening's issue of *Le Monde*. Then I window-shopped, quaking from the biting wind, which seemed to get colder every minute.

I had learned from my experience following Jane (and being followed by Inspector Perret) that surveillance wasn't among my talents. Even so, I was there, and watching, when Lucien rushed down the Rue Vavin and entered the front door of his building.

So now what? Just as he'd said, he'd come home to wait for a phone call. That call might come in five minutes or five hours. I contemplated staying where I was and gazing in a window at hand-knitted infant garments for five hours, but my interest in blue booties and bibs embroidered with "Bébé" wasn't that keen. The obvious thing to do was give up.

I gave up. At least, I told myself I was giving up. Yet in this case, giving up didn't mean going home, but going to a café on a corner half a block from Lucien's building, settling myself by the window, opening my copy of *Le Monde*, and ordering a *kir*. It was perfectly normal Parisian behavior and had nothing to do with hanging around to see if anything developed.

I puzzled my way through a seven-column analysis of French foreign policy, then decided I'd better start again at the beginning. By the time I'd gotten halfway through the second go-round it was time for another *kir*. My eyes stung from smoke, or foreign policy. I was getting hungry, and slightly dizzy. I had folded *Le Monde,* and was searching for the change to pay for my drinks, when Lucien Claude strode past the window, down the Rue Vavin in the direction of the Luxembourg Gardens.

I caught only a momentary glimpse of his face, but I could see he looked tense. This must be it. He was going to get the proof. I didn't have change, so I overpaid outrageously and plunged out into the street after him.

He was approaching the Luxembourg, but the garden closed at sundown, so he couldn't be going in. This stretch of the Rue Vavin was gloomy, lined with apartment buildings and shuttered shops. Lucien and I were the only pedestrians, but he didn't look back. Remembering Inspector Perret, *I* looked back, but nobody was there.

Lucien had reached the place where the Rue Vavin dead-ended into the closed gate of the Luxembourg. He crossed the street to the garden side and turned left, walking up the Rue Guynemer, along the high fence, black iron bars tipped with gold spikes, that enclosed the Luxembourg. I stayed on the opposite side of the street, well back, watching Lucien's head move under the street lamps, from one pool of light to another.

About halfway up to the next gate, he stopped. He seemed to be looking intently at the fence. Then he moved toward the fence, out of the light, and I lost sight of him as he bent down.

I didn't even have time to think of moving closer before a dark figure materialized, rising up between two parked cars on Lucien's side of the street. Its head had no definition, and I knew instantly it was wearing a ski mask. It moved a couple of steps toward Lucien, and then I heard the shots—two of them, just as there had been at the museum. I saw the figure move back, heard a car door slam, and in an instant a car with no lights pulled out of its parking place on the Rue Guynemer and drove away.

I heard a dog barking furiously, and a huge black poodle and the elderly man who'd been walking him reached Lucien at the same time I did. He'd fallen in a crouch, with one hand outstretched toward the fence. His eyes and mouth were open. Blood from the back of his head looked black in the yellow half-light of the street lamp.

"My God, it's like the war," the man whispered, his voice full of anguish. The dog barked and plunged at the end of its leash. I looked next to the fence, both on the sidewalk and in the bushes on the other side. There was nothing there, nothing anywhere around. Whatever Lucien had been reaching for, he hadn't been able to grasp it. Wind lifted the hair from Lucien's forehead, and the man with the poodle began to cry.

QUAI DES ORFÈVRES

I was sitting in an office at the Criminal Brigade headquarters on the Quai des Orfèvres. My dapper inspector, whose name I continued to repress, sat behind his desk, talking on the phone. It was midnight, or thereabouts, and he looked crisp and fresh in a blue pin-striped shirt with stark white collar and cuffs. On the floor beside my chair was my plastic shopping bag containing half a kilo of green beans, a goat cheese, a slightly used copy of *Le Monde*. When I looked down and saw it, the reminder of normal life made me want to cry, which was something I'd been trying hard not to do ever since I stood over the dead body of Lucien Claude on the Rue Guynemer.

I had told the police everything, including

the whole story of Madeleine Bellefroide's ransom offer and our negotiations. I had seen a number of members of the Criminal Brigade, including the relatively sympathetic Inspector Perret. When I talked with him about what had happened, he made a clucking sound and shook his head, his blue eyes grave. "This is terrible. The boss will be furious," he had said, and I thought he was right on both counts.

Most of the policemen I saw had one thing in common: they were highly irritated with me. They didn't trust me, either, and who could blame them? I was the one person they knew of who was closely connected to both murders. From the innocent bystander at the Musée Bellefroide, I had metamorphosed into a suspect.

I was wretched. When I closed my eyes, even to blink, I saw Lucien's dead face. I apologized over and over to the policemen, because I would never be able to apologize to Lucien Claude.

The dapper inspector put down the phone. Without looking at me, he picked up some papers from his desk and started to read. They were, I surmised, a transcription of my account of the evening's events. When he finally finished them and looked up, I could see I was about to get my tail kicked.

"This is astonishing," he said.

"I know. I know. I'm sorry."

"Do you realize what you've done with this ransom business?"

"Yes—" I had to stop and clear my throat.

He drew a box on a piece of paper and wrote something in it. "Madame Maxwell, have you ever heard of *garde à vue?*"

"No, I—"

"If we choose, we are legally entitled to put you under *garde à vue*. That means, we can hold you for twenty-four hours without charge while we continue our investigation."

"Look—"

"I am half inclined to exercise that option now."

Until you've been faced with a serious threat of being locked up, you can't imagine the panic it engenders. The thought of not being able to walk out of there, not being able to go home, sleep in my own bed, made me woozy. I pulled at my collar, as if I needed air.

Then I tried to imagine the reaction in Cross Beach when word got out I'd spent time in the Paris pokey, even if it was only twenty-four hours. Or, Lord help us, what

Loretta and the people at *Good Look* would think. None of them would understand about *garde à vue.* "Please don't. I've told you everything, honestly. I didn't kill Lucien Claude, and I don't know who did . . ." I continued in this vein while he drew another couple of boxes and wrote in them.

When I shut up, he said, "Naturally, we have called Madeleine Bellefroide."

Shame washed over me. On top of everything else, I'd let her down. "What did she say?"

"She corroborated your story." He acted as if this point in my favor were totally insignificant.

In the end, he let me go. It hardly needed to be said that he wanted me to stop meddling in the case, but he said it anyway. He also told me that *garde à vue* remained an imminent possibility. Chastened and miserable, carrying my shopping bag, I tottered out of his office.

I emerged into an anteroom to find Jack sitting there, reading a story about Princess Stephanie in a back issue of *Paris Match.* "Got time for coffee?" he said. "There's an all-night café on the Place St. Michel."

I was so touched to see him I had trouble

speaking. "You didn't have to wait. You must have filed your story hours ago."

"I did, but I thought I'd hang around to see if you made any surprise revelations." He stood. "Ready?" I felt too weak to move. The bliss of having the right person show up at the right time had taken away the remnants of my energy. He put his arm around my shoulders, I got my legs moving, and we walked to the elevator.

In the café, I broke down, hunched over my cup. "It's all my fault. All my fault," I sobbed. Steam from my café au lait drifted around my head. "He'd be alive if it weren't for me."

I was out of control, even though part of me was also ashamed of embarrassing Jack. He didn't sound embarrassed, though, when he said, "Bullshit, Georgia Lee. He'd be alive if it weren't for the person who shot him."

"But I made him—"

"You didn't make him. He insisted on being involved. Isn't that right?"

"He wanted out, and I offered to pay him."

"And he accepted."

"He didn't know he was going to be *killed!*"

"Well, neither did you."

I subsided, and with both hands managed to bring my cup to my mouth so I could take a swallow. "Poor Lucien Claude," I said, fresh tears dribbling down my cheeks.

"The innocent victim."

"Yes."

"The handsome man caught in a web not of his own making."

I blinked away some of the watery haze in my eyes and quavered, "What are you getting at?"

"I'm just thinking. Maybe Claude was the innocent victim. Or maybe he gave the person who killed him a reason to do it."

"That's like saying the victim of a rape was asking for it."

"You know, I must be psychic, because I knew you were going to say that." Jack lit a fresh cigarette with the butt that had been smouldering in the ashtray. "Nobody raped Lucien Claude. He was murdered. Now, did the man Claude was dealing with go to the trouble of setting all this up just to have a chance to shoot him? Or did he genuinely want the ransom money? Take a guess."

"I . . . I don't know . . ."

"A wild stab."

"O.K. Say he really wanted the money."

"In that case, by murdering Claude he has completely defeated his purpose, hasn't he? Couldn't it be that Claude gave him a reason for going so obviously against his own interests?"

I thought about it. "But if it's the same people, they killed senselessly once before— Pierre Legrand. Maybe they're maniacs who like to commit murder."

"Could be. I'm just raising the question."

I took another swallow of coffee, this time without as much difficulty. "They didn't tell me anything about tonight. What have you heard?" I asked.

He leaned back and laced his hands behind his head. "Not much. The ballistics people are working on whether the bullets came from the same gun that killed Pierre Legrand. Claude lived alone, separated from his wife. I understand they're checking to see if he's ever been involved in anything illegal or shady."

I finished my coffee. When I put the cup down, Jack reached over and took my hand. "Feel a little better?"

I nodded. He looked craggy, rumpled, kind, and very tired. He was smiling, and I liked his smile. I was so grateful to him for waiting for me and not letting me leave the

Quai des Orfèvres alone and in despair. I gave his hand a squeeze, and felt an unexpected tingly shock that I recognized all too well as that old devil, sexual attraction.

I reined myself in. The man was not only married, but a smoker. I told myself I happened to be feeling vulnerable right now. I extricated my hand with all deliberate speed and said, "Maybe I should go on home."

"I'll drive you."

The night was cold when we emerged, the Seine, under orange floodlights, pitch-black and moiling. "I shouldn't let you do this," I said without conviction as I pulled my coat around me. Jack lived in Neuilly, and my place was hardly on his way.

"What sort of cad would do less?"

As we rattled through the quiet Left Bank streets in Jack's aged Renault I said, "Let's go back by where it happened. Can we?"

Jack didn't reply but took a left at the next corner, and soon we were pulling into a loading zone on the Rue de Fleurus not far from the Rue Guynemer. We got out and walked the few steps to the corner. At the place Lucien had fallen, a portion of the sidewalk had been blocked off with barriers, and a couple of *gendarmes* wearing capes were loitering beneath the street lamps. As we

186

approached, Jack called out that we were from the press, and the *gendarmes* seemed willing enough to let us stand at the barrier and look at the black iron fence, bushes crowding it from the other side. I saw a dark patch or two that might have been blood or a trick of the light. I stared at the place, seeing Lucien crouched there, his hand out-stretched.

"He was bending down to get something, but nothing was there," I said to Jack. I was almost whispering, as if we were in church.

"Unless it was hidden." Jack's tone was as hushed as mine, his words blowing away on the cold wind.

I clasped my hands tight, looked at the dark patches, and tried once more to tell Lucien I was sorry. Then Jack and I turned away and went back to the car.

When we reached my place, I felt it was almost inhospitable not to invite Jack in for a drink or coffee, but I also felt it was a move to be avoided at all costs. "What on earth will your wife think? Will she be worried?" I said as I prepared to get out.

"Claire? She's used to it," he said shortly.

"Thank you, Jack. A lot."

I hugged his neck. There couldn't be any harm in that. I got out and climbed wearily up the stairs. By the time I reached my window he had already driven away.

A PHOTOGRAPH

"Please don't apologize," Madeleine Bellefroide said. She tossed restlessly on her sofa, where she was propped against a pile of silk pillows. A crocheted throw of ivory-colored wool was wrapped around her legs. She looked drawn and pallid, as if some harsh substance had leached the color out of her. When I'd seen her before, it had been difficult to believe she was seriously ill. Now, it was easy. Our failure to regain the mirror had literally knocked her off her feet.

It was the afternoon after Lucien Claude's murder. I had slept fitfully, gotten up late, and spent the morning at home. I felt achy, frayed, and depressed. I knew Madeleine Bellefroide and I should talk. I called, made an appointment, and took the bus to her apartment. When it was obvious that she wasn't angry with me, my explanations came easier.

"I thought he threatened to pull out so I'd offer to pay," I said. "But even after I offered and he accepted, he was afraid. There was more to it than the money."

Madeleine closed her eyes. "And now we're as far from getting the mirror as ever— or farther, perhaps."

I saw that in her way, she was as obsessed with the mirror as Bruno Blanc was. The fact that two men were now dead was secondary. The degree of her self-absorption was astounding, but I couldn't be sure that in her situation I would act or feel differently. "I wish we'd gotten it," I said, thinking how futile wishes were.

"Yes." The word was barely audible. Then, her voice a bit stronger, she said, "Madame Maxwell, the offer still stands. If there is any possible way—"

I shook my head. "I don't see how there can be. The police will have to know everything. I don't see how it can happen."

"I suppose not. But as I say, the offer stands."

I left her lying on the sofa, her eyes closed.

I supposed I should check in at the office, although my energy level was low and my enthusiasm nonexistent. When I got there Kitty was out, although she'd taken a couple of messages from newspapers wanting statements. I was beginning to comprehend what a nuisance press attention could be, but I was dutifully about to return one of the calls when the phone rang.

"Madame Maxwell?" It was a woman's voice, husky and familiar.

"Yes."

"It's Chantal Legrand. I was wondering—you're in your office now?"

"Yes, I am."

"I'm in the neighborhood. May I stop in and speak with you?"

"Well . . . sure. Of course."

"I'll be there in five minutes."

As I waited the five minutes for Chantal to show up I wondered what on earth she wanted and hoped it wasn't to berate me for trying to ransom the mirror from her husband's killers.

She arrived, dressed in a severe black suit that only made it obvious that she was bursting with life. As she spoke, she fiddled with the clasp of her purse.

"I read in the paper today about the death of Monsieur Claude. About you, and the mirror, and the ransom," she said.

"Yes. It was a terrible thing."

"Just like Pierre, you know?"

"Yes."

After an interlude of silence, she recommenced. "You had been dealing with Monsieur Claude, the newspaper said."

"That's right."

"I'm wondering—did he say anything about my husband, Pierre?" When that question was out, she picked up speed. "It haunts me, this mirror, the idea that Pierre might have been involved. I wanted to know if Monsieur Claude said whether the man—the one who wanted to sell back the mirror—whether he had mentioned Pierre?"

She took out a lace-trimmed handkerchief and carefully blotted her upper lip.

I shook my head. "As far as I know, your husband's name never came up in connection with the ransom arrangements. If the person who called Lucien Claude spoke of him, I wasn't told about it."

"I see." She gave a last blot. I was sure she hadn't gotten even a trace of her pale pink lipstick on her handkerchief. "I'm relieved to hear that. These implications—they're hard to forget."

"I'm sure they are."

I thought she'd be getting up to go, but she continued to perch on the edge of her chair. She said, "I don't suppose Monsieur Claude had any notion who these people he was dealing with might have been?"

"If he did, he didn't tell me."

"And you? You were there last night?"

"I was there, but I couldn't possibly have identified anybody. It was too dark, and it happened too fast."

She twisted her handkerchief. "I can only wait," she said.

Frankly, Chantal, with her tragic, semitheatrical air, was getting on my nerves. I knew she'd had a rough time, but I couldn't avoid the feeling that she was making the most of it. I was therefore relieved when she thanked me for my time and left.

I didn't stay around, either. I was so tired and discouraged that even sitting upright took effort. It was time to go home.

Dead on my feet, I pulled the afternoon mail from my box downstairs. There were the usual invitations to press previews, a bank statement that I didn't want to look at, a letter from Mama. And there was an envelope with no return address.

I opened it upstairs, in my apartment. The envelope contained a folded sheet of pliant cardboard. Tucked in the fold was a black-and-white Polaroid photograph. After one blank moment, I realized I was looking at a picture of Nostradamus's mirror.

ENLISTED

THE mirror had been photographed from above, lying on a white background that could have been a bed sheet or a piece of paper. It was eerily featureless and looked, I thought, more like a circular black hole than an object. Beside it was a battered-looking round leather case decorated with metal studs.

As I stared at the mirror, it seemed to expand and contract to the rhythm of the blood beating in my ears. Afraid I might pass out, I sat down and stopped looking at it until the pounding subsided.

Then I turned the picture over. Nothing was written on the back, and there was no message on the cardboard either. I looked at the envelope again. My name and address were printed in black ink, in capital letters. The postmark was four o'clock yesterday afternoon at the large post office on the corner of my street. That was odd. This photograph must have been the proof Lucien Claude had expected to pick up, yet according to the postmark, it had been mailed several hours before he was killed.

So here I was, still in the game. Or so the senders apparently thought. I went to call the Quai des Orfèvres, and when I got through to the Criminal Brigade I asked specifically for Inspector Perret.

He said he'd be right over, and he kept his word. When he arrived he was wearing jeans, running shoes fastened with velcro strips, a plaid wool jacket, and a soft cloth cap. A beige canvas book bag was slung over his shoulder, and he was carrying a *baguette*. I must have looked surprised at his outfit, because he said, "The arrival of the police should not be obvious, in case the building is being watched."

In case the building is being watched. Great. I felt compelled to look out the window. Across the street at the *charcuterie*, people waited in line to buy sliced ham, celery *rémoulade, pâté de campagne*, creamed potatoes. I didn't see anyone lurking, but who could tell? Inside the laundromat, a dark figure sat slumped in a chair. He could be waiting for his laundry, or for me.

I turned back to find Inspector Perret taking a waxed-paper envelope out of his canvas carryall. He slid the photograph into it while Twinkie stood on the table watching him. "Fingerprints," he said over his shoulder as he did the same with the envelope. When he had tucked them away he said, "Now," and looked at me expectantly.

I ran through the circumstances of receiving the photo, and for good measure repeated my version of last night's tragedy. He sat at the table, pulling bites from his *baguette* and chewing them meditatively. I hoped that when I finished he wasn't going to say he'd warned me, or he'd told me so, but I suppose only a saint could have resisted the temptation.

"I warned you, didn't I?" he said.

"Yes," I said snippily. I was tired of wallowing in blame.

"This is what happens when—"

"Would you like something to drink?"

"No, thank you. Nothing."

He pulled off and chewed another bite. I considered offering him jam. Every time I'd seen the man he'd been eating. He said, "The person who sent the picture will contact you. What will you say?"

I'd been wondering. I could say further inquiries would be handled by the police, but that hardly seemed productive. I evaded the question. "He may not call. He will have seen the newspapers."

"That's true. But the newspapers have made you look extremely suspicious. He may believe you want to proceed. For all he knows, you could have a great deal to gain."

And for all you know, too, I thought. I couldn't read his face. His blue eyes had an absent expression, as if he were looking forward to his next meal, but I thought there was more on his mind than that. "Surely he'll figure the police are watching me."

"Yes, he will. He will be cautious, and you must be also."

I was getting the drift. I sat down across from him. A couple of crumbs rode up and down on the corner of his munching mouth. "I must be cautious *how?*"

He swallowed. "You must be cautious if you decide to help us."

He'd finally said it. As soon as the words were out I was hit by a sneezing fit. After it ended ten sneezes later, and I'd blown my nose, I said, "Help you? You want me to pretend I'm still interested, something like that?"

His demeanor indicated that it was little enough to ask of someone who had caused as much trouble as I had. "That's right. Pretend you're interested. Set up a meeting to exchange the mirror for the money."

I rasped, "Would I have to go to this meeting?"

He shrugged. Details, details. "We would be backing you up, of course. The risk would not be great."

I had heard that one before. Not said to me but said in a zillion movies and TV shows right before everything broke open and went completely to hell. And the scene after that was the body-littered aftermath, with at least a few of the bodies being good guys. I was shy about asking my next question, but I forced myself. "What happens if I *don't* help?"

If he felt rejected, he didn't show it. "It may lessen your peril, but not a great deal. At this point you are involved, whether you want to be or not. Frankly, your best interests lie in helping to catch the criminals."

He stopped and thought. "And of course we would consider your cooperation an indication of good faith." Which meant, I took it, that they'd drop the *garde à vue* idea.

Naturally, I was going to consent. I'd only asked about other alternatives because I thought Mama would want me to. Now, when I told her about it afterward, I'd be able to say honestly that I'd been offered almost no choice.

And it would be great for the story.

"All right. I'll do it. Now what?" I said.

I couldn't tell if he were grateful or not. "If you'll allow me, I'll attach a listening device to your telephone," he said.

He had it right there with him in his canvas bag, a tiny black thing with a few wires attached. It was about as big as the palmetto bugs that used to get into my kitchen in Bay City. He had it hooked up in no time. "What will you do? Record my conversations?" I asked.

"That's right." He was reattaching the cover of the receiver. Twinkie was helping, standing by and giving his hand an occasional nudge with her nose. She adored men. She hadn't had this much fun in a long time. I couldn't tell from Inspector Perret's manner whether he liked cats or not. He hadn't made a fuss over how cute she was, but he hadn't shoved her out of his way either.

He hung up the receiver. "So there we are."

I had a bug on my phone. I remembered a few fairly specific phone conversations Kitty and I had had about our personal lives. We'd have to talk girl talk face to face until this was over. "What do I do?"

"You can only wait until he calls—if he calls," he said. "When he does, don't act too eager. That will make him suspicious. Let him see the money slipping away, and he will want it even more."

"But finally I consent?"

"Yes."

I glanced at the phone. I didn't know if I had the acting talent to bring this off. "I hope nothing goes wrong."

"We will be watching your apartment and listening to the calls. Go about your business. As far as he knows, you haven't contacted the police about the photograph, and that will be in your favor."

"Do I have to stay home or can I go to the office? There's a phone at the office, too."

His expression, I thought, was just a bit smug. "By tomorrow morning, one of these devices will have been placed on that phone, as well."

I imagined the police listening to reel after reel of Kitty's phone interviews about celebrity slipcovers. "Can I tell my office-mate the phone is bugged?"

He got serious to the point of grim. "No.

Don't tell anyone. Not about the photograph, or the plan, or anything at all."

I promised. After I had locked the door behind him, I noticed that he'd left his bread on the table. He'd only eaten a quarter of it.

In five minutes or so, I began to have that "What have I done?" feeling. Buyer's remorse. I'd bought Inspector Perret's proposition, and now I wondered if the price was too high. It wasn't much use to tell myself that I was the link to the money, and more valuable to the killers alive than dead. What if there were an angle I wasn't seeing, one that would make me more valuable dead?

"Go about your business," Perret had said, but I was afraid to leave the apartment, and I hadn't bought food for dinner. Checking my half-sized refrigerator, I found the beans and goat cheese I'd bought the night before. I also had a semi-gnawed *baguette*. These could make an adequate, if meager, repast.

Humming to keep my courage up, I started to get it ready. After a while, I realized I was humming "All Alone by the Telephone." I bit my lip and pulled the strings off the beans in silence.

AT THE CAFÉ DE LA PAIX

THE phone didn't ring all night. As time went on, I began to think about my junior year at Cross Beach High, when I'd been told on good authority that Junior Ellsworth was going to call and ask me to the prom. The phone didn't ring then, either. I finally went to the prom with Lonnie Boyette, which led to our romance and ill-fated marriage. The associations weren't good.

Anyway, here I was primed—terrified, but primed—for perilous, clandestine goings-on, and nothing went on. The phone was so silent I began to be embarrassed, imagining my police monitors making sarcastic cracks to one another about the deadness of my social life.

I went to the office the next morning and was glad to find that Kitty was out for the day, so I didn't have to feel guilty for not telling her we were bugged. By midafternoon, the edge was wearing off. I started to assume that the person who had sent the photo had changed his mind about dealing with me after seeing the papers. I felt let down but relieved and began to turn to other matters.

Before the murder of Lucien Claude I had been making unanswered telephone calls to the London residence of Clive Overton. I picked that up where I had left off, with exactly the same results. I wondered if the police knew Overton had checked out of the Christine and called Perret to ask, but he wasn't there and the person who answered claimed to be prohibited from giving out information of that nature. I called Overton's office at Art Services, Ltd. and was told blandly that he was in Paris at the Relais Christine. I started to contradict, then thought twice. If Overton were hiding out, it might be better not to let him know someone was searching for him. I thanked the secretary and got off the phone. I was stymied.

Being stymied, to a reporter, is like catnip to a cat. Nothing could have made me more determined to track Clive Overton than having the obvious ways of finding him cut off.

I mulled it over. My only two connections with Overton were Bernard Mallet and, possibly, Bruno Blanc. Since I'd discovered the possible connection with Bruno by going through Bruno's desk, I decided to try Mallet. My probing could be done in the guise of getting additional background for my story. I called the Bellefroide.

I didn't expect a friendly reception from Mallet and was therefore amazed to be put through immediately and greeted with unprecedented bonhomie. He still sounded jittery, but the hostility that had always been so noticeable was absent. He said he was tied up for most of the afternoon but that we could meet later, and we set an appointment for drinks at the Café de la Paix, not far from my office.

I was engaged in killing the afternoon and jumping at every jingle of the phone (mostly calls for Kitty) when Jack showed up. I hadn't seen him since he dropped me off the night of Lucien's murder, but that didn't mean I hadn't given him some thought. "The police just let loose a piece of info," he said.

"Yeah? What?"

"They've finished the ballistics tests. Pierre Legrand and Lucien Claude were killed with the same gun. Surprised?"

I felt as breathless as if it had been a shock. There went the faint possibility that the two killings were unconnected. Somehow, it made my own entanglement in the situation more frightening. "No. Not surprised," I said.

"You got pale. Do you need—"

I shook my head. "I'm off balance, that's all."

He looked at me keenly, but made no comforting moves, for which I was grateful. I felt a trace awkward with Jack now, although I realized that whatever had happened the other night had happened only in my overwrought psyche. Additionally, I had the burden of keeping my cooperation with the police a secret, and the upshot was that I felt tongue-tied. "How's the story coming?" he asked.

"Lurching along, I guess."

"Any new developments?"

"Nope, nope."

I'm not the world's greatest prevaricator. I can tell a good lie when I have to, but I need time to work up to it. I could feel my face reddening. Jack was leaning in the doorway, watching me. I managed to raise my eyes to his, and I saw he could tell that something was up. "So. Not a thing new," he said.

"Not a thing."

His smile told me I wasn't getting away with it. He left, saying, "If you need any help don't hesitate, Georgia Lee."

"'Thanks." God knows what he thought I was hiding. I wanted to be straight with him, and everybody else, again. If the criminals were going to call me about the mirror, I wished they'd get on with it.

They didn't. The afternoon crept along until it was time to meet Bernard Mallet. I walked the couple of blocks to the Place de l'Opéra. He was waiting for me in the glass-enclosed sidewalk section of the Café de la Paix that borders the Boulevard des Capucines.

He stood, light flashing off his glasses, when he saw me approach through the chattering crowd of late-afternoon drinkers, past such obstacles as tethered dogs, tray-toting waiters, and chairs draped with fur coats. He was wearing a nice three-piece suit of brown wide-wale corduroy, very French, but he looked worn out. I saw a tic at the corner of his eye that hadn't been there before. His fingernails, always ragged, were now practically nonexistent. He was drinking whisky. I ordered a white wine and we occupied ourselves with getting my coat off until it came. When the waiter left, Mallet said, "So the tragedy continues. Poor Monsieur Claude."

"Yes." I remembered the contempt with

which Lucien had spoken of Bernard Mallet. "Did you know him?"

He shook his head. "We never met."

"And did you know he was the descendant of Josef Claude, of J. Claude et Fils, who sold the mirror to the Bellefroides?"

His lips firmed into a prim line. "I know it now, of course."

He leaned toward me confidingly. I wondered if the whisky he was drinking were his first of the day. "I want to say something to you," he said.

What was coming? "Yes?"

"It will be too bad if the mirror is recovered now. Do you know why?"

"Uh . . . why?"

"Because if it is recovered, people will come to the museum only to see the magic mirror and will look at nothing else."

I couldn't believe it. "At least they'd come."

"But for the wrong reasons. Cheap, sensationalistic reasons."

If Bernard Mallet knew what was good for him, I thought, he wouldn't talk like this to other members of the press, who might not understand the strain he was under.

He continued, "So you see, even though I appreciate your efforts in our behalf, I would prefer that you not continue with the ransom attempt."

I goggled at him. Efforts in *our* behalf? Did the man really believe I had tried to ransom the mirror for the benefit of the Musée Bellefroide? The police had kept Madeleine Bellefroide's role under wraps, and she hadn't been mentioned in the newspaper accounts. I didn't suppose Mallet knew who had put up the ransom money, but he seemed less interested in finding out than in scotching the whole thing. "I don't think there's any possibility of going ahead now," I said, lying in my teeth for the second time that afternoon.

Mallet leaned back. "Good," he said.

He seemed more relaxed now, and I got out my notebook. "If you don't mind, I have a couple of additional questions," I said, and when he nodded the go-ahead I continued, "I was wondering how well you knew Clive Overton."

Mallet looked surprised. "Monsieur Overton is quite prominent in the field of art restoration."

"I mean personally."

He shoved out his lower lip, considering. Then he said, "Personally, I didn't know him at all. You see, not long ago we had an accident at the museum—a leak in the roof. The only work seriously affected was a fifteenth-century Flemish altarpiece."

I could hear Overton's laconic, "Altarpiece. Water damage," in my head. "So you called in Clive Overton?"

Mallet frowned. "Actually, no. As I recall, Monsieur Overton contacted us. He had heard about our misfortune somehow, and he wrote to tell me that he planned to come to Paris in the near future, and that he would be happy to be of service to us."

I was amazed to hear of these ambulance-chasing tactics. "Is that customary? For him to be in touch with you and ask for your business like that?"

"I suppose not, although I thought very little of it."

"Normally, would you have called him in? Or called somebody in?"

"Normally, I would probably have left it to our staff, at least in the preliminary stages. But when I heard from Monsieur Overton, whose reputation I knew well, I was eager to have his advice."

Mallet looked bemused, but so far was too polite to ask why I needed to know all this. I went on, "What would have been the procedure, if Overton had continued with the job?"

"The first visit, on the day you accompanied him, was diagnostic. Then, providing we agreed on a course of action, he would have gone to work."

"At the museum?"

"Possibly. Probably. It would be more convenient and would reduce the possibility of the altarpiece's being further damaged in transportation."

Mallet's glass was empty, and mine had only a swallow left. He said, "Are you asking these questions because you believe Clive Overton was involved in the theft of the mirror?"

I shook my head vigorously. "No, no. I'm filling in blanks, that's all."

Which made three lies in one day. If I kept up this pace, I might even get good at it.

A BROKEN ELEVATOR

MALLET and I finished our drinks, and I left him and started down the Boulevard des Capucines toward the Madeleine Church. If I got the Métro at the Madeleine station, I wouldn't have to change trains before getting home. I pushed along past travel agencies, tourist information offices, cafés, the Olympia Music Hall. A stiff breeze riffled newspapers and magazines at the newsstands. A government scandal had knocked "The Bellefroide Affair," as the press had christened it, off page one. The walk was colder than I'd anticipated. My winter coat, a camel wraparound that had been perfectly adequate last year in Bay City, might as well have been tissue paper. I turned up the collar. It was only October. I could barely afford a muffler, much less a coat that had actual buttons and maybe a heavy lining.

I thought over my conversation with Mallet. I was most struck by the fact that Overton had approached Mallet, apparently unusually eager to work at the Musée Bellefroide. A man of his reputation surely wasn't hard up for assignments. Could it have been a plot to get himself into the Bellefroide?

Suppose there was an elaborate scheme to steal the mirror, and Overton was in on it. Why, at the last minute, invite me along? Whatever the plan, the presence of an additional witness, a journalist to boot, hardly seemed an advantage. Yet it had been Overton who suggested freely that I come to the Bellefroide with him. And Mallet, I now recalled vividly, who demurred so strenuously at the door.

Shivering, I descended into the blessedly warm Métro. One of the souvenir shops in the station had, along with its Eiffel Tower key chains, plastic coasters with views of Montmartre, and *"J'aime Paris"* T-shirts, a display of cheap wool scarves. I bought a chocolate brown one and wound it around my neck, and was almost thawed by the time we reached Montparnasse. I was vaulting up the stairs to my apartment, glad for once to have the opportunity to get some circulation going, when I heard the familiar sound of rattling metal that meant somebody was stuck in the elevator. The elevator had several levels of disrepair. The worst was the hopeless case when the situation had to be dealt with by elevator professionals. Sometimes, though, if a person outside pushed one of the call buttons, the mechanism spontaneously repaired itself and worked perfectly until an unforeseen time when problems began again.

I reached my floor and pushed the button to rescue the caged person, who continued monotonously shaking the door. I heard grinding clanks that meant the strategy had worked this time, and the elevator slowly ascended to my floor. As it did, an American female voice cried, "Oh, thank God! Thank God!" and the wrought-iron cage came into view with its captive occupant, Bruno Blanc's white-haired girlfriend, Jane.

I didn't much like this development. Jane hadn't seemed smart enough to be sinister, but I wasn't ready to trust her. What was she doing here? And had the police, supposedly watching my every move, seen her come in?

If I could've slipped into my front door undetected I would've done it, but she was already fumbling her way out saying, "Oh, God! Let me out of here!" She emerged and fell into my arms.

I had once been stuck in the elevator, which is why I take the stairs, and it wasn't great, but I thought Jane was laying it on a bit thick. "I have claustrophobia. My therapist says it's birth trauma," she half-sobbed against my shoulder.

I was in a quandary. The obvious move was to take her into my apartment and settle her down with a brandy, both for her own good and in the interest of whatever she might let slip, in her upset condition, about Bruno and the Speculatori. Yet maybe she was trying to get me to do just that. Her breathing was slowing down and I was going to have to say something. I was halfheartedly patting the back of her black leather jacket when I heard rapid footsteps coming up the stairs. The wild notion occurred to me that she had me immobilized, and now her confederate was arriving to do me in. I was considering shoving her downstairs and running for it when the climber came into view and I recognized Inspector Perret. He was wearing his plainclothes outfit of yesterday, minus only the *baguette*.

Jane was standing upright now, hand against her brow. Her white hair hung limply under the black beret and spread on her shoulders like moulted feathers. "I was coming to see you about your story," she said.

Perret had almost reached us. I couldn't introduce him as an inspector in the Criminal Brigade without possibly blowing everything. At least he knew who Jane was, since he'd followed both of us from the Rue Jacob to the Porte de Clignancourt. I was staring dumbly at him when he reached the top step, took me by the shoulders, and kissed me on each cheek in the French manner of greeting between friends. Then he repeated the performance for two more kisses, which meant we were special friends indeed.

If I hadn't been immobilized already that

would've stopped me, but then he proceeded to smile dotingly and say, *"Bonjour, chérie,"* which pretty much means "Hello, darling."

I can take a hint, especially if I'm bludgeoned with it. I gave him the kind of look I might give a hulking blond boyfriend five or six years my junior and said *"Bonjour"* back. I turned to Jane, who had recovered and was looking at Perret with noticeable interest and said to her, "This is my friend—"

Well, I didn't remember his first name, but before I had time to make one up he jumped in, offering his hand and saying, "Gilles Perret."

It no longer seemed risky to invite Jane in, and soon I had poured medicinal brandy for all of us. Jane eyed Perret and said to me, "I kind of wanted to talk with you privately."

He was standing by the window, arms folded, watching the street. "It's O.K. to talk," I said, in a moment of inspiration. "Gilles doesn't speak English."

"He doesn't?" She gazed at him. Then she leaned toward me and said, "Geez, he looks like a pistol. Is he as good as he looks?"

Perret didn't quiver, and it was too far away to see if he was blushing. Maybe he *didn't* speak English. "Fantastic. The best," I said.

"Lucky you." Jane sat in my armchair and rolled her head back. "God. That elevator. Can't you sue or have a rent strike or something?"

I didn't want to discuss my elevator or her birth trauma. "What did you want to talk with me about?"

She sat up straighter. "Listen. Are you still working on that story? About the mirror?"

"Yes."

"And you were dealing with Lucien Claude, the one who got killed, weren't you?"

"That's right."

"I was with him that afternoon, before it happened. If I tell you, will I get my name in the paper? Can I get paid?"

There was a whispered *"Zut"* from the window. Inspector Perret had dropped a lighted cigarette and was bending to pick it up. He got it, stuck it in his mouth, and gave me a piercing look before he turned away.

"What do you mean, you were with him?" I asked.

"I mean I was *with* him. Something strange

was going on, believe me. Wouldn't you like to know about it for your story?"

I had to carry the ball here, and it seemed important that I not start gibbering. I said, "Have you told the police?"

She looked at me disdainfully. "The pigs? I don't want anything to do with them. But are you interested?"

There was only one possible answer. "Sure. Sure I am."

"I've heard you can get paid for an exclusive story. Can you work out something?"

I glanced at Perret. He was leaning against the book case, leafing through an issue of *Good Look*. I wondered how he'd react if I said what I wanted to say, that I considered paying for a news story even tackier than pleated plastic rain bonnets, and that while I lived I would never do such a thing. Instead, I said, "It might be arranged. I can't exactly promise."

"But I'd be in the story? My name?"

"Sure. Absolutely."

I could see she wasn't going to press the money issue. Glory was what she wanted. I got out my notebook, flipped to a clean page, and said, "Go ahead."

She looked gratified. Her moment had arrived. She leaned forward and started to talk.

216

JANE'S ROMANCE

"You knew Lucien Claude," Jane said.

"That's right."

She paused for a moment of what I presumed was silent respect for the dead. Then she said, "Wasn't he *the* most gorgeous man you'd ever seen?"

"He was good-looking."

"Bruno introduced me to him, out at that antiques stall Lucien had at Port something. The minute I saw him I thought, 'This is for me.' Bruno's O.K., you know? He's really spiritual. But this guy was outstanding."

"Did Bruno have business with Lucien Claude?"

"I guess. They talked in French. While they talked, I stood there thinking, *Wow*."

Jane's face was a moony tribute to the toothsome Lucien. She continued, "So that night, all of a sudden Bruno tells me he's going out of town the next day, and so—"

"Wait a sec. Where did he go?"

She shrugged. "No idea. He's been full of

business, but he never tells me anything. Besides, I was thrilled he was going. I thought, *Great*. The coast is clear." Her face fell. "Little did I know, huh?"

"So, Bruno went out of town . . ."

"He left the next morning. As soon as I was sure he was gone, I called Lucien and asked if I could see him."

I'm no shrinking violet, but I found this brassy. "What did he say?"

"His English wasn't great, but I gathered he was busy."

I imagined Lucien fielding calls from lovesick Jane and the mirror thieves at the same time. "Where did you reach him?"

"At his place. I'd found out he lived on the Rue Vavin."

She hesitated, glancing at Perret. He was sitting now, still leafing through *Good Look*. "Aren't you afraid he'll get bored?" she asked.

"Oh, he never gets bored. Never."

"He's so cute."

"Thanks. Now, you say Lucien told you he was busy."

She nodded. "I was *wild*. I thought, when will Bruno ever go away again? I meditated, I chanted, but I couldn't put Lucien out of my mind. So I decided to go over to his apartment and convince him in person."

"You're persistent, aren't you?"

"You can't let rejection get to you. Sometimes men put up a big front of saying no when they really mean yes."

I'd have to remember that. "What did you do then?"

"His building has one of those dumb code locks, and I couldn't actually get in, so I found a phone booth and called him. I said I was in the neighborhood and wondered if I could run by."

"What did he say?"

"I thought he was going to refuse again. He even sounded kind of pissed off. But he stopped and thought about it, and then he said why didn't I come on up."

I felt a pang of envy, I admit it. Down South, we were taught to be relatively subtle. Who would've imagined those guerilla tactics would work?

Jane slumped down on the sofa. "I was so happy when he said that," she whispered, and her pale blue eyes filled with tears.

I got up to get her a tissue. The box was in the bookcase, at Inspector Perret's elbow. When I passed him, he gave me an intense

219

look, and an almost imperceptible nod of his head.

After a modest interlude of sniffling, Jane continued, "He had a gorgeous apartment: white walls and sofas the color of mushrooms. He had a big balcony, too. I was standing there looking out, and he came up behind me and sort of nuzzled my neck. That drives me wild."

"Yeah. Me, too." It really does.

"And he said, 'What are we doing? This is crazy. What will Bruno think?' And I said something like, 'Screw Bruno—' "

She puddled up again at the memory of this magic moment. I sneaked a sidelong glance at Perret. He was actually peeling the foil wrapper off a chocolate bonbon. He must've had the damn thing in his pocket.

"I thought I'd gotten really lucky," Jane went on plaintively. "He was the most fabulous kisser. He gave a new meaning to 'French kiss,' you know? And then, just when I thought we were moving in exactly the right direction . . ."

She exhaled a long breath, which seemed to deflate her totally. She had slid so far down in the chair that her beret was knocked askew. "Something went wrong?" I asked.

"You might say. He started talking about

some appointment he had. He said we'd have to get together another time. And he asked me to do an errand for him, because he was running late."

I leaned forward. "An errand?"

"Yeah. He had an envelope, and I was supposed to take it and leave it next to the fence at the Luxembourg Garden. He gave me specific instructions. The fence is divided into sections. I was to go to the fifth section past the gate at the Rue Vavin and stick this envelope down inside the fence between the concrete and the bushes. I figured maybe it had to do with buying drugs."

The thought didn't seem to disturb her, "So you did it?"

"I didn't want to leave, but he kept promising we'd get together soon, and he said he had someplace important to go. I walked over to the Luxembourg and did just what he said. I didn't peek into the envelope, either. I was so absolutely snowed by him."

The location she'd described was undoubtedly the place where Lucien had been killed that night, reaching toward the fence. But nothing had been there. I'd looked myself.

"That's when the upsetting part started," Jane said. She looked petulant, now, rather than sad.

"What happened?"

"I left the envelope, just like he'd asked. Then I just—hung around the park. I was so depressed about leaving Lucien. And then guess what?"

"What?"

"Lucien showed up. He walked right into the Luxembourg, with a newspaper under his arm. I was in shock."

"Did he see you?"

"Not then. He strolled in, all the time in the world, and took a chair next to that building where all the green metal chairs are, and people sit in the sun—"

"The Orangerie."

"I guess. He sat down and opened the paper. I thought, *This* is the important appointment? He can't be with me because he has to go read the paper in the park? I couldn't believe it."

"What then?"

"I thought maybe he was waiting for somebody, so I took a chair and watched. He's sitting there reading. A lot of other people are doing the same thing: reading, playing checkers. This went on for quite a while."

"And did someone come to meet him?"

"Nobody. Finally, I thought, this is ridiculous. He'd been reading the same page in his paper for about an hour. So I walked up, plopped down beside him, and said, 'Hi, there.' "

"Was he glad to see you?" I guess it was mean to ask.

"Are you kidding? I thought he was going to have apoplexy. He said, like, 'My God, what are you doing here?' and I said, 'Passing by,' and he said, 'You *must* go away. You *must.*' His eyes were bugged out. He said, 'Go away!' Can you imagine?"

I could. "So you left?"

"Sure. I know when I'm not wanted."

Sure. "So that's it?"

"Not quite. I went off, but I sneaked back. I thought, if he's meeting a woman I want to see what she looks like. He kept reading the paper for another long time. And then, all of a sudden, I saw him looking toward the fence, toward the place where I'd left the envelope. I looked, too, and I saw a man crouching there on the other side, the street side. Then whoever it was hurried away. Lucien walked to the gate. He was sort of hiding behind his paper. When he got to the gate, he took off after the guy, and that's the last I saw of him."

Inspector Perret stirred, and I looked

around at him. He was doodling on a piece of paper. Twinkie was asleep in his lap. He said in French, in a casual tone, "Darling? Ask her for a description of the man."

"Give me a chance, Gilles," I said in French, and then, in response to Jane's quizzical look, switched to English: "He wants to know if you'd like more brandy."

When she refused I said, "You didn't get a good look at the other person?"

"Not really. It was a guy wearing a cap. He was just a blur behind the fence and the shrubbery."

"You didn't see where he went?"

"Up the street. Away from the Rue Vavin."

"And you never saw Lucien again?"

The tears welled. "No. He didn't treat me right. I know that. But I still can't believe he's dead, and we'll never get a chance to . . . to . . ."

"To finish what you started."

"Yeah."

She stared glumly into space. The silence in the room was broken by Inspector Perret's breathy, almost tuneless whistling between his teeth. He could possibly have been attempting "Frère Jacques."

"Well," I said.

She looked up. "What do you think?" Her spasm of grief had given way to other considerations.

"Fascinating."

"Can you use it? And if so, do you think—"

"I'll have to see. Can I reach you at Bruno's?"

"Yeah, I'll be there."

She would gladly have stayed, but I hustled her out. I closed the door after her and leaned against it. Inspector Perret and I had time to exchange a glance, but not to say anything, before the telephone rang.

TWO CALLS

IT was Loretta, at the *Good Look* office in New York. I sank down on the bed. Unpleasant as ransoming the mirror promised to be, I'd have preferred that call to this one. Loretta and I had spoken after the incident at the Bellefroide, and she had been genuinely concerned for my welfare. This time, her tone indicated that she thought I'd gone too far.

"Georgia Lee, I'm hearing the strangest

things. I keep getting calls asking me whether our columnist is a thief and a murderer."

"You can't tell me you believe I am."

The hesitation before she said "Of course I don't" was a shade too extended, I thought.

"Loretta, I've had some problems here, and—"

"I should say! I understand you've been involved in a shady deal about that mirror and somebody *else* has been killed and the police questioned you. What *is* this?"

"It was unavoidable. It will blow over, believe me."

"When I consented to let you do 'Paris Patter' I never dreamed of contending with anything like this!"

"Well, I've got news for you. Neither did I."

There was a short silence. I thought I saw the axe descending. "I have to make something clear to you," she said.

I gritted my teeth. "Yes?"

"We cannot have *Good Look* dragged through the mud. We've worked too hard—"

"*Good Look* will not be dragged through the mud."

"Having a thief and murderer on the payroll is not the image we want to project."

"I am *not* a thief and a murderer!"

"It's the image I'm talking about."

Maybe I was going to escape this time. "Look. You know you like 'Paris Patter.' This will blow over, Loretta. Trust me."

She finally agreed. "But if I see one more word about you in the *Times* . . ."

"You won't. Promise."

We hung up, and I punched the pillow a couple of times with my fist. Dragging *Good Look* through the mud, indeed! I wasn't a thief and a murderer, but still I was about ready to kill Loretta. Inspector Perret wasn't there to inquire what was the matter, because halfway through the conversation he had disappeared into the kitchen. If he was looking for something to eat, he probably felt as let down in there as I did out here. I walked to the kitchen door and found him drinking a glass of water, which was about the only thing I had, besides cat food.

I said, "Sorry about the phone call. It was my boss."

"There is trouble?"

"Yes. She doesn't like my being mixed up in these murders. She thinks it's bad for her magazine's image."

He chuckled. "It's not a crime magazine, then?"

I gave a weak smile. "No. And if she fires me, I'll probably have to leave Paris."

He looked stricken. Obviously, he thought leaving Paris was a fate too horrible to be contemplated. "You want to stay?"

"It's a funny thing, considering all the trouble I've had," I said, "but I really do."

On this wistful note, the phone rang again. This time I knew, somehow, that it was the call I'd been waiting for. The man's voice was muffled and far away, as if he were speaking from underneath several layers of bedcovers. "Georgia Lee Maxwell?"

"Yes."

"You received the proof? Are you interested?"

"Yes. Yes, I am."

"Have you told the police?"

"No. I haven't said anything."

"Go to the Gare Montparnasse. On the arrivals side, on the platform level, are three telephone booths against the wall. Wait at the middle booth."

I had my mouth open to say something, although I'm not sure what, when the connection was broken. I hung up and turned to Perret, who was standing behind me. "I have to go to the Gare Montparnasse. Middle phone booth on the arrivals side," I said. My own telephone was nicely bugged. I'd assumed I'd carry out this transaction in the comfort and privacy of my home. Darling Perret wouldn't send me out to the Montparnasse train station, would he?

"One of my colleagues will follow you to the station," he said. "I'll leave here before you. I may have been seen coming in."

When I didn't reply immediately he said, "All right?"

"Sure. Fine."

"Good. We'll be with you. I'll see you here afterward." He looked jubilant. He gave me a brisk "buck up " pat on the shoulders and, as if we were friends who met frequently, kissed me perfunctorily on each cheek. Then he was out the door.

I said, "Come back," but it was too late. By that time, he must have been halfway down the stairs.

FOLLOWING DIRECTIONS

THE Gare Montparnasse is a monstrosity of modern design located behind the equally hideous Tour Montparnasse, the tallest building in Paris. These blights on the neighborhood were about ten minutes' walk away.

Outside, the early-evening winter darkness had descended. I was bundled to the eyeballs against the cold but felt so exposed I might as well have been naked. I crossed the Boulevard Montparnasse to approach the station by the Rue de l'Arrivée. Scurrying along the shadowy arcade of the shopping center in front of the Tour Montparnasse I kept my eyes straight ahead. I fervently hoped my police shadow was with me, but I couldn't look around to check, for fear of alerting whoever else might be watching.

I emerged on an uninviting, windswept concrete plaza. Across it was the station, home-going throngs surging through its plate-glass doors. Those people were intent on catching the train, getting a good seat, arriving home, having a decent dinner—reasonable and enviable concerns. *My* main concern was not to forget or garble my instructions. Arrivals side, platform level, middle booth. I wasn't sure exactly what it meant, but hoped it would be clear once I was inside.

I was hyperventilating by the time I pushed through the doors and joined the stream to the up escalator. At the top was a huge, brilliantly illuminated room furnished with ticket machines, news vendors, coffee stands, information boards, and all the other elements you'd expect to find in a train station. Escalators and stairs mounted another half-flight to the left and right, and signs indicated that you had to go up to get to the platforms for arrivals and departures. I turned right, toward arrivals, and as I got off the escalator saw the three booths, across a wide expanse of polished marble floor. They were against the wall, under a huge decorative graphic of red and blue cubes, next to vending machines, a coin-operated photocopier, and one of those cubicles where you can take your own picture. To the right, on the perpendicular wall, was a bookstore. A few people were standing around the phone booths in a ragged line. I crossed the floor, feeling like the perfect target.

All the booths were occupied. I was supposed to wait for the middle phone, but there was only one waiting line. If it looked like I was trying to go out of turn I'd be risking mayhem on yet another front. I stood at the end of the line, shifting my weight every three seconds and craning my neck toward the middle booth. Suppose the person in there, a jowly, red-faced man in an overcoat who seemed engaged in a long harangue, finished his conversation. Was I meant to take possession of the booth then?

231

People in the other two booths finished their calls. I moved up in line. The jowly man talked on. If it got to be my turn and another booth came free, I'd have to go to that booth. I'd pretend to make a call, then get in back of the line and try again. Why did these idiots give out such hard-to-follow instructions?

I surveyed the nearby scene. A uniformed *gendarme* gazed at the self-service photos. An Arabic-looking boy went by with an armload of yellow roses in cellophane cones. A rat-faced man in a loden coat consulted a Métro map. A woman in red leather pants browsed at the window of the bookstore. I moved up to first in line.

The jowly occupant of the middle booth slammed the phone into the receiver and stalked away. All my limbs jerked, I rushed forward and shut myself in. By the time I got the door closed, the phone rang. I grabbed it and panted, "Hello?"

"Georgia Lee Maxwell?"

"Yes. Yes."

"On the Rue St. André des Arts you will find the Bar St. André. Go downstairs to the telephone and wait."

"Wait a min—" Of course he'd hung up.

I slammed down the receiver with at least

as much force as the jowly man had used. I had nerved myself up to this point, but not to going through the same thing again. Would I have to run all over Paris before we talked? And where the hell was the Rue St. André des Arts?

I was never without my pocket street atlas. I checked it and discovered that the Rue St. André des Arts was in the Latin Quarter, one of the streets running into the Place St. Michel. It was only a few stops on the Métro, which I could go downstairs and catch here in the station.

I had to walk for what seemed miles underground—over moving sidewalks, past flower-sellers, candy-sellers, jewelry-sellers, an accordion player, a guy who would laminate personal papers—before I reached the right platform. Once there, I studied my companions, trying to figure out if the police were still with me. Could these giggling teenage girls in down jackets be members of the Paris S.W.A.T. team? Or was my protector the hunched old man in the beret who was heavily loaded with shopping bags? Or had Inspector Perret's colleague lost me after all?

I got out at St. Michel and found the Rue St. André des Arts without difficulty. It was narrow, funky, and clogged with students.

The Bar St. André, a block or so from the Place St. Michel, was similarly populated. None of the clientele was over the age of twenty, and they were all drinking beer, playing pinball, and shouting above the combined noise of jukebox and television set. I made my way to the staircase leading down to the bathrooms and telephone.

The phone booth was in an alcove outside the men's room and smelled of toilets that should have been scrubbed a couple of weeks ago. The dimly lit area was deserted, although reverberating with noise from above. I had visions of a masked figure with a gun stepping out of the men's or ladies' room and blasting away. As this thought, or fear, formed itself, I heard footsteps on the staircase and a woman with a shoulder-length black pageboy, wearing a coat of fluffy white fur, swept past me into the ladies' room. She was searching for something in her purse. I caught just a glimpse, underneath her coat, of red pants that might have been leather. As the door swung to behind her the phone rang.

I picked it up and said, "Talk now. I'm not going to another booth."

"The proof is satisfactory?"

"The proof is fine, but I'm worried about what happened to Lucien Claude."

"What happened to Lucien Claude has nothing to do with you, or with our negotiations. Do you want the mirror?"

"Yes. We've offered one hundred fifty thousand francs."

"Get the money. We will make the transfer tomorrow."

"Look. How do I know—"

"Get the money. You must handle this yourself. We are watching, and we know you."

"Listen—"

"We will know if you tell the police. If you do, you will be in trouble."

I was paralyzed. The line remained open a couple of seconds before he hung up, but I couldn't think of anything to say. Then he broke the connection. *We will know if you tell the police.*

The woman in the white fur came out of the ladies' room and ascended the stairs. I didn't know if she was the woman in the red leather pants at the bookstore in the Gare Montparnasse. A policewoman, maybe. *We will know if you tell the police.* I had to get out of here. The smell was getting to me. I climbed the staircase and shouldered my way through a bunch of kids with no worries other than their next exams and went out into the cold Paris night.

INSPECTOR PERRET

"I have said already, there is no way they can know." Inspector Perret sounded weary. He *had* said it, several times, but I could still hear the hateful voice: *We are watching. We know you. We will know if you tell the police.*

We were in my apartment. He had come back with the French version of a pizza: a small round crust, a smear of tomato sauce, a couple of artichoke hearts, and a thin slice of ham. It was infuriatingly inadequate.

"He told me to get the money," I said.

"We will get the money."

"Real money?"

"Why not? They won't have it for long."

He was a blond, barrel-chested, picture of imperturbability. There were no furrows in his broad brow, no tremors in his oversized hands. Why should there be? I, after all, was the one who'd be executing the fancy maneuvers. And I was both furrowed and trembling.

"I hated the sound of his voice. *Hated* it,"

I said. I was working myself up into a snit. Lonnie, my former husband, could have told Inspector Perret that this was a good time to escape—grab a shotgun and go out to kill squirrels, or turkeys, or whatever was in season.

"Nevertheless—"

"He sounded completely cold-blooded. What's to stop him from shooting me?"

Inspector Perret smoked and rubbed Twinkie behind her ears. She was purring loudly. I said, "Considering my cat loves you better than me, I hope you'll keep her if I get killed during this lunatic scheme."

"I couldn't possibly. I have a dog," Perret said.

This was too much. Because my apartment was a studio, there was no bedroom to stalk into and slam the door, so I stalked into the bathroom and slammed the door. I sat down on the toilet seat, put my head on my knees, and cried.

Eventually Perret did the gentlemanly thing and knocked discreetly, inquiring if I were all right.

"I certainly am *not!*" I bawled. "I'm scared to death of being *killed!*"

"But Madame—"

"Why does everybody call me Madame?

I'm sick of it! Can't you call me Georgia Lee?"

I thought I heard him clear his throat. He said, "Georgia Lee," stumbling over it badly. Then he said it again, getting the hang of it.

"Georgia Lee? Will you come out now?"

I was mollified. The man knew how to wheedle, an admirable trait. I splashed my face with water and came out, just in time to catch the ringing phone. I had the dreadful feeling it was going to be Ray, but it was Bruno Blanc.

"Something is moving. The mirror is moving. I can feel it," he said, sounding agitated.

I wondered if Jane had prompted this call somehow. "I don't—"

"What do you know? You must tell me."

"Nothing . . . nothing."

My disclaimer didn't stop him. He said, "I see the mirror, and I see you. The mirror is rolling toward you like a shining black wheel, and the closer it gets the larger it grows."

Bruno's visions were so reassuring. "I don't know anything about it. Ask the police."

"They will tell me nothing."

"I can't help you." Firmness worked best

with Bruno, and in this case it got him off the phone.

I told Perret, "Bruno Blanc says he can feel the mirror moving. He says it's rolling toward me like a wheel." I didn't know if Bruno was clairvoyant, but I had no doubt he knew about psychological manipulation. I recounted the rest of the conversation to Perret, who made no significant comment. I finished by saying, "Bruno and Jane. What a pair. What did you think of *her* story?"

"I think she admired Lucien Claude very much, and he used her."

"What was Lucien up to in the Luxembourg?"

"It seems clear that he wanted to see who picked up the envelope. This must have been a prearranged way to communicate secretly."

"And he got Jane to leave the envelope so he couldn't be identified himself."

"I suppose so. She must have horrified him when she sat next to him and talked to him afterward. That would have ruined his chances of remaining incognito, if anyone were watching."

So Jane, unwittingly, might have fingered Lucien for his killer. How ironic.

Perret said, "I must go. There's a great

deal to do. If you like, I can ask a woman officer to stay with you for the night."

I shook my head. I didn't feel like being hospitable to a woman police officer. I felt like getting in bed and staring hollow-eyed into the darkness for the next eight hours.

At the door, Perret turned. "I almost forgot," he said. "Jane said to you that I looked 'like a pistol.' I don't know that expression. Can you explain?"

His wide, tough-guy face expressed polite curiosity. I sorted through a couple of possible responses before saying, "I took it to mean that you looked like an extremely good lover."

Perret looked flabbergasted, but not displeased. He said, "I see," and left, and Twinkie and I were alone.

WAITING

I got up at dawn and made coffee, then opened my curtains and looked up and down the Rue Delacôte. Across the street water was sluicing through the gutter, and a man was sweeping the trash out with what looked like a picturesque bundle of twigs. I knew from watching other street cleaners that it *was* a bundle of twigs, but the twigs were plastic. I had spent some time trying to decide whether this represented progress or not.

Nobody was stirring except the street cleaner, but someone must have been watching my window because soon the phone rang and Inspector Perret announced his imminent arrival.

He came in burdened with a white paper sack and an Air France flight bag. He placed the bag carefully on the bookcase.

"What's that? Your lunch?" I cracked nervously.

His expression said humor should be restricted to appropriate occasions. "The money."

I gulped and offered him coffee. The white sack proved to contain half a dozen croissants, and he was generous enough to share them with me. We had a breakfast that was as congenial as a meal can be when one party is suffering from a near-terminal attack of nerves and the other is lost in the joy of chewing.

"When do you think he'll call?" I asked.

He shrugged. He had the French talent for shrugging.

"Do you think I'll have to run around

town to different phone booths, like last night?"

His shoulders went upward again. He helped himself to the raw honey, cream-colored and thick as peanut butter, that I'd put out to go with the croissants.

"Do you think—"

The phone rang. So early? I bit my lip and got up to answer.

It was a woman who said she was Madeleine Bellefroide's nurse. She was calling on behalf of Madeleine, who wished to speak with me. I said to put her on, and in a minute I heard Madeleine's voice, which sounded distant and slow, almost drugged.

"Madame Maxwell? Is that you?"

"Yes. How are you?"

"I'm not well. Not at all."

"I'm sorry."

"I had a dreadful night. I woke this morning with the idea that I must see you."

"Um. Would tomorrow—"

"Today. Now."

"Well . . . Could you hold on for a minute?"

I put my hand over the receiver and told Inspector Perret what was going on. He nodded. "Go. But don't be long."

"What if it's a trap? Will somebody be following me?"

"Of course. Always."

I told her I'd be right over and hung up.

She had sounded terrible, and the sight of her didn't reassure me. Looking shrunken in her armchair, she leaned slightly to one side as if trying to avoid some persistent pain. She was wrapped in a dressing gown, yards of dove-colored velvet with satin cuffs and lapels. Her lips were pale, and when I took her hand in greeting her fingers were cold and limp. "So here you are. Is there news?" she said, and in spite of her condition I saw her hunger, still ferocious, for the mirror.

I couldn't possibly reassure her. "No. Nothing," I said.

She closed her eyes. "I dreamed you had gotten it and were bringing it to me."

Wretchedly, I shook my head. "I don't have it. I wish I did."

I could see her gathering her strength, preparing her assault. She looked at me, pleading. "Madame Maxwell, I'm desperate. Desperate."

"I wish—"

"I reinstate my offer. I implore you to get the mirror for me."

What a hellish situation. I was going to try

to do what she wanted, but I couldn't tell her. My face was burning. "I just can't."

She sat forward, suddenly energized. "But something is happening. Yes, I know it is. I can see it in your face."

"No. Not—"

"Yes. Soon you will have the mirror. I know it."

"No! The police—"

She fell back and shaded her eyes with one hand. "The police. They will regain it and give it back to Bernard Mallet, to be locked away from me forever." Her voice was desolate.

I couldn't stand this. "Please listen," I said. "I can only say that *if* the mirror is regained, and *if* I have any influence, I will make sure you see it before it goes back to the museum." Inspector Perret could grant me that favor at least.

Her tongue slid over her lips. She said, "Do I have your word?"

"I can only promise to try."

She took my hand and her grip, so lifeless before, was strong enough to hurt. "You will get it."

I lowered my eyes, unable to meet her gaze. When she released me, her cheeks were pink. "You will call me soon. Very soon."

"As soon as I can." I had to get out. I said good-bye.

On the Avenue de Suffren, in front of a flower shop, a woman in dark stockings and a tight black skirt was paying for an armful of peach-colored roses. Her hair was piled on top of her head in a messy bun. I wasn't sure what made me think she was the woman I'd seen last night, her hair in a page boy, wearing red leather and white fur, going into the ladies' room at the Bar St. André—my policewoman companion. She didn't glance at me, but I noticed that the animated conversation she was having with the shopwoman terminated just as I passed.

Back at my place, I found Perret wadding up pieces of paper and tossing them for Twinkie to bat around. She had never shown any interest in such activity before, but she'd apparently regressed to madcap kittenhood under the influence of her love for him. As she scrambled around, sliding into corners and galloping from one end of the room to the other, he said, "Nothing is happening. The phone hasn't rung."

"What do we do now?"

"Wait."

I had a deck of cards somewhere. We could play honeymoon bridge, or maybe poker. The idea didn't appeal, though. The atmosphere was too fraught. When Twinkie tired of frisking about, Perret settled down to read a secondhand copy of *Maigret et la Vieille Dame* that I'd bought hoping to improve my French, and I tried to work on "Paris Patter."

Sitting with ransom money at your elbow, waiting for the crucial phone call, can make most concerns fade into insignificance. Under these circumstances "Paris Patter" seemed laughably trivial. Who in God's name *cared* that you could get adorable umbrellas at Madeleine Gély? Or fun jewelry at Comptoir du Kit? Or exquisite notebooks at Papier Plus?

By lunchtime, Perret was halfway through *Maigret et la Vieille Dame*. I had accomplished exactly nothing. Twinkie was deep in comatose slumber.

One of Perret's colleagues delivered sandwiches to the door, and Perret and I talked as we ate lunch. I told him about Cross Beach, and the beautiful bay, and the swamps, and the pine woods. I told him how I used to write the society column for the Bay City *Sun*. I talked a little about my marriage to Lonnie.

"And now you've come to Paris," he said.

"Yes. Here I am."

"You came for no reason? Just like that?" He snapped his fingers.

"I . . . needed a change."

He looked at me acutely. "It had to do with a man, I think."

"Why do men always think everything has to do with a man?"

He smiled. "I'm not wrong, am I?"

"Not totally."

He told me about himself, too. He'd grown up in some industrial town I'd never heard of, moved to Paris, become a policeman. It had been his dream to be part of the Criminal Brigade, and he achieved it. He had lived for some years with a woman named Marie-Luce, but at the moment they weren't together. His dog was a boxer named Willy.

At last, toward midafternoon, the phone rang.

Same man, same muffled voice. "You have the money?"

"I have it."

"You've told no one?"

"No."

"The police?"

"No."

"All right. Put the money in a plastic bag.

247

Something that looks worthless. Do you understand?"

"Yes."

"Take the bag and walk up the Rue de Rennes to the Rue de Vaugirard. Proceed on the Rue de Vaugirard to the Luxembourg Gardens. Repeat."

"Up the Rue de Rennes to Rue de Vaugirard, then on to the Luxembourg Gardens." The Luxembourg was where they'd killed Lucien Claude.

"Enter the garden by the gate next to the palace. At the statue of Pan, climb the steps to the terrace. Near the railing you will see a bench, a waste container, and a tree lined up in a row. You will put the money in the waste container. Repeat."

I repeated. Then I said, "What about the mirror?"

"When you leave the money, you will find further instructions."

"Are you kidding? I can't—"

"Do it this way or give up the mirror."

"I—"

The phone was dead.

I hung up and sat on the edge of the bed. "I think it's a trick," I said, and told him the arrangements. "What's to stop them from taking the money and leaving false instructions about the mirror?"

"Nothing," Perret said. "But if they pick up the money, we will have them, and once we have them, we'll have the mirror, too."

I still wasn't crazy about it, but Perret was getting the flight bag from the bookcase. "The money has to be in a plastic bag," I said. "There are some under the sink."

He went into the kitchen, and a few minutes later emerged with a reasonably full bag. It was white plastic with burgundy lettering that said "Au Bon Marché" and had come from the big department store of that name nearby. I looked inside, but he had wrapped the contents in newspaper.

I got my coat. I was dressed for the occasion in green corduroy pants, a white sweater, comfortable shoes. I told him exactly what the man had said to do.

"You must follow the instructions without deviation. You understand that."

"Yes." There was so much I wanted to say, but I felt choked. I managed, "They killed Lucien Claude there, at the Luxembourg."

"Lucien Claude was almost certainly trying to cheat them in some way."

"Right." And what had *I* done? Betrayed them completely by telling the police.

He started to say something, but I was turning away. If I were going, it was time to go. I picked up the bag and went out the door.

IN THE LUXEMBOURG

THE Rue de Rennes is a major thoroughfare: broad, congested, and not especially pretty. Buses and cars roar up and down it, dispersing fumes over the numerous pedestrians. Holding my Au Bon Marché bag in what was meant to be a casual grip, I turned into it and started on my assigned route.

Because the sun was out again, the street was busier than ever. People seemed to flood toward me, and all I could think about was somebody grabbing the bag, or knocking it out of my hand so that hundred-franc notes went swirling, causing a riot.

I could barely feel my feet hitting the pavement. I tried to concentrate on what I was passing: the sidewalk bins of Tati, the cheap department store that was once bombed by terrorists; FNAC, a huge book-record-camera emporium; boutiques selling shoes and clothes, where I sometimes browsed. All of it kept fading in and out.

There's a crêpe stand at the intersection where the Rue de Rennes crosses the Rue de Vaugirard, and as I waited there for the light to change I watched the vendor spread jam on two of the thin pancakes, roll them up, and hand them to customers. My mouth watered, but it was fear rather than hunger. I crossed and continued on the Rue de Vaugirard.

Within ten minutes, I was crossing the Rue Guynemer. I didn't even glance toward the place where Lucien had been shot but continued toward the Luxembourg Palace, the beige-gold stone edifice that houses the French Senate. Crossing the entrance to the palace courtyard where the senators and staff parked their cars, I turned in at the gate to the gardens on the other side.

Even in my present state, I noticed that the gardens looked magnificent. It was the perfect setting for an autumn stroll, and I only wished that were my purpose. I proceeded along the wide, sandy walkway beside the palace. The flower beds were bright with gold, ocher, and magenta blossoms, bordered with white stone urns containing bursts of chrysanthemums, alternating bronze and yellow. I clasped the bag more tightly. I was passing the Medici Fountain. At the end of its shaded, urn-bordered pool bulked an ornate grotto where a pair of white marble lovers were shadowed by a giant who intended them no good.

A short way beyond the fountain was the statue of a carefree, posturing Pan, and beyond him the steps to the terrace. As always in the Luxembourg, there were people around: joggers, mothers with toddlers, tourists sitting down to consult guidebooks, students daydreaming over textbooks, citizens of all descriptions strolling, striding, and wandering on their various ways. There were also plenty of *gendarmes* guarding the palace. It took real audacity—or real stupidity—to set up this crime at the scene of a previous murder, and in such a stronghold of the law.

I looked toward the stone railing and immediately saw the lined-up bench, trash can, tree. The sight was like something I'd seen already, in a dream, and as if in a dream I floated toward it. I was rolling the bag up, wadding it up, as if it were garbage. The trash can was a basketlike contraption of curved metal slats, with a solid metal lining. Behind one of the slats, near the ground, a piece of white paper fluttered. I jammed the hundred and fifty thousand francs into the can, reached down, and retrieved the paper. Printed on it in black ink were the words: "The mirror is in the right-hand urn at the end of the Medici Fountain."

I turned. It might be true, or it might be a way of getting me clear of the money. Whichever it was, I had no choice but to go back to the Medici Fountain and look. I returned to the steps and descended.

The pool of the fountain was lined with urns and bordered by swags of ivy. The two urns at the end, though, were wider and shallower, the shape of a candy dish rather than a vase. Both contained a profusion of yellow chrysanthemums. I moved to the one on the right and peered in. There, camouflaged nicely among the leaves, was a circular case of green leather, decorated with metal studs. I slid my hand under the flowers and took hold of it. When I pulled it out, I felt a throb of relief.

The relief lasted approximately a half-second, which was how long it took me to turn and see two young men approaching me, very purposefully. One was burly, with a small mustache, and the other had lank, shoulder-length brown hair and wore wire-rimmed glasses. Police, I thought, coming to congratulate me, protect me, take charge of the mirror. I almost smiled at them before I realized that the police wouldn't be showing themselves so soon. They wouldn't give themselves away until they'd pounced on whoever picked the money out of the garbage can. Besides, there was a threatening look to these guys.

I didn't stop and think about it. I ran, propelled by instinct more than logic. I caught a glimpse of their startled expressions as I took off, scampering along the pool and dodging behind the baroque-style bulk of carved stone at the end.

Somebody called out from the terrace. The police might have seen me start to run. Breathless and disoriented, I huddled momentarily in the scraggly bushes. I wasn't hiding, because there was nowhere to hide. I didn't think my chances of evading pursuit were very good.

I thought: They may get me, but they're not going to get the mirror. I pulled the case open and took it out. It was round and black and cold. I slipped to the other side of the leaf-speckled pool, then darted forward. Kneeling. I dropped the mirror into the murky water. It made the tiniest plopping sound as it went in. I backed away.

This had taken almost no time. It was one of the few occasions in my life when getting an idea and carrying it out were almost simultaneous. I could hear a snarl of excited voices as, once again, I started to run.

CAPTIVITY

THE Luxembourg is a French formal garden, not a jungle where a person could hunker down and hide in the undergrowth. My options were few, and soon exhausted.

I dodged back behind the fountain and started for the nearest way out, a gate leading to the busy Place Edmond Rostand, just off the Boulevard St. Michel. I was focused on my destination—the opening in the black iron bars, the crosswalk, the red awning of the café across the street. When the mustached man appeared on the path in front of me I was going too fast to stop. I careened into him, he grabbed me, and I saw from the corner of my eye the other one running out the gate and flinging open the back door of an illegally parked black Renault. I cursed myself for making it so convenient for them as they hustled me across the sidewalk and stuffed me in the car.

My captor and I were inside, and the door had slammed, before I had a chance even to squeak. Then the one wearing steel rims got into the driver's seat, and we took off down the Boulevard St. Michel. Through the back window I got a brief impression of people on the sidewalk staring after us, looking baffled. I would guess the entire episode, from the time I picked up the mirror, had lasted two minutes.

Next, a jacket was thrown over my head and I was pushed to the floor of the back seat. I curled around the mirror case, making myself into a ball like the armored bugs I used to play with in the dirt as a child. When the man tried to take the case away I scrunched up tighter, and he gave up. "We will have it soon enough," he said in a cold voice.

It was dark inside the jacket and smelled like perspiration and male cologne. I stayed curled up on the floor. I couldn't possibly overpower my captors, and I wasn't anxious to make them madder. As we maneuvered through the streets of Paris, I tried to figure out what had happened.

Maybe I'd been double-crossed, and the intention had always been to take the mirror back after I'd let go of the money. But why do it so clumsily? They could have tricked me in a million ways that would have been easier than this.

A scarier possibility was that they didn't want the mirror, they wanted me. Or they wanted the mirror, but they wanted me, too. Still, the same reasoning applied. They could have gotten me whenever, instead of at such a dangerous moment.

But of course it wasn't supposed to be dangerous. I wasn't supposed to have told the police.

I ground away at these questions through innumerable stops at traffic lights and the squeals of brakes that were par for the course for Paris driving. There was no indication that we were being pursued. Eventually, we picked up speed and I realized we must have made it to the *périphérique,* the superhighway that runs around the edge of town.

I didn't like this development any more than the ones immediately previous. It smacked of being taken to a lonely road, shot in the head, and having my body discovered next spring by bird-watchers. In Paris, there were people around, so if you yelled, somebody would probably hear. There were taxis, buses, the Métro, in case you needed to get away fast. Outside of Paris, there was—what? Aside from obligatory day trips to Chartres cathedral, the palace at Versailles, and Monet's home at Giverny, I'd hardly been outside the city limits.

We were zipping along. I could hear the roar and rattle of speeding trucks, the whizzing of other cars. My companions weren't given to conversation, and when they did exchange words it was in tones too low for me to distinguish anything. I began to feel queasy. The smells inside the jacket intensified. I had to pee. I clung to the mirror case.

I wondered what Inspector Perret was doing and feeling right now. I hoped he was remembering how he'd assured me I was in no danger, and was so sick with guilt that he couldn't even stuff his face with whatever food was handy. He'd probably say that my running away was contradictory to his orders, and not in the game plan. So what? I would say. What would *you* do, Perret, if a couple of bad-intentioned thugs came at *you?*

I hoped that damn dog-loving Perret would have the decency to go to my apartment and feed Twinkie, who would soon be wanting her dinner. Or Kitty could do it. Kitty had a key. She could do it, if she knew what had happened. And speaking of what had happened—what *had* happened?

Above all other hopes, I hoped I would get out of this alive.

And then there was the mirror. Clutched in my hands was an empty case. I had a vision of the mirror itself, lying on the bottom of the Medici Fountain, cushioned on dead leaves and other gunk.

The mirror was my weapon. If I used it right, it could get me out of this. I saw it again, through the cold, brownish water. I thought, I hoped, that there were flickers in its depths.

A ROOM WITH LACE CURTAINS

I would guess it was an hour before we turned off, and the car seemed to be on a small road again. Since I didn't know what was in store for me when we stopped, I wasn't overjoyed.

Now, the two of them had a conversation. The few words I caught were about directions, a typical exchange being:

"It's here, isn't it? No, no, the next one!" from my companion in the back.

"What's wrong with you? Can't you read a map?" from the driver.

"Turn here, Louis. *Here*, fool!"

So the driver, the steel-rims wearer, was called Louis. The name meant nothing to me.

Eventually, we got on a bumpy surface. I bounced around, bracing myself as best I could with my feet. This might well be the lonely road I feared. I tried to compose my mind for imminent demise, but it was difficult when my head was constantly jarred by my teeth being knocked together. Then the car turned, went along a smooth but crunchy surface for a short time, and stopped. The motor cut off. Wherever we were, we had arrived.

The car door opened, and they pulled me out. I said, "What's happening?" and then, gathering steam, yelled, "Let me go! Help! *Help!*" Inside the jacket my voice sounded enormously loud. Outside, it was probably whisper volume.

"Shut up," one of them muttered in my ear, and his pressure on my arm increased. My legs were so stiff I had trouble standing. I was pulled forward over what seemed to be gravel. A few grassy, country-type smells drifted up under the jacket. I heard a door opening, but whoever opened it didn't say anything.

"Steps. Up," one of my captors said, but

I dug my heels in and screamed, "No! Let me go! Help!" and I don't know what else.

I locked my knees, and one of them said, "Let's go." They dragged me up several steps, bumping my shins painfully, and over a threshold. I continued to shriek, thinking all the time that if I'd had the sense to create such a scene in the Luxembourg Garden I might not be in this fix.

The mirror case was snatched from my hands, and then I was pulled around a corner and, I thought, into another room. A door closed behind me. I heard a key turn, followed by retreating footsteps.

I was so amazed to be left alone that I stopped screaming. I realized I could take the jacket off my head. I threw it on the floor and felt enormous relief, my eyes dazzled by the daylight. I took deep gasps of air, shaking my head.

The shouting started just about then—a hoarse, crazed-sounding bellow. I couldn't understand the words but the emotion was unbridled fury. They had opened the mirror case.

While the ranting continued, I looked around. I was in a bedroom. There was a single bed with an iron headboard and a faded mauve spread, a braided rug on the floor, dingy lace panels in the windows. A beige metal gooseneck lamp sat on a chest of drawers that had been given an amateurish brown paint job. The walls were covered in cheap-looking wood veneer paneling. Through the windows I could see a field with tall grass, the rutted clay road by which we must have approached and, across the road, a stand of trees. In the distance beyond the field, more trees and what might have been a railroad crossing. In other words, it was remote. No wonder they'd let me scream my lungs out.

The screaming had now been taken over by someone else, and he continued while I tried the windows and found, not to my surprise, that they were jammed shut and I couldn't budge them. They were also heavy, double storm-window types that would be hard to break. I tried the door, more as a ceremonial gesture than through any real hope that it had spontaneously unlocked. It hadn't.

So here I was, captive in a dreary bedroom in the boondocks, listening to a venting of maniacal anger that might, at any moment, be directed at me. I didn't know what else to do, so I lay down on the bed, still wearing my coat and shoes. The afternoon light was dimming to gold, and a rising wind buffeted the house.

The shouting eventually subsided. It was a relief not to have to listen.

I didn't have long to relish the quiet before the door opened and Louis, with the steel rims, came in. He didn't look as substantial as he had before, as if he'd been withered by the blasts of fury. He wore jeans and a green V-necked sweater with a white shirt beneath. He picked up the jacket, leaned against the chest of drawers, and crossed his arms. "Where is the mirror?" he said. His voice was reedy. Over all, he wasn't an impressive character.

I had expected the question. "You have it. You, or whoever grabbed the case away from me."

"Where is the mirror?"

"You have it. You took it."

He straightened and seemed about to leave when I said, "I want to go to the bathroom."

He walked out and locked the door behind him, but in a few minutes he was back. "Come with me," he said.

Surprised that I was being treated so well, I went with him a few steps down a hall, to a cubbyhole with a toilet and sink. He made me leave the door open, but I rose above the embarrassment. Feeling much better, I tried to look around on the short walk back to the bedroom. I didn't see much. A closed door, probably another bedroom, at the other end of the hall. A rapidly glimpsed living room with the same lace curtains and drab furniture, and maybe a kitchen beyond. The place had no personality and didn't look like anybody's beloved home.

Then I was back in the bedroom. As he went out, my captor said, "We want the mirror."

I didn't respond. The door closed, the key turned.

I lay down on the bed again. I'd make a plan to get out of here. While I was debating how to begin, improbable as it may seem, I dozed off.

I know it sounds ridiculous. I guess I wanted so badly to escape that I took the only immediately available route. I drifted in and out of consciousness until the door opened again. It was almost dark. I sat up to see Louis coming in again. He switched on the lamp and said, "Have you thought about the mirror?"

"Sure, I've thought about it."

"Where is it?"

This could go on forever. "Look. We aren't getting anywhere being so cryptic. Are you telling me it wasn't in the case, where it was supposed to be?"

He turned around and left. He must have to consult with his boss every other instant. Much as I would've liked to think I'd be leaving soon, I decided to take off my coat. The room had no closet or armoire, so I hung it on a knob of the chest of drawers. He returned. "No. It wasn't in the case," he said.

"Then your business is with the people who had it, not with me. I paid the money. They promised me the mirror. I didn't look in the case when I picked it up. There wasn't time."

He looked dubious. He was quite young, I realized. Pimples dotted his chin, which wasn't surprising considering the greasy state of his hair. He looked like a slightly repellent nonentity, which is probably what a lot of criminals are in the beginning.

I went on, "If I didn't think it was in there, why did I hold on to the case? Why didn't I just let you have it?" I wasn't sure of the answer myself, but it made a presentable argument. He started to pick at his chin but still didn't reply. I said, "Go talk to the people who set up the exchange. They can tell you what you want to know."

Naturally, he went out again. He was back soon. He said, "We don't believe you. You hid it somewhere."

"I hid it? I was hardly out of your sight. I didn't have time to hide it."

"You hid it. Where did you hide it?"

"I didn't."

"Where?"

"Nowhere."

His popping in and out was beginning to seem ludicrous. As he was leaving this time, I said, "I'm hungry."

After a while, he returned carrying a tray holding bread, cheese, a Bosc pear, a glass of red wine. He put it on the foot of the bed and said, "You will have to tell us sometime. You will stay here until you do."

I shook my head, and he left. I ate and waited for him to come back and pick up the tray. He didn't come. I didn't hear noises or voices. Were they still here? What were they doing? I watched the door, expecting it to open any minute. I began to feel very lonely without him.

BREAKFAST

ALL through the night, the wind roared across the field and broke around the house like a wave. Propped against the thin pillow, the lamp burning, I listened to it and stared out the window into the darkness. Once or twice a train went by, a fast-moving string of tiny lighted windows in the distance, and I put my face against the glass. At other times I lay back and studied the lace curtain, with its motif of flowers entwined in an oval frame around a bird. The bird, the train, even the wind became symbols, mocking symbols, of freedom. As the hours passed, I began to loathe the room with the tired loathing that comes when unpleasant situations continue too long. It was a feeling I used to have about my relationship with Ray. I slept fitfully and woke. I worried about Twinkie. When the first light broke I got up shakily, went to the door, and began beating on it with my fist.

No response. I kept hammering. My hand

hurt, but the thuds sounded good to me. Then I thought: Why shouldn't I hit the door with something else, something harder, and make a louder noise? My eye had fallen on the gooseneck lamp, with its round metal base, when I heard footsteps. I screamed, "Open up! Open up!" The footsteps stopped on the other side of the door. I resumed pounding. Moments later the steps receded down the hall.

"Don't go," I said. "Please don't go." The steps died away, and the only sound left was the wind.

I would make him come back. I would batter the door, batter the lock until it gave. I unplugged the lamp. My fingers were closing around the neck when I hesitated. They were screwing me around, and they were winning. If I battered the door, even broke it open, they would catch me before I could get away. If I used the lamp to smash a window, they would hear. Whatever I did, if it went wrong they would take the lamp away.

I had read in a magazine somewhere that if you were in a stressful situation you should stop and take ten deep breaths, concentrating on each one. This seemed an appropriate occasion to try it. I sucked in air. Sure enough, by breath six or seven my mind was clearing. By breath ten I was close to getting hold of myself, but I decided not to let my captors know that.

I flung myself on the door, slamming both fists against it, screaming, "Come back! Please! Come back!" in a fair imitation of hysteria. When the emotion seemed about to become real, I stopped to breathe. Then I started again.

During the second breathing pause, the steps returned. I cried, "Let me out!" and in a moment a voice, I thought it was Louis, said, "Are you ready to talk?"

"Yes! Yes!"

The door opened, and he stood there with a self-satisfied smirk on his face. He looked even greasier and less savory than yesterday, and the pouches under his eyes indicated he hadn't slept much better than I had.

He accompanied me to the toilet. While I was there, I rinsed my face and hands, the cold water almost painful on my oversensitive skin. I tried to avoid looking in the mirror, where a pallid creature with shocked eyes made poking motions at the bird's nest on her head.

He didn't take me back to my bedroom-cell, but through the living room to the kitchen, where his mustached cohort, in socks, pants, and a webbing undershirt, was pouring steaming water from a kettle into a filter-style coffeepot. He glanced at me and grunted. I didn't grunt back.

The kitchen had a breakfast nook, built-in benches on either side of a formica-topped table, and Louis seated me on one of the benches and asked if I wanted coffee. While he was getting it, I gazed out the window at a desolate and overgrown backyard enclosed by a ratty hedge. In the middle of the yard was one of those clotheslines shaped like an inside-out umbrella. A couple of dish towels on the clothesline were whipping in the wind, which was still high. There were no houses in sight. I wondered what had possessed somebody to build this suburban villa in such an isolated and unpleasant spot. I could imagine the ad: "Location perfect for kidnapping and other clandestine operations."

Louis set a plate in front of me on which was a hunk of bread (yesterday's, I ascertained by trying to tear off a bite) and a little plastic tub of strawberry jam. The coffee was soon ready, and I chewed the stale bread with the gusto of one who isn't sure where her next meal is coming from, or if there will be a next meal at all. The mustached man took a mug of coffee and left, but Louis stayed with me. His body odor wafted across the table and my appetite started to flag.

After a few minutes he half-rose from the table, his eyes on the doorway. I followed his gaze. Standing there in black turtleneck and black trousers, his grizzled hair wilder than ever, was Bruno Blanc.

So Bruno was behind this. I should've known the ranting despair I'd heard yesterday had come from him.

I put down my cup. Bruno glanced at Louis and said, "Leave us," in a tone that showed who was in charge. When we were alone he took Louis' place on the bench opposite me. His eyes were bloodshot, and the skin of his face hung in folds. He had the air of a man barely able to hold himself in check.

"So the mirror brings us together again," he said.

"Right. The mirror abducted me, held me prisoner . . ."

His shoulders twitched. "We want the mirror. When we have it, you may go."

"I told your . . . your henchman—"

He leaned across the table, grabbed the neck of my sweater, and pulled me toward him. "You told him a lie."

I tried to free myself. "I didn't."

"You did. When you picked up the case in the Luxembourg, the mirror was in it."

"Let me go!"

"You had the mirror." He held on for a moment longer, then shoved me back against the bench, which rattled as my body thudded against it. He leaned over the table, glaring. "Where is it now? Where?"

"I don't know."

"Liar!" He threw himself back on his bench. "Your lies are useless. I know it was there."

Was he bluffing? "How are you so sure?"

His tone was venomous. "How I'm so sure is not your business. Consider this: If I didn't think you know where the mirror is, I might as well have killed you yesterday."

That angle had occurred to me. Stonewalling could reach the point of diminishing returns. If I convinced Bruno of my ignorance, my next stop could be a windblown grave under the clothesline.

I said, playing for time, "You would kill me for the mirror? Jane said you thought life was sacred."

His reply was incantatory. "Anyone who stands in the mirror's way is in danger."

"Pierre Legrand and Lucien Claude stood in its way?"

The corners of his mouth jumped. "It would seem so."

It would seem so. He went on. "I want the mirror. Tell me where it is, and I'll let you go."

I doubted it. Why should he set me free, when I was able to incriminate him? He leaned forward. "Tell me. Now."

Although he hadn't touched me again, I felt pushed to the wall, squeezed until I couldn't breathe. I said, in a petulant tone, the only remark that entered my head: "It isn't fair. I paid the ransom."

To my astonishment he laughed, a derisive bark. "You paid the ransom!"

"I did! I—"

"You paid nothing. You alerted the police. The Luxembourg was swarming with them. The ransom was never picked up." A smile contorted his features. "Don't you understand? You are in serious difficulty. And now you must tell me where the mirror is."

REACHING AGREEMENT

My first reaction to Bruno's news was fury at Inspector Perret. So the police had blown it and shown me up as a stool pigeon or whatever the expression was. Bruno might be demented, but he was right about the difficulty I was in. If I ever—*ever*—got my hands on Perret, I'd . . .

"The mirror," Bruno said.

I had to concentrate, or I wouldn't live to take horrible and appropriate revenge. "Yes. I know where it is," I said.

I pressed against the back of the bench, trying to escape his avidity. He reached out, his fingers scrabbling at my arm. *"Where?"*

I shook my head. "I have to show you."

"Why?" Although the word was an explosion of frustration, I thought he had expected it.

"I want to be sure of getting back to Paris. The only protection I have is my knowledge of where the mirror is."

274

"You think I couldn't kill you in Paris, just as easily as I could here?"

I thought of Pierre Legrand and Lucien Claude. Being in Paris hadn't kept them alive. But I wasn't about to give up my one advantage. "You'd never find it without me."

The obsessive, hungry look passed over his face. "I could torture you. Force you to tell me."

When he said "torture," my head swam. I hate even the sound of the word. But I couldn't lose control now. "You could torture me, but I might hold out a while. Or faint, or something." (I meant "die," but I couldn't say it.) "If you take me to Paris, I'll tell you where it is. It's simpler that way."

I could see him thinking about it.

"I promise. Swear to God," I said.

He gazed at me a minute more, then turned and called, "Louis!" When Louis appeared, Bruno said, "We're leaving for Paris. Take her to her room and then wait at the car." He left, walking rapidly through the living room, and Louis and I followed him toward the back of the house.

I had no faith in Bruno's intention to let me go. I don't usually break my word when I swear to God, but I thought under the

275

circumstances God would understand. It was time to resort to violence.

Bruno had told Louis to take me to my room and then wait at the car. He hadn't mentioned reporting back after I'd been locked in. That meant, providing Bruno and the man with the mustache didn't see anything, all they'd expect to hear was my room door closing and somebody going out the front as Louis went to the car to wait as ordered.

The door to the other bedroom closed as Louis and I entered the hall. As I thought he would, Bruno had closeted himself. I might have a few minutes, although considering how anxious Bruno was to get the mirror I thought they would be few indeed.

I decided what to do as we walked through the bedroom door and I saw my coat hanging on the knob of the chest of drawers. I brushed past it and deliberately knocked it to the floor saying, with great distress, "Oh, *God!*"

I had thought he'd look down, which would give me a chance to grab the gooseneck lamp and whap him. In fact, he was polite enough to stoop to pick the coat up, which gave me a twinge, but only a twinge, of guilt when I brought the lamp down on the back of his head.

The crack a lamp base makes when hitting someone's skull is a nauseating sound, but I would have been more nauseated if Louis hadn't done what I intended, which was drop senseless. His eyelids fluttered as I searched his pockets, but that was all. I had a momentary, insane hope that I'd find the car keys, but that was too much to expect. I did find the room key, solitary on a ring. He was lying on my coat, but I jerked it out from under him. I closed and locked the door behind me.

I strode, but did not run, down the hall and through the living room. I had some trouble figuring out the several front door latches, but I was outside soon enough. It may not have been the perfect getaway, but it was a getaway.

LYING LOW

I stayed on the front stoop during a two-second search for possible cover, looking over a couple of stunted rosebushes, the car in the gravel driveway, the road in front, the field to either side, and, across the road, a stand of almost leafless trees. The trees weren't a thick, concealing wood, but they were the best alternative.

I ran across the yard, and the bumpy clay road, and only then saw a ditch, steep-sided and filled with withered leaves, that ran between the road and the trees. I missed my stride and fell, slithering into it, my breath knocked out. Dry leaves crackled around me and underneath them were more leaves, sodden and compacted. Dampness soaked through the knees of my pants and my hands sank into mold. In a moment or two I had recovered my bearings and decided I wasn't seriously hurt. I eased myself up to the rim of the ditch until I could see the house. The front door was opening.

I lay still, breathing through my mouth, and watched them come out: Bruno Blanc, in a sheepskin jacket; the mustached man; and behind them, in the doorway, leaning on a cane, a figure in a black overcoat and hat, whose face I couldn't see.

Bruno stopped, taking in the fact that Louis wasn't at the car, where he was supposed to be. His head swung slowly from side to side and then, wildly, around toward the house. He pushed his way past the black-clad figure and back inside.

This wasn't the head start I'd hoped for. As desperate as Bruno was, he'd get into that bedroom somehow, and then—

Bent practically double, I moved cautiously along the side of the ditch. The wind was rushing, so there wasn't much danger that they would hear me. I clambered over the rocks and fallen branches and stepped in water up to my ankle. When I looked again, I'd put a fair distance between me and the house. The mustached man was still in the yard, and the figure in black had moved out to the stoop. I didn't see Bruno. I hunched over and continued.

By the time I stopped for a breather, the house looked small. The car was still there, but I couldn't see any people. They might have spread out to comb the area. I started moving again. Where could I hide? For a few insane moments, I considered climbing a tree. I saw myself perched in the leafless branches, visible for miles. I could burrow under the leaves in the ditch, though. I could burrow like a mole, a rabbit, deep down so I was completely covered up. I scrambled along in my humped-over crawl. They would know by now I had gotten away, that I wasn't in the locked bedroom.

I heard a motor. At first I barely noticed

the sound, a deeper drone below the noise of the wind, but then it got louder. I glanced up and saw it was their car, the Renault, coming slowly up the road in my direction.

If I didn't do something, they would see me. There were no convenient boulders to hide behind, no big drainage pipes, no underbrush, no caves. I could only dig into the leaves, so I dug. I pushed my way through the dry drifts into the mold, and then I lay still and prayed I was covered.

There was a pleasant, earthy smell under the leaves, so strong it was almost a taste. I thought I felt a bug crawling over the back of my neck. I wished my coat were golden brown, instead of camel. The car noise got louder as I squeezed my eyes closed and moved my head to get a twig out of my nose. They were even with me now. They were looking, straining their eyes. What did they expect to see? Surely not a messy leaf pile with patches of camel showing through.

The sound passed, faded. When it was almost gone I raised my head. The Renault was approaching the railroad crossing. As I watched, it seemed to pick up speed. They had given up. They were going back to Paris, probably. Where they would surely be waiting to intercept me.

When they had disappeared, I climbed out of the ditch and sat on its edge. They would be in Paris before I was. They might break into my apartment. They might be so mad with me they would hurt Twinkie.

The thought brought me to my feet. The police, the police, I told myself. Surely they'll be watching the apartment. They won't let that happen. But if it weren't for the police, for Inspector Perret, I wouldn't be in this fix.

I brushed the leaf mold off my coat as best I could and started off, staying in the trees. The road would have been easier walking, but the wood offered more protection. I didn't see anybody—neither Bruno and his minions nor anyone else. The railroad crossing, so utterly distant, grew gradually, gradually, nearer.

I reached it at last and was standing forlornly, looking up and down the empty tracks, when a miracle happened. A truck rattled up. Behind the wheel was a woman with a square, plain face, a flowered kerchief tied around her head. She didn't look French, and I could barely understand her accent when she said, "Do you need help? A ride?"

Her eyes were blue, the loveliest shade I'd ever seen. I nodded several times before I could say, "Please. Is there a train station nearby?"

She nodded, and I got in the truck. The radio was on very low, playing a bouncy accordion tune. I looked sideways at her, but she simply put the truck in gear and we took off. Neither of us spoke. In ten minutes, we had entered a village, steep-roofed stone houses bordering narrow streets, and she was pulling up at a white clapboard station with a sign that said, "Chateau Josse."

I got out of the truck. I said, "I can't . . . Thank you. Thank you."

I probably would have kept saying it, but she drove away. I turned to the station, to find out when the next train for Paris was due.

BACK TO PARIS

THE village of Chateau Josse was not a major stop on the railroad. The only train to Paris left around one in the afternoon, which meant I had several hours to kill after I bought my ticket. The one-room station had a few upright benches, timetables on the walls, a dozing clerk at the window, and a couple of shiny snack-vending machines. It also had the one thing I had most hoped to see: a pay telephone. I fell into the booth, pressing coins in the slot with trembling fingers, and soon was listening to the short buzzes that meant the phone was ringing in Kitty's apartment in Paris. She answered, sounding breathless and abrupt.

"Kitty? Kitty?"

"Georgia Lee! Georgia Lee, where are you?"

"Kitty." I started to snivel. "Don't hang up."

"No, of course I won't hang up. Are you all right?" She sounded near tears herself. We were a fine pair.

After a few tries, I managed to tell her I was in Chateau Josse, which I had ascertained was to the southeast of Paris. Then I said, "What's happening there?"

"What's *happening?* The papers are saying you and your gang double-crossed the police and stole the mirror yesterday. Jack is *so mad* with you for not telling him."

Oh, no. *I* stole the mirror? Bubbles of hysteria rose in my throat. Choking them down, I said, "What about the ransom?"

"Nobody picked it up. Too much commotion. They're saying it was a smooth and ruthless operation!"

I leaned against the wall of the booth, gasping with out-of-control spasms that might have been laughter or sobs.

"I tried to tell that inspector, Gilles Perret, that you'd never do a thing like that, but I don't know if he believed me."

"Ah—ah—"

"Are you all right?"

"Whoo."

"And then the other thing—"

I couldn't believe there was another thing. "What?"

"Somebody broke in and trashed our office last night."

That sobered me. *"No."*

"Yes. Jack called not long ago. He walked by the door this morning, and he knew something was up because he smelled Sphinx all the way out in the hall. They poured it over everything—my slipcover samples, the typewriters—he said the place *reeks.*"

I didn't say anything. It seemed likely that this was retaliation for my having alerted the police and foiled the ransom pick-up. That made a clean sweep: Bruno Blanc, the police, unknown office-trashers, all out after Georgia Lee Maxwell. Were any of them closing in, even now, on the Chateau Josse train station?

"Georgia Lee?"

"Yes?"

"Forgive me for asking this, but—"

"No, Kitty, I did not double-cross the police and steal the damn mirror. I was abducted by Bruno Blanc. Give me a break!"

"I said forgive me."

"For crying out loud!"

I thought I heard sniffling at the other end of the line. Then it broke over me: "What about Twinkie? Did somebody feed Twinkie?"

Her reply, I thought, held a trace of moral superiority: "I went and got Twinkie last night. She's here with me. She seemed upset, so I gave her some *foie gras*. She's asleep in front of the fire."

I was overcome. Twinkie was safe, warm, and stuffed with *foie gras*. After I thanked Kitty profusely she said, "What are you going to do now?"

I didn't know. I was a fugitive. The police felt burned, and I didn't know whether they would belive me if I tried to explain. If they didn't, the simple solution would be to lock me up. My recent experiences in that line didn't make me more eager to be locked up. "I have a ticket for Paris, but—" I began.

Kitty broke in. "You can't go home. You'd better come here."

"Do you realize what you're saying?

"Yes."

"Everybody in the world is after me. They may be watching your place, too."

She must have been thinking about it, because she said, instantly, "So this is what we'll do. When the train comes in, take a taxi to Chez Adele"—the café around the corner from Kitty's place—"and I'll meet you there with one of Alba's uniforms. If you wear that, you can walk right in and they won't look at you twice."

Alba was Kitty's Portuguese housekeeper. Surely Kitty was right. A slightly disheveled housekeeper would be the last person they'd scrutinize. Still, I felt constrained to say, "Are you sure? You could get in real trouble."

"What time does the train arrive?"

I didn't argue anymore. We made our final arrangements and hung up, and I had nothing left to do but wait for the train.

This I did without incident. The time passed slowly. I sat on one of the benches, drinking coffee and eating cookies from the vending machine. I was afraid to expose myself by leaving the station. In the warmth of

286

the waiting room, fatigue began to win out, and I kept waking myself up when my head dropped over. I got up and wandered outside, walking up and down the windswept platform. It looked like rain.

People began to drift in about an hour before time, and when the train arrived a knot of us, maybe ten in all, stood on the platform. After I boarded, found a seat, and saw the last of the Chateau Josse station, I could no longer keep my eyes open. I slept heavily all the way to Paris, rousing from my stupor only occasionally, to see this or that platform sliding by through a rain-streaked window. When the train pulled in I roused myself and went to find the taxi line. Soon, I was on my way to Chez Adele. I was in Paris. I had made it back.

REUNION

KITTY lived on the Avenue Gabriel, near the Rond Point of the Champs-Elysées and a mere stone's throw, if that were your political inclination, from the presidential palace. Chez Adele, around the corner, was filled with babble and smoke. Its decor was as upscale as the neighborhood, with hanging

Tiffany-style lamps, red plush upholstery, and stained-glass panels. Harried pink-uniformed waitresses bustled through the crowd of late lunchers.

I found Kitty at a dark corner table, a white porcelain teapot and cups in front of her and a shopping bag from Hermès on the floor at her feet. She was wearing thigh-high boots, tight suede pants, and an oversized jacket with braid trim, epaulets, and frogs that looked like part of a band uniform. I sat down, and she looked at me and said, "Good Lord. Do you want a brandy?"

I'd done my best in the ladies' room on the train, but I was well aware that a dab of lipstick wasn't going to salvage what abduction, sleeplessness, and leaf-burrowing had done to my appearance. "I'll take tea. Break out the brandy at your place, assuming I make it there."

She poured and said, "I went to the office. The police wanted me to see if anything was missing."

"And *was* anything missing?"

"Nothing of mine. I couldn't tell about your stuff."

We sipped. She indicated the Hermès bag. "The uniform's in there. I brought one of Alba's cardigans, too. And a string bag with some apples in it, so you'll look like you went shopping."

"Alba doesn't mind?"

"She's not there. Today isn't one of her days. She leaves an extra uniform at my place. The sweater she forgot, I guess."

"I hope this works. Have the papers been running my picture?"

"No. You're lucky the Ministry of Defense scandal broke. You're not getting the play you would have normally."

"Fickle fame." I was dying to get to Kitty's. I wanted to see Twinkie. I picked up the bag and went to the ladies' room.

In one of the stalls, I took off my disgusting garments. Putting Alba's starched white dress on my unwashed body seemed like a desecration. I buttoned it and slipped on the pale blue cardigan with puffs of white angora on it. The ensemble was completed by Kitty's artistic touch of the string bag with apples. I didn't know whether I looked terribly Portuguese—I'd never heard of a Paris cleaning lady who wasn't Portuguese—but surely I could pass at a distance. I shoved my discarded clothes into the Hermès bag and returned to the table.

When Kitty saw me she said, "Swell." I didn't ask what the comment implied. She picked up the loaded Hermès bag and, looking like she was going home after a multi-thousand-dollar shopping spree, left me to sip dregs and wait till she got there.

The café was so jammed it was unlikely that my transformation had been noticed. I allowed Kitty a full ten minutes, then followed her.

A light rain was falling, making it reasonable for me to keep my head lowered. From the corner of my eye I tried to see if anyone was lurking in the park across the street. I saw a few people rushing by, sheltering under umbrellas, and a couple of dog-walkers, and that was it. I turned my gaze to the drops hitting the sidewalk. I was somebody's nurse, cleaning lady, housekeeper, caught in the rain during an apple-buying excursion. Either the uniform conferred anonymity or nobody was watching, because soon I was inside Kitty's place, giving her a shaky, but triumphant, hug.

Kitty's apartment is posh. When her estranged husband, Luc de Villiers-Marigny, decamped for the Riviera to indulge his dissipations and perversions, he more or less gave it to her, although he remains the legal owner. She lives in fear that he'll straighten himself out and return to claim it. In the meantime, she has french windows and a long balcony with a view of the Champs and the Grand Palais, marble fireplaces in every room, ornate plaster mouldings, and Luc's collection of sexually explicit pre-Columbian statuary. When Kitty is squeezed for cash, she has been known to sell a statue, although she prefers to pawn them.

I looked around for Twinkie. She was crouched on the coffee table, eyeing me sullenly. When I picked her up and held her close, crooning, "Here I am, Twinks. Here I am, girl," she squeaked in protest and twisted her body out of my grasp. She landed on the floor, shook herself all over, sat down with her back to me, and began washing her face.

"She's mad at you for leaving her," Kitty said soothingly.

I was nettled. "To hell with her," I said, and collapsed into a chair in front of the fire.

Kitty brought me a brandy and a pile of newspapers with my story in them. I glanced over a few. Nobody seemed entirely sure what happened in the Luxembourg, but nobody was anxious to give me the benefit of the doubt. In speculation, I was everything from a weak-willed dupe to the mastermind. "Innocent" was not a cornerstone of anyone's theory.

I wondered if Loretta and the *Good Look* people had yet heard of my latest go at dragging *Good Look* through the mud. While I was living it up in Chateau Josse, "Paris Patter" may have petered out. Which would be a serious problem only if I avoided jail.

Enough was enough. I tossed the papers aside. "Tell me about the break-in at the office," I said to Kitty.

She had settled on the sofa. Twinkie, still ignoring me, marched to the hearth and lay down with her nose practically in the fire. "The police had the building under surveillance, but of course there's a lot of coming and going," she said. "Jack said maybe somebody went in late in the afternoon and hid. Because of Worldwide, there's plenty of nighttime activity, too."

"Has there been any more word on it? Did Jack call again?"

She flushed. "Yeah, he called. Nothing new."

I looked at her closely. "You didn't tell him you'd heard from me, did you?"

Looking surpassingly guilty, she said, "No, I didn't."

"Come on, Kitty."

"I didn't! Really! But—"

"But—"

"But I think he guessed."

"For God's sake! How?"

"He just . . . knows my voice. I'm afraid he could tell."

I put down my brandy and lay back. It was meant to be a gesture of disgusted resignation, but it felt so good I could hardly muster the energy to say, "He'll be over here any minute, battering the door down, looking for a scoop."

"Give him some credit, Georgia Lee. He's awfully worried about you."

I wanted to argue. I thought of a great riposte, but my mouth wouldn't form the words.

In a few minutes I woke up enough to stumble to the bathroom and turn on the shower. I shucked off Alba's dress and stood under the steaming water a long time. When I got out, I found a lace-trimmed nightgown Kitty had hung on the door. I put it on, went to the darkened guest bedroom, and slid between crisp sheets. Just as I was falling asleep, the bed shook gently. A cold nose nudged mine. Emitting breathy purrs, Twinkie curled up next to me, and the two of us settled down for a nap.

IN THE OFFICE

When I woke, it was dark. Twinkie was gone. A light was on in the living room, and I could hear voices. I found a man-sized navy terrycloth robe in the closet, put it on, and crept out to see what was happening. Kitty was on the sofa, legs stretched out and ankles crossed. Sitting in a chair, with Twinkie curled up on his knees, was Jack. On the coffee table was a bottle of red wine, glasses, and a plate of pâté and sliced bread.

I stepped into the room and said, "Fancy meeting you here, Jack."

He grinned. "You can lead a newshound around the block a few times, but you can't put him off the scent."

"I had to let him in," Kitty said. "He was threatening to flash your whereabouts to all parts of the globe if I didn't."

"Hardball, eh?" I was ravenous. I spread pâté on a piece of bread and took a bite. Duck liver mousse. The wine was a Bordeaux. I poured myself a glass.

"Tell me something," Jack said.

"What?" I sat down. The mousse was fabulous. I spread some more.

"Where's the mirror?"

I gave a gigantic shrug and kept chewing.

"Sure you know. Come on, kiddo."

I sipped my wine. Delicious. "Sure I know. And I'm not about to tell you, or Kitty, or anybody else. Take my word for it, I'm saving you a lot of aggravation."

Kitty said, "What about the cops? Wouldn't they forgive you if you gave it back?"

"So far, they've jumped to believe the worst. And even if I gave it back, would that exonerate me? I have to decide what to do."

Jack pointed a finger at me. "When you decide, don't forget Jack. A five-minute head start on the story is all I'll need."

"You can lead a newshound around the block, but you can't teach him sensitivity," Kitty said. "Don't browbeat her, Jack. The woman was *kidnapped*."

"She's a pro. She understands."

I understood. I said, "So you discovered the break-in at our office."

"How could I not? I walked by the door and caught a whiff of a suffocating odor. I thought, either a herd of musk oxen is in there grazing—"

"Camels," Kitty said. "A herd of camels."

"—or something is wrong. I went in. I actually thought about putting a handkerchief over my nose and mouth, but I couldn't see why that would help."

"Was it a real mess?"

"A mess, anyway. Pieces of cloth strewn all over the place—"

"My slipcover swatches," said Kitty mournfully.

"Papers thrown around, your Bay City mug and Kitty's teacup broken. But the worst was the smell. They'd poured that Sphinx stuff all over—into your typewriters, on the extra ribbons. I found the empty bottle on the floor. Two hundred milliliters."

We fell silent. I was stricken at the thought of our vandalized office.

"So that's that," Jack said. "Practically the entire Criminal Brigade came to check it out, including a bruiser named Jacques Perret—"

"Gilles Perret."

"—who seemed to be either a special friend or a special enemy of yours. I couldn't tell which."

"I don't know myself." I felt terribly depressed.

We all stared into the fire. At last I roused myself to say, "I wish I knew if they'd taken anything of mine."

"We could go and look," Kitty suggested.

I shook my head. "The place will be watched."

"They're through in the office by now."

"Yeah, but outside."

We lapsed into silence again until Jack said, casually, "This is where I make you happy you let me in. Or do you already know about the back door?"

We looked at him. I wasn't about to give him the satisfaction of saying, "What back door?" He yawned, scratched Twinkie's head and said, "This sure is a nice cat."

"Stop screwing around, Jack," Kitty said.

He smiled sweetly and said, "There's a back door. Nobody uses it except the janitors. But guess what?"

"You know how to get in it," I said.

"I have a key. A few years ago, I did some interviews with a man who had hit squads out after him. Political stuff. He was afraid I'd lead them to him if I went to his place, so he came to me. I finagled a key to the

297

back door so he could go in and out in secret. And I never gave it back."

I stood up. "Then let's go."

We didn't leave immediately. I was constitutionally incapable of putting on my slacks, sweater, and camel coat again, and I didn't particularly want to wear Alba's uniform, so we had to find an outfit of Kitty's for me. Since she's taller and thinner than I it was a complicated matter, made more complicated because we had diametrically opposing views about what would look good on me.

"Those stripes are *great*, Georgia Lee."

"But it hangs like a sack. Look at the way it hangs."

"It's supposed to be that way. It's made that way."

"I could never in my life go out looking like this."

"Try this one, then."

We continued, with Jack in the living room yelling "Are we going or what?" until we settled on a getup neither of us liked: a rhinestone-studded olive-green velour sweatshirt that reached almost to my knees and skintight silver pants. Then we all trooped down to Jack's car.

The drizzle had let up, but the streets were damp and glistening, the streetlights fuzzy-looking in the saturated air. It was about ten o'clock at night. The Rue du Quatre-Septembre, so busy during the day, was almost deserted. The glass fronts of banks and office buildings looked shadowy and hostile.

Jack whipped around a corner, pulled into the alley behind our building, and parked next to a row of garbage cans. Despite the darkness, the sinister echoes, the sudden terrifying rattling of discarded newspapers, we got into the building and up to the office without incident. As Kitty unlocked the door I caught the smell of enough musk and patchouli to dab on the pulse points of several harems. Then the door opened, and the unmistakable odor of Sphinx rushed out. It settled in the back of my throat and wrenched several coughs out of me.

"It was worse this morning," Jack said.

Kitty switched on the lights and I rushed to the window, bent on flinging it up for air. I had it halfway raised when I stopped dead. Standing next to the automatic teller booth at the bank across the street was a figure in a black overcoat and hat, leaning on a cane. I had last seen that person on the front stoop of the house near Chateau Josse. "Turn out the light!" I cried and dropped to my knees.

"What is it?" said Kitty, but the lights went out.

"Look!"

They joined me at the window, in time to see the figure turn and start limping toward the Place de l'Opéra. When I babbled out where I'd seen him before Jack said, "I'm going after him," and started for the door.

Kitty and I both yelled "No!" at the same time and I added, "The others might be around somewhere, Jack!"

He said, "Oh, for Christ's sake," but turned back.

I sat down at my desk chair. I had known they'd come back, known they'd be watching. All around me was the pathetic jumble that our minuscule place of business had become. Unrolled typewriter ribbons festooned the desks. The coatrack, never stable, listed to one side with a broken leg. Letters, press releases, and slipcover swatches littered the floor along with shards of my mug and Kitty's cup. Desk drawers gaped open, and clean typing paper had been saturated with Sphinx. The scent hung over everything like a noxious fog.

"Do you still want to search?" Kitty asked in a tentative tone.

"Might as well."

She pulled the blinds and turned the light back on, and I turned grimly to the task. In half an hour or so I'd been through it all and hadn't found anything missing. My typewriter would surely reek forever. "Time for that word processor," I joked feebly, although there wasn't a damn thing funny about it. I hated this entire situation, and most of all I hated the smell of Sphinx.

I sat at my desk feeling defeated, trying to wind up an unwound typewriter ribbon. I had never before realized how full of enemies the world could seem.

AFTER DINNER

"WHOEVER tore up the office was in Paris last night. Bruno and his friends were in the country," I said.

"It's not that far. Couldn't they have driven back here and done it?" said Jack.

I considered. "I'm pretty sure they didn't. The wind made a lot of noise, but I would have heard the car. I hardly slept at all."

"Research has proven that often when people think they hardly slept at all they really slept quite a bit."

"Jack, I know damn well I would have

heard the car. It was outside my window, practically. Besides, we're not talking plain old insomnia. We're talking massive fear, serious—"

"All right. You would have heard. Where does that leave us?"

It was around midnight—in other words, the shank of the evening for many Paris restaurants, including the one not far from the Opéra where Kitty, Jack, and I had just had dinner. We were sitting at a banquette table, the mirrors that lined the wall behind us reflecting a dining room with every place occupied. Glasses clinked, smoke drifted, conversation and laughter flew around us at lubricated volume. Late diners were still arriving. After a long and at times furious debate at the office about whether to risk leaving the building, Jack had finally announced that no mysterious person in black was going to keep him from eating dinner. Kitty and I had fallen in line with his point of view, and we were now mopping our plates, finishing the wine, and waiting for coffee.

"Who wanted this mirror?" I said, counting on my fingers. "Bruno Blanc, Madeleine Bellefroide—"

"Hey! Maybe it's Madeleine Bellefroide,"

said Kitty, who'd been looking sleepy. "She hired a couple of thugs to steal it, and they panicked and killed Pierre Legrand. Now she's joined forces with Bruno. *She's* the one in black with the cane."

"And the ransom offer?" I asked.

"Camouflage. Cast suspicion elsewhere."

"Very cagey. And to evade suspicion even more thoroughly, she sticks the mirror into an urn in the Luxembourg Garden and loses it."

"There could be a reason. Keep an open mind. You have a soft spot for Madeleine."

She was right. I wanted to trust Madeleine Bellefroide, although if I thought about it I couldn't see why I should.

Jack expelled smoke, thickening an already heavy atmosphere. Kitty patted back a yawn. "What about Lucien Claude?" I said.

"Mr. Adorable? What about him?" Jack remained touchy about Lucien's looks.

"Why was he killed? I can see why they got rid of Legrand—"

"You can? Why?"

"Because they wanted the mirror, and—"

"They *had* the mirror. Pierre Legrand was lying face down on the floor. He wasn't stopping them, any more than you were."

"Yeah, but suppose he had reason to know

who they were, because of some prior approach or deal."

"O.K."

"So they kill him because of that. But why Claude?"

Jack let smoke drift slowly out of his nostrils. Then he said, "The same reason, maybe."

"Then why get involved in trying to ransom it back?"

"Say he was going to double-cross them."

Just for argument I said, "He seemed so sincere."

"I never said he wasn't a good con man."

The coffee arrived. Kitty said, "Look. You saw the people who killed Pierre Legrand. Why don't you go through the suspects and decide who *couldn't* have done it?"

I threw my mind back to those awful few minutes in the storage room at the Bellefroide. "It couldn't have been Bruno Blanc or Lucien Claude. They're too tall," I said. "It couldn't have been Bernard Mallet or Clive Overton, because they were with me. It couldn't have been Madeleine Bellefroide—"

"But the killers could've been hit men hired by any of those people," Jack said.

I ignored his excellent point. "It could

have been the two guys who abducted me. Louis and the other one. They're about the right height."

"Which is—"

"Medium. And medium build."

"Maybe they're the ones, then," Jack said.

I shook my head. "They're in with Bruno Blanc, and Bruno didn't have the mirror. Bruno *wanted* the mirror. If his friends had stolen it, he'd have had it, wouldn't he?"

"Unless something completely misfired," Jack said.

"I have the feeling a lot of things misfired, up to and including the ransom transfer," I said. "The only problem is, I can't figure out where the divergence is between the way things went and the way they were supposed to go."

Waves of laughter from the next table washed over us. Everybody was having a wonderful time. "You know who's fishy?" I said.

"Yeah. Chantal Legrand," said Jack.

"Chantal? I was going to say Bernard Mallet."

"Look at Chantal. Look at all the dust she kicked up, calling a press conference to clear her darling husband's name."

"Well, she—"

"Instead of doing that, she made him look worse."

"*Cherchez la femme,* huh? The woman is always wrong?"

"Sweet little wife, ha!" Jack's tone, I thought, was edged with real bitterness.

I tried to pull us back to the realm of speculation. "Yeah, but what does Chantal have to do with Nostradamus's mirror?"

"Oh, who the hell knows." Jack slid down in his chair, staring at the bottom of his espresso cup.

"Well, I think Bernard Mallet is fishy," I said.

When Jack didn't answer, Kitty said, sleepily, "Why?"

"He seems to hate the mirror. He doesn't want it back. Did I tell you he asked me not to proceed with the ransom plans?"

Jack roused himself. "So he stages a robbery at his own museum and has his guard murdered so he can get rid of an artifact he considers a piece of junk," he said sarcastically.

I was irritated. "Look, Jack. It's easy to be negative and piss on everything."

"Good suggestion." He stood up. "Excuse me for a second."

As he made his way toward the toilets, I said, "What's the matter with him?"

Kitty ran her finger around the top of her glass. "I think talking about Chantal put him in a bad mood."

"Obviously. But why?"

"Something to do with husbands and wives."

"You mean . . . Is his marriage shaky, or something?"

"Something. I don't really know."

"What's his wife like?"

"Claire? Gorgeous. French. She comes to his office every now and then. They have a couple of kids who are almost grown."

"But what—"

"Who knows? Jack stuck it out when you and I didn't. Maybe he's sorry."

I was swept by sadness. "What a life. You're sorry if you do, and sorry if you don't."

"That's about it."

"Let's go home."

We didn't talk much on the way. Jack seemed to be driving faster than usual. Kitty yawned repeatedly and leaned her head against the window.

When we pulled up on the Avenue Gabriel,

Kitty said, "Let me go first and get the door open, Georgia Lee. Then you hurry in."

"Right."

She slipped out of the car. Nervous, I looked up and down the dark, quiet street and inspected the park across the way. As I watched, a dark figure rose from a bench.

I stared, immobilized. The person in the black overcoat and hat hovered there like the manifestation of a nightmare. A moment later, reanimated, I grabbed Jack. "Look! Over in the park!"

He saw. "God *damn* it," he said fiercely. He pulled the hand brake, jumped out of the car, and sprinted across the street. Before I could decide whether to follow him or go to the door, where Kitty was beckoning, Jack had grappled with the shadowy form and they both fell flat.

Some flailing ensued, but it didn't look like a fierce contest. No reinforcements emerged from the bushes, either. I jumped out of the car and ran toward them, with Kitty close behind.

Jack was getting to his knees, dusting his hands, by the time we reached him. The man in black was writhing, moaning with what sounded like serious pain. A hat and cane lay near him on the gravel. In the light from the street lamps, I could see his face plainly.

"It's Clive Overton," I said. "Overton, the art restorer. Remember?"

Overton groaned. We got him under the arms, dragged him to his feet, and hustled him across the street to Kitty's before somebody alerted the police.

CLIVE OVERTON

OVERTON lay wheezing and grimacing on Kitty's sofa. The three of us stood looking down at him, Kitty holding a glass of water.

"What if he *dies?*" I hissed to Jack.

"Don't be ridiculous," he said, but I thought he looked scared.

Kitty knelt beside Overton. "Would you like some water?" she asked.

He didn't respond, but the wheezing lessened. In a few minutes he motioned for water. After she'd moistened his lips he lay back with his eyes closed, and eventually the heaving of his chest slowed down. When he opened his eyes, it was to look at me. "I beg you," he croaked.

Maybe he wasn't going to die. If not, I was plenty pissed off with him. "Where are

Bruno and the boys?" I said. "Are you here to drag me back to Chateau Josse for another go-around?"

"So you know," Overton said.

"Yes, I know. I saw you out there. I saw you watching the office tonight, too."

He looked tearful. "None of this is right," he said.

"You're telling *me*."

He struggled to sit up. "Yes, I watched the office. I was desperate to find you. When I saw you at the window tonight, I knew you'd returned to Paris. I thought perhaps you'd stay here instead of at home."

"How did you know about Kitty?"

"Bruno met her at your office, and remembered her name. I found her name and address in the telephone directory."

Bruno, no doubt, could do the same. I no longer felt so safe here.

"We never intended to harm you," Overton was saying.

"Is that so? Is that why your friends grabbed me, and locked me up—"

"None of it was supposed to happen!" Overton's face was bright red. "Hear me out. Hear me out, can't you?"

I didn't want to push him into a stroke. "All right. I'm listening," I snapped.

He took out a handkerchief and mopped his forehead. "I came to beg for the mirror. The mirror is all we want."

" 'We' being—"

"The Speculatori. Students of the art of divination."

Jack put in, "A secret society?"

Overton shook his head. "We have no occult rituals. We are nothing more than a group of people with an interest in the subject. Our most talented member by far is Bruno Blanc, who is truly gifted."

"What about art restoration?" I asked. "Are you really an art conservator, or is that just a cover for the Speculatori?"

"Of course I'm an art conservator. That's how I make my living. And until recently the Speculatori had no need for a 'cover.' "

"But now?"

"Now we are in difficulties. And still we don't have the mirror we've gone through so much to obtain."

Overton had gotten hold of himself, and although he looked ill he was now much more the pudgy and proper Englishman I had accompanied to the Bellefroide. He was, in fact, a good deal more loquacious than he had been on our taxi ride. He said, "I can only tell you what happened."

"Go ahead." We gathered around, like children waiting for a bedtime story. Kitty stayed on the floor beside him, Jack leaned against the mantel, and I sat in the chair next to the long-dead fire.

Overton said, "I looked into the mirror. That was the beginning."

The chills came, wave after wave. "You looked in Nostradamus's mirror? How did you manage that?"

"It wasn't difficult at all." His lips moved, suggesting a smile. "Bernard Mallet wasn't always the director of the Musée Bellefroide. It was a tragedy for the Speculatori when he was named to the position five years or so ago, after the previous director died. Mallet's predecessor was considerably more lenient in his handling of the mirror."

He leaned back, his eyes fixed on the luxuriant plaster garlands that surrounded Kitty's fireplace. "Some years ago, perhaps fifteen, I paid my first visit to the Musée Bellefroide," he said. "At the time I was an assistant, something of an apprentice, in the workshop of a widely respected expert in art conservation. He had been called to the Bellefroide for a minor consultation and he brought me along, more to look after his

312

travel arrangements than for any other reason.

"It was a time of extreme turmoil in my personal life. Without going into detail, I will say that questions concerning my direction and identity had become so pressing, and so seemingly unresolvable, that I thought constantly of killing myself. I had, some time before, a suicidal accident, when I walked into traffic without looking where I was going. I escaped with a broken leg. When I'm under stress, the leg still aches terribly. It's aching now.

"The man I worked for and the director of the Bellefroide were old friends. When our work was done, they wanted to disappear for coffee and gossip together. So that I would be occupied and out of their way, the Bellefroide's director, Mallet's predecessor, took me to the storage room and invited me to look at the works that were not on display. He was a jolly fellow, as unlike Mallet as you can imagine. He pointed out several items he thought might interest me, and as he was leaving he said, 'And if you'd like to see your future, have a look in Nostradamus's mirror.' He opened the drawer where it was kept, showed me the case, and told me about Josef Claude, the man from whom the

Bellefroides bought the mirror. He said, 'I think the later members of the family thought owning such a thing wasn't quite dignified, and they refused to have the mirror displayed. But have a look, if fortune-telling interests you at all.'

"I had never, at that point, given a thought to divination or the occult, and I had no intention of wasting my time looking into Nostradamus's mirror. I was so engrossed in my own troubles that I gave only perfunctory attention to the contents of the storage room. Soon I was staring out the window, caught once again in my ever-descending spiral of self-hatred."

Overton massaged his leg slowly, frowning. I thought of the cold, slippery weight of the mirror, the way it had felt before I dropped it into the Medici Fountain.

"I don't know what made me turn from the window," Overton continued. "When I did, I saw that the drawer where the mirror was kept was still open. I thought I would close it, so the director wouldn't realize how uninterested I'd been in his treasures. But instead of closing the drawer, completely without premeditation, I picked up the mirror case.

"I remember telling myself not to be foolish, even as I was opening the case and taking the mirror out. The mirror was cold to the touch, and its surface was perfectly brilliant, perfectly black. It was like an object in a hallucination. I bent over it and looked."

He'll say he didn't see anything at first, I thought. Then there's a stirring in the depths.

"Although my face was directly over the surface, I saw nothing, not even my own reflection," Overton said. "I began to feel a sort of panic, but was unable to look away. And then, deep in the blackness, there was a sign of movement."

Overton's voice was rough with emotion. I could hear his breathing.

"In the mirror's depths I saw the figure of a man, naked, walking toward me," Overton said. "He was stumbling, at times almost crawling, and I soon saw that this was because he was bleeding copiously, hideously, from a number of wounds.

"It was a dreadful sight, sickening. I didn't know how he could continue to move, yet he came closer. When he was close enough, even though his face was distorted with pain, I recognized him as myself."

Overton ran his hands over his heavy jowls. "I felt the most ungodly despair," he said.

"I wanted to take the mirror and smash it against the wall, but I couldn't. In the mirror, the man's gaping wounds had poured out so much blood that he was wading through it, ankle deep, and as I watched, the stream grew deeper, up to his knees, and deeper yet. He was wading, painfully, laboriously, through a river of his own blood, and then he sank into it.

"I cried out, I think, but I could not stop looking, and as I watched his head reappeared and he began to swim. He swam strongly, carried along by the dark river that had emerged from his own wounds. I saw that he was in his element. I saw that his wounds hadn't healed, but that he might make use of them."

"But that's awful!" Kitty burst out. "It would have been so much better to see him get well!"

"Perhaps it would. But that isn't what the mirror showed me." Overton paused. "What I saw gave me hope. The man—my image—wasn't engulfed, after all. He continued, and progressed, in his way. And so did I."

Kitty shuddered and turned away. Overton said, "I put the mirror back in its case and replaced it in the drawer. A short time later the director and my mentor came for me, and my visit to the Bellefroide was over. I didn't return until you and I, Mrs. Maxwell, went there together a little more than a week ago. And this time I knew the mirror had brought me back."

BRUNO'S OBSESSION

SILENCE fell. Overton took a drink of water. The rest of us stirred, as if during intermission in the theater.

"How about coffee?" Jack said. "Anybody want some? I'll make a pot."

"That would be lovely," Overton said.

Kitty's face was still somber. "Sure," she said, almost inaudibly.

Jack said, "Do you still keep it in the same place, Kit?" and when she nodded, he went into the kitchen. In a minute or two, I heard water running.

Overton lay back, massaging his leg. I got up and moved around the room, pulled back the curtain and looked down on the empty and peaceful Avenue Gabriel. Neither Kitty nor Overton spoke. Eventually, I went to the kitchen to see if Jack needed any help.

The water was boiling. The coffepot, all prepared with the paper filter in place and

317

the coffee in it, sat on the counter. Jack was leaning next to it, scribbling in his notebook.

"What are you doing?" I said.

He glanced at me. "Just want to get a few points down before he goes on."

"Why? A few points for what?"

"Hang on a sec." He continued to write.

I poured the water into the top of the pot and inhaled the aroma as it started to drip through. "Don't do this to me," I said.

He stopped writing. He clicked his ballpoint, closed his notebook, and turned to look at me. "Do what?"

"You know what."

His gaze was level. "No, I don't know what. Tell me."

I felt as if all the awful things that had ever happened to me were flying at me at once. "Don't take this story away from me, Jack. Don't. I know you can do it. You've got the outlet. I've told you everything, and—"

"Oh, shit," he said.

"I'm just asking you—"

"—not to do my job. Is that right?"

"No! No, it isn't. But you know I've been involved in this from the beginning!"

He crossed his arms. His tie was loosened, the sleeves of his white shirt rolled up, just like a newsman's should be. "Let me tell you something," he said. "Your story is your story. I can't possibly take it away from you, because you're the only one who can write it. But two murders and the theft of this mirror are news, too. You can't expect me to keep a complete hands-off attitude, and you shouldn't ask me to, either."

"I wish I'd known how you felt before I told you everything."

"Jesus Christ!" He slapped the counter with his open palm, making the coffeepot jump. "I'm not a thief, Georgia Lee. I'm not going to rip you off. Do you understand what I'm saying? I *can't* write your story. Only you can write it."

I slumped against the wall. I didn't know what to say. He turned his back to me and leaned heavily on the sink. I heard a movement behind me, and Kitty's voice said, "Uh, how's the coffee doing?"

"Ready," said Jack. I went back to the living room, and in a minute he came in with a tray.

When everyone had a cup, Overton said, "I'm sorry to be making such a long job of this. It's only that I want you to understand fully what's happened." He stirred his coffee and put down his spoon. "You may find it difficult to credit, but during the following years I rarely thought about my experience with the mirror. I accepted the lesson it had given me, and in time my life became easier and happier. I was more interested in fortune-telling, crystal-gazing and such than I'd been before, but it wasn't a dominant part of my life. It became so only after I'd met Bruno Blanc."

Overton's face softened. He said, "Bruno and I were introduced by mutual friends here in Paris several years ago. Before long, I became aware of his remarkable gift for divination. I was more and more fascinated by it, and seeing this he introduced me to the Speculatori. Bruno and I became close friends, and at last I told him about my experience, years ago, with Nostradamus's mirror.

"My story had an extraordinary, and not very healthy, effect on him. He questioned me, over and over, about every detail of the episode. When we were together he talked continually about the mirror, and what a person of his gifts might do with it. Around this time, Bruno made his first petition to Bernard Mallet, who by then was director of the Bellefroide, asking if he could see it.

"Mallet refused, but we hoped he might

be persuaded. Bruno became more involved with the mirror. He searched out Lucien Claude, and heard his story about his ancestor Josef. He read, meditated, honed his powers in order to be ready for his opportunity with the mirror, which he had convinced himself would surely come. And he continued to approach Mallet, and Mallet continued to refuse.

"I could have, and perhaps should have, intervened and used my own position as leverage with Mallet. But frankly, because of my career I was reluctant to be associated with something that would be suspect in so many eyes."

Overton put down his cup. "Now comes the thing that is hardest to explain," he said. "And that is why, when Bruno suggested out of frustration that we try to steal the mirror, I consented."

He looked around at us. Nobody moved. "I can only say that between the time I looked into the mirror and the time I met Bruno, my life had been rational, calm—and a bit constricted. It was productive, but not exciting. I didn't know people like Bruno, people who cast themselves so willingly into the unknown. If Bruno was obsessed with the mirror, I became obsessed with Bruno."

His face pinkened. "If he wanted the mirror, I wanted him to have it," he said softly.

I was astonished. I said, "You mean the day we went to the Bellefroide you knew—" but Overton held up his hand to stop me.

"No. Let me explain," he said. "Bruno had done everything. He had begged Mallet. He had tried to buy the mirror. At last, crazed with frustration, he approached the guard, Pierre Legrand, and offered to pay him to steal it. And, perhaps the ultimate frustration, Legrand refused.

"Bruno didn't tell me about this until after his encounter with Legrand. I was horrified, most of all at what the situation was doing to Bruno. I begged him not to take any more action on his own. I told him I would find my way into the Bellefroide and reconnoiter, that I might be able to get the mirror for him myself. Would I have done it? I can't say. Someone else was bolder and quicker than I."

He looked steadily at me. "Now we come, Mrs. Maxwell, to the visit you and I made to the Bellefroide. I had heard of the damaged altarpiece and had contacted Mallet—who, naturally, knew nothing of my connection with Bruno. The purpose of my visit was not only to look at the altarpiece, but to see if the mirror were still in the same drawer. I would have to return to the Bellefroide to work on the altarpiece, so would have had several opportunities, probably, to take the mirror. This first day was to be a general survey. Magazines have often featured me and my work, and in fact, this time I was glad enough to have you along, as I thought bringing a journalist with me would establish my lack of ulterior motive.

"Then, to my utter shock, the mirror was stolen and Legrand was murdered while we were there. My first thought was that Bruno had gone mad, disregarded me, and arranged it himself. When the police arrived I collapsed, quite genuinely, and by the time I was able to speak with them I had also spoken with Bruno, and gotten his assurance that he wasn't behind it. As soon as I was well enough, I went with Bruno to the house where you were later taken."

"You were in the other bedroom," I said. "The one with the door always closed."

"I was badly upset, and needed seclusion. I hardly bargained for what happened next."

"You mean Georgia Lee's kidnapping?" said Jack.

"Yes. During that time I was frequently sedated. I know only that Bruno came to me, very excited, and said we now had a chance to get the mirror, that he would have it within twenty-four hours. He didn't explain the arrangements he'd made, or how he'd made them. The next afternoon, when you arrived, he burst in and said, 'The fools have taken the woman, too.' I think, you see, that his plan was for the two young men, who are disciples of his and members of the Speculatori, to take the mirror away from you. You were more alert that they expected, and they felt the best course was to take you as well."

"I ran when I saw them coming toward me," I said.

"Yes, well, that threw them off, you see. Bruno was practically beside himself already, and then, when the mirror case was empty—"

"I heard him."

"His distress was terrifying. I began to think he might be capable of killing after all."

"But Pierre Legrand? And Lucien Claude? He all but admitted he'd killed them. He threatened to kill me, too."

"He would threaten anything, if he thought it would bring him the mirror. He wanted to frighten you, but I feel certain he wouldn't commit murder. You see, Bruno has a sense of mission. He wants to combine his power and the mirror's in the cause of greater understanding. To begin such a project by killing two people would be a perversion of his purpose."

"But to begin it by stealing the mirror would be O.K.?"

"You're being ironic, I realize, but yes. I agree with Bruno that the mirror must never go back to the Bellefroide, must never return to the clutches of Bernard Mallet. This is the case I've come to plead."

He leaned toward me. "Bernard Mallet is an unfit custodian," he said. "He admits that he cares nothing for the mirror. Why return it to him? It has been taken. He need never know it was found again. You could say the case was empty when you got it. You owe him nothing. Do you see?"

"I see your point—"

"Of course you do. Give the mirror to those who appreciate it, who are equipped to use it. With the mirror, Bruno will do stunning things. He will be a tremendous force for good."

When I didn't reply, Overton continued, "I said I'd come to beg you, Mrs. Maxwell, and I have. I beg you. I implore you. Give us the mirror."

WHERE THE LIGHT FALLS

I lay in bed with Kitty's down comforter, in a *broderie anglaise* cover, tucked up around my chin. The bedside lamp cast a mellow and restful glow, but even without the last round of coffee I wouldn't have been able to sleep.

I hadn't given Overton an answer, and he'd gone quietly without one. Hat in hand, he said as he left, "You will think it over. You must promise me that."

I promised, and we closed the door after him. He was an unhappy man, I thought, and yet he'd seen his vision and he'd found the love of his life. Maybe he'd had more than most of us got.

Now, I was trying to calm the continuing caffeine rush and sort out his story. According to Overton, Bruno had expected his helpers, Louis and the man with the mustache, to grab the mirror away from me in the Luxembourg. That meant Bruno was privy to the arrangements for the ransom transfer. How could he have been? Nobody but the police and I had known the final plan, and we had known it only a short time before.

So Bruno must have found out from the other side.

Sure. If *I* didn't tell, and the *police* didn't tell, *they* told.

Well. Why?

Because it didn't matter to them who got the mirror. They only cared about the money.

But everybody cared about the mirror. The mirror was the mystic center, the motivation, the fatal attraction.

Right?

Across the room, hanging on the wall, was a framed pen-and-ink drawing of a house sheltered by two trees. It was a picture of Kitty's childhood home in Ames, Iowa. I stared at it, my mind churning. I couldn't see it very well, because the light from the lamp didn't reach quite that far.

A voice said: *You are standing in a dark place, holding a light. You refuse to look where the light falls, but persist in searching the shadows.*

I lay there thinking about Bruno's words. They seemed to push against my brain until they produced an idea.

I got out of bed, wrapped the comforter around me, and went to the living room, where Jack had insisted (for our protection and, no doubt, in the interest of being where the action was) on bedding down on the sofa. I shook the snoring, motionless pile of quilts and said, "Jack!"

After the predictable complement of "Wha?" and "Whassamatter?" he sat up, shaking his head.

"Jack, tell me about the ransom transfer in the Luxembourg. I never heard exactly what went on."

"Sure, Georgia Lee," he said groggily. "Why wait till morning when we can discuss it right now?" When he lit a cigarette, I caught a glimpse of him. His hair was standing up every which way, and he was wearing a V-necked T-shirt that showed a puff of gray chest hair. I suddenly felt tender toward him, sorry we'd quarreled earlier, and sorry that relationships have to be complex instead of simple, and sorry—

"What do you want to know?" he asked.

"What happened? Did anybody try to get the money?"

He heaved a deep sigh. "Let's see. According to the police, you put the ransom in the trash can, picked up a note, and proceeded back to the Medici Fountain. They're stationed all around the trash can, waiting for the pickup, but of course there are other people around the trash can, too. I think the cops may have had somebody taking pictures surreptitiously. Then there's an unexpected commotion by the fountain, and the next thing anybody knows you and two guys are jumping into a Renault."

"They were *shoving* me into a Renault."

"All a matter of perspective. The cops break cover and run after you, and that's it."

"Nobody approached the ransom?"

"Not close enough to be suspicious. But as I said, they'd have been watching whoever was hanging around."

"Right."

My idea was with me, burgeoning. Jack exhaled a drag and put the cigarette out. I felt his hand on my back, rubbing just the right spot between the shoulder blades. So I wasn't the only one who'd felt the current flowing between us. Knowing it would be better not to, I leaned my head back and closed my eyes. "You've forgiven me?" he said.

"Oh, hell. You know you were right."

"I know you care a lot about this story."

"It's . . . in a way, it's all I've got." I don't know why I said something so pitiful, but it's how I felt at that moment.

"It's like that, sometimes," Jack said. "Takes over. Carries you."

"Until nothing else matters?"

"Nothing."

He put his arms around me, and I leaned against him. Chest hairs tickled my nose. I could hear his heart. "What's wrong, Jack?" I said.

He didn't answer for a while. Then he said, "It's too boring to talk about. Been written so many times Loretta wouldn't even want it for 'Paris Patter.' "

"I'm sorry."

"Nah."

His kiss tasted strongly of cigarettes, so when I say I responded anyway, instead of pulling away gagging, you'll know how powerful it was. My arms went around him before I knew they were about to, and it was several kisses later before I could make them let go.

When I did, I said, "Jack, I don't know exactly what you're going through—"

"Jesus, Georgia Lee—"

"But I can't, I really can't—"

"I'm not—"

"I can't play it through with you. I haven't got the resources. I can't."

There was silence. Then, "All right. I don't think you understand, but all right."

It wouldn't have been polite to tell him I'd heard this kind of thing before, so I just stood up, said "See you tomorrow," and went back to bed. I lay awake a long time.

In the morning, we found a note on the dining table:

Ms. Kitty and Ms. Georgia Lee—
    Morning has broken and so, the office tells me, has the Rue de Castiglione bombing case. I've got to go. On the way out, I'll tell the concierge that Kitty's ex is back in town and that nobody, repeat nobody, is to be allowed upstairs.
    Will call later.

> Love and smooches,
> Jack

"Typical," Kitty said as we ate croissants and strawberry jam. "He'll protect us until a hotter story comes along."

"Has he always been this way?"

"Can't you tell? He was *born* this way."

"Is that why your relationship with him didn't last?"

She raised her eyebrows. "He told you? What a beast."

"He didn't say a word. I already suspected, and when last night he asked if the coffee was in the same place, it was a clue."

"Yeah. Well, 'relationship' is hardly the term to use. 'Fling' is more the term."

I wish I could say I didn't feel jealous, but I did. Kitty had everything: a gorgeous apartment, a fling with Jack, a cute pastry chef, Marc-Antoine, languishing after her. I had— I had Twinkie, who at this moment made a flying leap onto the table, skidded on a place mat, and upset the milk pitcher. As I mopped up I said, "You must be dying to get her out of here, with all these priceless statues around."

"Not at all. Stay as long as you like."

"Thanks, but I'm pretty sure we'll be back at my place tonight."

She consented to let me try another outfit today, and by searching far in the back of her closet I managed to put together an ensemble of apricot silk blouse, rust-colored pullover, and beige corduroy skirt which, although Kitty considered it hopelessly conservative, was more in keeping with my self-image. "At least wear a belt—no, not there, hip level," she said. As I complied, she looked at me dubiously. "You're sure about this?"

"Personally, I think rust is one of my better colors."

"I don't mean the clothes. I mean, are you sure you should go out?"

I wasn't sure at all. If it worked, though, it would be the quickest way out of my dilemma, and I wanted to get out quick. "I'll be fine," I said, trying to sound convinced. "Can I borrow a pocketbook, too? The biggest one you've got."

The biggest pocketbook Kitty had was a pigskin whopper the size of carry-on luggage. I put on my coat and slung it over my shoulder. I was ready. Once more into the breach. Then I could go back to Montparnasse, back home.

COUR ST. JEAN

I got out of the taxi on the corner of the Rue Charonne. I told myself I was taking a risk, but not a huge risk. If I'd called the police, they'd want to interrogate me, press me, maybe put me under *garde à vue*. Why would they listen to a bizarre theory that, from their point of view, was probably concocted to draw attention from my own guilt?

The weather was glorious, as beautiful as the day Overton and I went to the Bellefroide, although colder. Winter would begin soon, and from all reports it would be gray, freezing, and long. Maybe I could do a "Paris Patter" about the joys of winter here, if I could discover what they were.

Soon I was crossing the cobblestoned courtyard of the Cour St. Jean. The bright sun seemed to accentuate its dilapidated appearance—the sagging drainpipe and peeling paint. The furniture-maker's workroom was closed. Before I entered the gloomy hall I glanced up. I thought a lace panel moved in one of the windows above, but I wasn't sure. I climbed the staircase and knocked on the door.

In a minute or two, Chantal opened it. Her black hair had its usual just-rolled-in-the-hay look, and she was wearing her typical severe white blouse, this time with khaki pants. She looked dewy and fresh. Whatever toll recent events had taken on everybody else, Chantal didn't seem to have suffered.

She said, "I'm astonished to see you," and she looked it. She continued, "I read in the newspaper that the police want to question you."

I waved it aside. "That's been cleared up. I've just spoken with them. As a matter of fact, the entire case is cleared up. That's what I've come to tell you."

She stood still, watching me. I peered past her shoulder. "May I come in?"

She didn't move. "What do you mean, cleared up?"

"Why, they've arrested Bruno Blanc," I said. I could feel my manner getting chirpy, as if we were talking over a back fence in Cross Beach. "He's a member of a group called the Speculatori. He's the one who approached your husband about stealing the mirror."

"I see." She stepped back. "Come in."

In most respects, the room was as it had been before. The ugly sideboard was in place, as was the muddy brown furniture. The Virgin Mary was gone from the television set, though, and over the couch was a fringed throw printed with huge red poppies. She took my coat and hung it in the closet, and when we were seated she said, "Please. Tell me everything."

I repeated essentially what I'd said at the door, with some expansion and embellishment. When I finished, she said, "So Bruno Blanc stole the mirror and killed Pierre?"

"His confederates did. You see, Pierre knew Bruno was after the mirror. Bruno asked Pierre to steal it. Pierre hadn't told you who it was, right?"

She shook her head. "No, he never said."

"So I guess Pierre was killed to keep him quiet."

"I . . . what does Bruno Blanc say? Does he admit everything?"

"He's claiming he didn't do it, but the police believe they have a strong case."

Chantal's eyes were lustrous. "This *is* a relief," she said. She stood. "May I offer you coffee?"

I was overcaffeinated, but this was one cup I wasn't going to refuse. I had hoped she'd be cordial enough to offer, although if she didn't I was prepared to demand it. "I'd love some. Thank you."

As soon as she left for the kitchen, I crossed to the sideboard. I remembered from my previous visit that she'd taken the family album out of the top left-hand drawer. I pulled on the drawer. Stuck. Water was running in the kitchen. She might get the coffee started and then come back. Was the drawer locked? I jiggled it. No. Stuck.

I heard her footsteps moving across the kitchen. I heaved on the damn drawer and got past the rough place. There was the album. Cups and saucers clinked. I took the album out and got the drawer shut somehow. I'd heard, maybe read in Heloise, that candle wax on the runners would fix that kind of thing. I was back on the couch, having slid the album into Kitty's capacious pocketbook, by the time Chantal returned with my fortieth cup of coffee in the past twenty-four hours.

Now, when all I wanted was to get the hell out, she unbent enough to chat. I told her, distractedly, how Bruno had abducted me. I said he had practically admitted the two murders to me. I said the desire for the mirror had driven him insane. All the time, I was scorching my tongue trying to get the coffee down so I could leave.

When the cup was empty I put it down and stood briskly, to forestall an offer of more. "I have to run," I said, crossing to the coat closet. "Is this where you put my—"

I had the closet door open by that time. I stopped, reeled back. A tiny waft of Sphinx had hit me in the face. I gave her an involuntary and unwise glance of realization and started to cough.

I had blown it. I didn't know whether the smell came from shoes, gloves, a scarf that had trailed in the cologne, but that odor was unlike anything else. And since Sphinx wasn't yet on the market, she could only have picked it up in one place. The office, when she trashed it. She and—

She came up behind me, efficiently bent my arm back and clamped her hand over my mouth and called, medium loud, "Armand!"

He emerged from the hall, handsome and square-jawed, a cleft in his chin, tousled brown hair: cousin Armand, whose photograph with Chantal's wedding party was in the album now reposing in Kitty's bag. That was the photo I wanted to show Perret, to see if Armand had been lurking near the ransom, and to Jane, who'd gotten a brief glimpse of a man picking up an envelope from Lucien near the Luxembourg fence.

"Why couldn't you have stayed away, you fool?" Chantal whispered savagely in my ear.

Since her hand was over my mouth I couldn't reply, and indeed I was asking myself the same question. It had seemed relatively easy. It had *been* relatively easy, until Sphinx felled me once again.

They didn't talk. An exchange of glances was enough. They obviously had a contingency plan worked out. I hated to think of the implications for me.

They taped my wrists behind me, exactly as they'd done at the Bellefroide, and then gagged me with a large white handkerchief that must have been Armand's, or maybe Pierre's. By this time, Chantal was holding one of the black guns I remembered from the Bellefroide. They sat me at the dining table. Armand put on a jacket and a cloth cap and started for the door.

Chantal, watching me, said, "Wait." Her face and neck were pink. She crossed the room to Armand and kissed him. It wasn't a "Hurry back, dear," peck, either. As I watched her press her hips against him I thought, She loves this. She wanted to get rid of her husband, but she stumbled across something that turns her on more than Armand or any man.

He finally disentangled himself and said, "Soon." He went out and she returned to me. She slid into one of the other dining chairs and propped her elbow on the table, pointing the gun at me. She blotted her upper lip.

I sat still. I knew she'd shoot if I didn't. I felt sure she was the one who'd pulled the trigger on both Pierre and Lucien. Especially

Pierre, her husband. *You refuse to look where the light falls, but persist in searching the shadows.* Maybe it was just a lucky guess, maybe he really had a gift, but Bruno Blanc's reading had given me the clue. I'd been looking, we'd all been looking, toward the mirror. We hadn't stopped to consider the most simple possibility: that what had taken place at the Bellefroide was the premeditated murder of Pierre Legrand.

"I tried to be faithful to Pierre. I really did," Chantal said.

I'll just bet she had, but I wasn't able to argue.

"Armand and I have loved each other since we were children," she went on. "We've been lovers since we were, oh, ten or eleven. I've never loved anyone else."

I gurgled, but she wasn't interested in a response from me. "I thought Pierre would be good to me, but he was so harsh, so strict," she said. "He was so—*old*. I loathed him." She shivered, and I watched, cross-eyed, as the black hole at the end of the gun barrel moved rapidly back and forth.

"So I went back to Armand." Her voice was insubstantial, a sigh. And she and Armand had plotted to kill Pierre. Chantal would inherit Pierre's money, and all would be well in the Cour St. Jean.

"Pierre used to hurt me," Chantal said. "He whipped me, when I was bad." Her eyes widened. "Oh, I was happy to kill him. I assure you I was."

It was painful to think what hell her relationship with Pierre might have been. Maybe when she'd shot him, she'd found out for the first time what power meant. But I didn't want to be part of the ongoing process of discovery.

She didn't speak again. In about ten minutes I heard a car below, and footsteps on the stairs. Armand came in, looked at her, and said, "It's downstairs."

She stood and pulled me to my feet. She said, "Get her coat," to Armand, and in a moment she was draping my camel coat, which now smelled ever so faintly of Sphinx, over my shoulders. She put on a jacket and said, "I will remove your gag now, Madame Maxwell. We will go out to the car, the three of us together. If you scream, I will shoot you. Do you understand?"

I nodded, and Armand untied the handkerchief. I moved my aching jaw back and forth. I doubted that any pleading I might do would bring about a change of heart.

We left the apartment and descended the dusty staircase. Outside, a dark green car was parked in the courtyard. The sun was almost blinding. Our shadows glided over the cobblestones.

We were approaching the car. Armand was in front, Chantal close behind me, holding my arm. The door to the furniture-maker's workroom stood ajar. It had been closed, hadn't it, when I came in? I was almost positive it had.

We had just passed the workroom door when it burst open and banged against the wall. Two men carrying rifles rose from behind the car. A voice I recognized, in a conversational tone, said, "You will drop your weapons."

The three of us turned. Standing in the furniture-maker's doorway, his own gun drawn, the sun blazing down on his blond hair, stood Inspector Gilles Perret.

FROM THE MEDICI FOUNTAIN

DAWN the next day was gray and windy, and in the Luxembourg Gardens yellow and bronze chrysanthemums swayed in stone urns. Dead leaves rode the ripples on the surface of the Medici Fountain. The fountain was cordoned off, and *gendarmes* stood on its perimeter, their capes fluttering. The few passersby at this early hour seemed anxious to get to other places. Kitty, Jack, Inspector Perret, and I stood near the rope, watching a young man in a wet suit talking to one of the *gendarmes*.

The atmosphere was subdued, tense. Perret was passing the time while we waited by telling us, in a low voice, what he had learned since he showed up and saved me, having made an informed guess about where I was. Kitty had called him, so I now owed her my life, along with various other debts.

"Chantal has said nothing, but Armand"—Perret made a gesture of contempt—"He is so weak. The instant we separated them he began babbling, blaming her for everything. He says it was her idea, that she did the shooting, that if he didn't do as she asked he thought she would kill him, too."

It was a sad end, I thought, to Chantal's great love affair. "So killing Pierre was the purpose behind everything?" Jack asked.

"Yes. The mirror was the excuse. Bruno Blanc had asked Pierre to steal it. Pierre refused, but he told Chantal the story, including the fact that it was Bruno who had asked him. Chantal recognized this as an opportunity.

"She found out from Pierre where the mirror was kept. When he told her that on a particular morning he had to be at work early because a visitor was coming, she thought that would be a perfect time. The museum would be open. Pierre would be there, but few others would. Chantal and Armand made their plans, with the result you know."

I was watching the man in the wet suit. He didn't seem in a hurry to get into the frigid-looking water. Why did everything always take so long?

Kitty said, "But if they just wanted to kill Pierre, why all the business with the ransom?"

"Money," Perret said. "They got rid of Pierre, which was the main purpose, but they also gained an artifact Bruno Blanc wanted badly enough to propose stealing it. They contacted Bruno, anonymously of course, and offered to sell it to him. They arranged for him to contact them by leaving messages at the Luxembourg fence. Bruno was desperate to have the mirror, but he had no money. He went to Lucien Claude to see if Lucien would help him, and he told Lucien everything. At that point, you, Madame Maxwell, entered with your offer of ransom from Madeleine Bellefroide."

"And muddied the waters," I said, looking at the waters of the fountain.

"Yes. Now two people wanted the mirror, but only one of them could pay for it. Bruno knew he couldn't compete, but he also expected that the sellers didn't care who got the mirror as long as they got the money. He asked them to tell him the details of the transfer, so he could seize the mirror himself. They agreed, thinking a diversion at that time was a good idea—which it did not prove to be."

The man in the wet suit was moving toward the steps at the pool's far end.

"What about Lucien Claude?" Jack said.

"Lucien wanted money, too. He thought he could get more if he found out who he was dealing with and tried to blackmail them. He had Jane leave a message about the ransom by the fence in the Luxembourg. Then he went there, waited until Armand picked it up, and followed him back to Chantal's house. It was his misfortune that they spotted him and realized what he was doing. They called Lucien and told him to pick up the proof at the accustomed place, then waited for him and killed him. Meanwhile. the photo was already in the mail to you."

Kitty said, "And the break-in at our office?"

"Chantal and Armand, enraged at losing the ransom."

"Then what—" Kitty began, but at the same time a *gendarme* called, "Madame Maxwell!"

I ducked under the rope barrier and walked to him. "Can you show us exactly the place?" he said. He glanced at the man in the wet suit, who was descending the steps. "She will show you!" he called.

I went to the spot, between two urns, where I'd dropped the mirror in, and said, "Right here." If it were down there in the murk, there was no sign of it now.

The *gendarme* said, "Thank you. Stand back now, please."

I moved away. The wet-suited man was wading now through thigh-deep water. He reached the place I'd indicated and began walking slowly from side to side, feeling around with his feet. I thought, What if it broke? Or could somebody have found it, fished it out? I said, "It would be close to the edge." I could hear the anxiety in my voice.

He continued to move back and forth and then he said, "It's here. I feel it."

He sank into the water and felt around with his hands. A moment later, his head disappeared below the surface and then he came up sputtering. He shook his head vigorously, like a dog, and water drops flew. Then he brought his hands up. He was holding a round black object.

"Here it is!" one of the *gendarmes* shouted, and they crowded to the edge of the fountain to see. I wanted to run toward it myself, but I felt Perret's restraining hand. "We will have it soon," he murmured, and I remembered our bargain.

The atmosphere was like a party, with shouts of congratulations to the man in the wet suit and, when he emerged, pats on the back, a blanket around his shoulders, and a drink of brandy. Then Perret left us to join the bureaucratic huddle at the fountain's edge.

I was trembling from both cold and nerves. Jack put his arm around my shoulders. "Take it easy," he said.

"After all this—"

"Right. Right."

Kitty turned to me and said, "I'm still wondering."

"What about?"

"That phone call you got while I was there, remember? The one accusing Mallet?"

"Bruno, in a fury. He did blame Mallet for the whole thing."

"But then the anonymous letter. Was that from Bruno, too?"

I considered. "I guess it was," I said, but somehow I didn't feel sure.

It was about twenty minutes before Perret broke away. Jack left, heading back to the office to file his story. I watched him go out the gate and dash across the Rue de Vaugirard, on his way to the Odéon Métro station. My feelings about him were complicated, and I thought the balance between us was fragile. For now, though, it was holding.

Finally, Perret came toward me. He was carrying a briefcase. "Let's go." he said.

I waved to Kitty and followed him and a uniformed policeman through the gate to a car parked nearby. The policeman got behind the wheel and Perret and I got in the back seat. My eyes kept turning to the briefcase on Perret's knees.

"So there it is," I said.

He patted the briefcase. "Yes. At last."

"Did you . . . see it? Look in it?"

He smiled. "To be honest, it isn't impressive. Would you like to see?"

Would I like to see? I wasn't sure. And yet I thought, if I pass this up won't I worry about it forever? So I said, "Yes. I would."

He opened the briefcase. The mirror was wrapped in layers of soft beige jeweler's cloth. He unwrapped it and handed it to me.

I was surprised. It was black, and the surface was glossy, and it was cold in my hands. But I got no impression of depth, of the limitless blackness those who had looked into it described. There seemed to be clouds below the surface. No matter how long I gazed, I knew I would never see a vision there.

I kept it for a minute or two and then, with puzzlement and relief, handed it back to Perret. Whatever the mirror had shown to others, it had nothing to show me.

As we passed the École Militaire, Perret said, "I want to return this." He reached in his jacket and pulled out a dog-eared paperback and handed it to me. It was my second-hand copy of *Maigret et la Vieille Dame*. "I hadn't finished it, so I took it with me. I didn't think you'd mind."

I chuckled. "Was it good?"

"Very enjoyable."

I handed it back to him. "I'd like you to keep it. A souvenir."

He looked immoderately pleased and tucked it away again.

By this time, we had reached the Avenue de Suffren. This was the bargain: I would tell Perret where the mirror was, and he would let me show it to Madeleine Bellefroide before we gave it back to the museum. We pulled into her street. The Eiffel Tower, beyond, was almost lost in early-morning gloom.

Someone would have called by now, and we would be expected. In fact, Madeleine herself answered the door. She was dressed in white, a loose, long-sleeved dress. Her hair was brushed back, and she wore her pearls. Hawk-nosed and pale, she looked wonderful, as beautiful as she'd been the first day I met her. When we came in, she put her hands on my shoulders and kissed me on either cheek.

I introduced Perret. Then I said, "We have it. We got it back this morning."

As my own eyes had, hers drifted to the briefcase. I said, "Inspector Perret consented to let you look at it."

"I ask you not to tell anyone we have

350

done this," Perret said. "I'm not sure Monsieur Mallet would approve."

Madeleine nodded. "I'm quite sure he wouldn't. I have no intention of telling him or anyone."

Perret opened his briefcase and handed her the mirror, wrapped again in cloth. She took it and said, "Do you mind—Could I look at it in private? In another room?"

I saw Perret hesitate, and she said, "I certainly won't steal it. I'm grateful enough to be given this opportunity."

"All right. But for a very short time," Perret sounded wary.

Holding the mirror against her bosom, she left the room. Perret paced nervously. Everything was very quiet. I wondered what she was seeing, whether it would bring her hope or despair.

Ten minutes passed. Perret smoked and bit his knuckle. Even I started to wonder if Madeleine had gone down the fire escape with the mirror under her coat.

"This is too long. I must interrupt her," Perret said, but before he reached the door she entered the room, the cloth in one hand and the mirror in the other. She looked paler than before, but steady. "I'm sorry to have kept you," she said. "As a matter of fact,

I've spent this time trying to decide what to do, what to tell you."

Perret reached her, took the mirror. "What to tell us?"

"That's right." She shook her head. "You see, this is not Nostradamus's mirror. It isn't the same mirror at all."

MAGIC MIRROR

BERNARD MALLET sat at his desk in his elegant office at the Bellefroide, his face buried in his hands. Through the window behind him I could see branches tossing, the last leaves being stripped from the trees in the garden. On the desk in front of Mallet lay the mirror, in a nest of its beige wrapping.

Perret, next to me, shifted in his chair. Since he told Mallet what Madeleine Bellefroide had said, Mallet had made no sound at all.

Perret leaned forward. "I must ask you—" he began, but Mallet shook his head.

In a moment or two, he lowered his hands. His pinched face looked like an unhappy child's. "It's over, anyway," he said.

"And this—" Perret gestured to the desk.

"Madeleine Bellefroide is right. It isn't the real one."

"This is a substitute? It was exchanged?"

Mallet looked at the mirror wearily. "It's a substitute, of polished black marble. A maker of grave markers created it for me. I didn't tell him, of course, to what use I intended to put it."

"You yourself carried out the substitution?" Perret sounded appalled, but it was beginning to make sense to me. This explained, fully, Mallet's seemingly paranoid reluctance to show the mirror to anyone, much less to put it on display.

"What happened to the real mirror?" I asked.

Mallet shook his head. "It's—gone. I don't think it will be found again."

"It was stolen, you mean? Before this?" Perret demanded.

"No. It wasn't stolen."

We waited. Mallet got up and turned to look out at the garden. His back was to us, his hands clenched behind him. "It happened some years ago, soon after I became director of the Bellefroide," he said, his voice thin and lost-sounding.

"I was very proud," he said, turning toward us again. "I had been at a small museum in the provinces. To have been named to this post was a coup. I was determined to do the best possible job. Fairly soon after I arrived I made an inventory of our holdings, a survey of the works for which I was now responsible. In the course of it, naturally, I came across the mirror.

"My attitude toward the mirror was exactly the one I have expressed. I considered it an unimportant part of an interesting collection. I found out what I could about it, which was not much, and went on to other matters.

"I wish I could tell you, now, what made me decide to look into it. At the time, it seemed a harmless impulse. I was here, working late. I felt stimulated by my new responsibilities. And the idea came to me that I should look in Nostradamus's mirror. Once I had thought of it, I found myself leaving my office and going downstairs.

"I was a bit ashamed of what I was doing, but I told myself no one would ever know. I took the mirror from the drawer and removed it from its case."

As Clive Overton had done years earlier, I thought.

Mallet sat down again, as if his legs had given under him. "Somehow, the experience began to be more compelling than I anticipated," he said. "The sight of the brilliant black surface made me feel breathless. I tried to tell myself it was the late hour, the extreme quiet, but it wasn't only that. I felt myself drawn in as I bent over it.

"The surface was completely dark. There was no reflection of my face or the light in the room. I found this frightening and was about to pull back when I saw movement in the blackness. Deep within the mirror there appeared the image of a man moving toward me. When he came closer, I saw he was holding something in his cupped hands. The object was shining with a soft, luminous glow. The man was bending over it, and from the illumination it gave off I saw that the man was myself. The expression on his—my—face was one of tremendous joy, of beatitude.

"As I watched, the same joy filled my own heart. This was a man who had gained what he treasured, who held in his hands exactly what he needed. I associated that glowing light with my recently acquired position, my move to Paris, my new life. What a wonderful omen it seemed!"

Mallet's eyes reddened. "Forgive me," he whispered, and stopped speaking. After a few moments he resumed. "I was so happy, watching my fortunate image. And then, to my horror, everything changed. The light in my hands seemed to pulse. Without warning, it flew up and away, a streak so quick and so bright I couldn't see what it was. In the residual light, though, I saw my face. It was filled with unutterable grief. My image sank to its knees and stretched out on the ground in despair.

"Do you wonder that I couldn't bear it!" Mallet burst out. "In an instant, I had seen myself deprived of everything that mattered! You can see, can't you, how I must have felt?"

I was sick with Mallet's loss and grateful, at the same time, that I hadn't looked into the real mirror.

"I was overcome with the most ungodly combination of fury and terror," Mallet continued. "My first impulse was to smash the mirror, but even in that state of emotion I couldn't do such a thing, destroy an object that was in my charge." He gave a half-sob. "I put the mirror in my pocket and rushed out. I needed to move, to escape.

"I walked through Paris, my new home, seeing nothing but the image of my despair and loss. The mirror seemed to drag on me, pulling me toward my knees, my defeat.

After walking a long time, I found myself beside the Seine, near the Mirabeau Bridge.

"I walked out on the bridge. The night was quiet, the street lamps and the city around me glowing, the river rushing beneath. I thought of throwing myself over the railing. It seemed worth it to be rid of the image that still haunted me. And yet, I thought: Perhaps I could forget if the mirror were gone. I took the mirror from my pocket and threw it as far as I could, downstream into the Seine.

"I saw it strike the water, and I felt some ease. I turned away and went home. By the next morning, I was concerned only with concealing the fact that I had irresponsibly destroyed part of the Bellefroide collection. I arrived early and put the mirror case back in the drawer, and later that day I arranged to have the replacement made. When it was finished I put it in the case. I refused all inquiries about the mirror, even those from Madeleine Bellefroide. Over time, I became convinced that the light, after all, need not fly from my hands. But of course it has, as the mirror had shown me it would."

Mallet closed his eyes briefly. Then he said, "I was shocked and horrified when the mirror was stolen. I did everything in my power to discourage the efforts to find it. I was afraid Madame Maxwell, as a journalist, would investigate on her own, and I'm ashamed to say I wrote her an anonymous letter to try and dissuade her." He looked at me. "I apologize if it frightened you."

I nodded, and he went on, "None of it did any good. And now, everything I fought to prevent has happened."

Mallet stared at the piece of marble on his desk, the pseudo-mirror that had served its purpose so long. The atmosphere in the room was so heavy with sorrow that I didn't want to stay, to hear what punishment Perret might exact. I murmured, "I'll call you," to Perret, said good-bye, and left.

The morning remained chilly and overcast. I wandered in the general direction of the Seine. Perhaps I was retracing, in some measure, Mallet's steps that night. Storekeepers cranked down their awnings. Water sluiced through the gutters. Two men with squeegees were washing a phone booth. On a street corner, dead leaves spun in a tiny, momentary whirlwind.

The walk to the river took a while, but at last I came to the Place de Barcelone. Across the way was the Mirabeau Bridge, with its green-painted wrought-iron railings, its huge statues of sea denizens jutting out over the Seine. Morning rush traffic roared across.

I crossed and walked out on the sidewalk on the downstream side. In the middle of the bridge, I leaned on the railing for a long time. The Seine was very broad at this point, muddy yellow-green. The ripples and pulls on its surface indicated strong currents beneath. The mirror could be rescued easily enough from the Medici Fountain, but never, surely, from here. It was ground to pieces, buried in silt, or rolling along the sea bottom, miles away. And yet, perhaps it would survive. Some day it might wash up, be fished out by an unsuspecting person who would gaze in it and see—what?

In the meantime, I, too, had a new life, and no divining mirror to show me it wouldn't be everything I hoped.

I took the Métro at the Mirabeau station, and in half an hour was at the office. Kitty wasn't there, but the window was open and the smell of Sphinx much abated. My typewriter had aired out, too. I flicked the switch and it came on. I wound a piece of paper into it. I started to write.

A note on the text
Large print edition designed by
Pauline L. Chin.
Composed in 18 pt. Plantin
on a Xyvision 300/Linotron 202N
by Tara Casey
of G.K. Hall & Co.